'The other night you mentioned there was something you needed to tell me. Maybe you should tell me now.'

Cooper dreaded the truth. The truth wasn't going to set him free; it was going to sink him. 'Kelsey, I'm...I'm not sure this is the time—'

'Don't lie to me, Coop,' she said, cutting him off. Breathing deep, she looked him square in the face. 'Is there another woman?'

The question hit him like a glass of iced water. Of all the things he'd been concerned about, that was the last thing he'd expected her to ask. 'Why would you think there was someone else?'

'Because...' Her voice had started to quiver. 'Because since the accident, things have been *different* between us.'

Coop felt a knotting in his stomach. Of course things had been different. They were divorced. They hadn't been together as man and wife in over two years...

Dear Reader,

June is definitely a hot month! Our latest HEART-BREAKER title, *Prime Suspect*, comes from Maggie Price, a woman to watch—she's new but she's very special. Maggie herself once worked as a crime analyst for a police department so she really knows what she's talking about.

Fans of hers will be pleased to see Beverly Bird return with a new set of linked books and these are unique; set against the background of the traditional Amish community and centring on the hunt for missing children. Look out for *Loving Mariah*; we thought it was terrific!

Mind Over Marriage is a very moving and emotional tale of a marriage granted a second chance when a wife *forgets* that she's divorced her husband! And finally, don't miss the latest instalment in Maggie Shayne's novels featuring the Brand family, *Badlands Bad Boy*. Wes Brand is part Comanche and a real lone wolf.

Enjoy them and come back next month, when Nora Roberts is kicking off a brand-new mini-series!

The Editors

Mind Over Marriage

REBECCA DANIELS

SILHOUETTE

Sensation

First published in Great Britain 1998
Silhouette Books, Eton House, 18-24 Paradise Road,
Richmond, Surrey TW9 1SR

© Ann Marie Fattarsi 1997

ISBN 0 373 07765 3

18-9806

Printed and bound in Great Britain
by Mackays of Chatham PLC, Chatham

REBECCA DANIELS

will never forget the first time she read a Silhouette® novel. 'I was at my sister's house, sitting by the pool and trying without much success to get interested in the book I'd brought from home. Everything seemed to distract me—the kids splashing around, the sea gulls squawking, the dog barking. Finally my sister plucked the book from my hands, told me she was going to give me something I wouldn't be able to put down and handed me my first Silhouette novel. Guess what? She was right! For that lazy afternoon by her pool, I will forever be grateful.' That was years ago, and Rebecca has been writing romance novels ever since.

Born in the Midwest but raised in Southern California, she now resides in Northern California's San Joaquin Valley with her husband and two sons. She is a lifelong poet and song lyricist who enjoys early-morning walks, an occasional round of golf, scouring California's Mother Lode region for antiques and travelling.

Other novels by Rebecca Daniels

Silhouette Sensation®

*Tears of the Shaman
*Father Figure

**It Takes Two*

TYVMFE! - 797
SDS OOPS!

Prologue

Thursday, 10:01 a.m.

"Hi, Mr. Reed, this is Barbara Reynolds from Continental Casual. Isn't this rain something? Hope you're managing to stay dry. Just wanted to call to remind you your policy is coming due next week and I'd like to set up a time when we can discuss a renewal. Call me when you can. I'm at 805-555-8100. Bye."

Friday, 2:33 p.m.

"Hey, Coop. It's Dale McCannon. Time to renegotiate the lease again. Hope the place is still standing. Give me a call—you know the number."

Tuesday, 6:56 p.m.

"Cooper, hello, it's Morris Chandler. Been a long time, I know. I tried the house, but must have missed you—left a message on the machine, though. I was hoping I'd catch you at work, but no doubt this storm has you grounded. Coop, I...I need to talk with you—don't know quite how to say this. Something's happened—to Kelsey, I mean. She's in the hospital, Coop and...and, well, she needs you. Please call me as soon as you can, as soon as you get in. If there isn't someone at the house, I'll be at Community General in Santa Ynez. Please, Coop, it's really important.''

Wednesday, 7:55 a.m.

"It's Mo Chandler, Coop—looks like I missed you again. I'm still at the hospital in Santa Ynez, Community General. I could really use you up here, Coop, as soon as possible. I know it's a lot to ask, but I'm desperate.''

Wednesday, 11:27 a.m.

"Mo again. Coop, it's bad here. Kelsey needs you, Coop. Please come. *Please.*''

Chapter 1

They were calling it the storm of the century, but as far as Cooper Reed was concerned, that was just so much media hype. He'd weathered a lot of storms in his thirty-nine years—from Mother Nature as well as a few of his own making. And while the severe weather system that had moved over the state of California eight days ago and pelted coastal communities with raging winds and fierce rains had been bad, it wasn't the worst he'd seen.

Still, the storm had managed to disrupt his life pretty good, not to mention the toll it had taken on his well-being. His helicopter flight service had ground to a dead stop, and he could count on one hand the number of hours of sleep he'd had since volunteering with the rescue efforts that had begun seventy-two hours ago. His chopper had been in the air almost constantly in the past three days, so to say he was exhausted was an understatement.

Coop stumbled into his small, cluttered office and collapsed in the squeaky chair behind the desk. As offices go, it wasn't much, with its bare floors and cramped space, but that was okay. He wasn't there much, anyway. He spent most of his time piloting his helicopter back and forth between the airport and the huge offshore oil platforms that dotted the waters off the Santa Barbara coast. On four scheduled flights each day, he would ferry people, equipment, supplies—and just about anything else anyone would pay him to deliver—over the turbulent waters of the Pacific.

He leaned back, resting his head against the slick green vinyl and gazing through the small, grimy window beside the desk. The main runway of Santa Barbara's small airport was quiet now, but that hadn't been the case seventy-two hours ago. The place had been abuzz with activity then, air ambulances and transport planes landing and taking off one after the other, and emergency vehicles screaming back and forth, sirens blasting. It had been crazy—but then, like everything else since the damn storm had hit.

Starting eight days ago with a light drizzle, the storm had intensified over the California coast. For four days the calm waters of the Pacific had turned into a teeming caldron of destruction and death. Swells offshore rose as high as sixty feet and created a tide that swallowed up beaches and brutally pounded cliffs.

The aftermath had been no less brutal—a harsh testament to the fury of Mother Nature's hand. Injuries up and down the state had been bad, and some areas had experienced devastating destruction. Every pilot, seaman, heavy equipment operator, truck driver, search-and-rescue squad, law-enforcement agency, emergency medical team and able-bodied soul with two steady hands had pulled together to work the massive rescue campaign Coast Guard and Red Cross officials had organized.

Coop rubbed his scratchy eyes. He'd lost count of the number of trips he'd made between the airport and the offshore drilling platforms since the rescue began. With considerable storm damage to many of the platforms, and critical injuries, time had been of the essence in getting help to the stranded workers. He'd spent the past three days picking up and delivering injured workers to area hospitals, carrying supplies and equipment to repair damage, transporting work crews to storm-ravaged areas and assisting in search-and-rescue missions up and down the coast.

The wind shifted suddenly, sending a smattering of light rain against the windowpanes. It hit the glass with a crackling sound, a feeble reminder of the gale-force winds that had ripped through the area only days before. Coop gave his eyes another rub, stifling a yawn, and reached for the stack of mail Doris had dutifully left piled on his desk over a week ago.

Doris DeAngelo called herself his receptionist—probably because she sat behind the small counter out front— but to anyone who knew Coop and his aversion to anything resembling paperwork, she was the heart of Reed Helicopter Service. Coop might be the pilot and owner, but Doris was the reason the doors stayed open for business. She saw to it schedules were met, phones were answered and bills were paid on time.

Except the offices were empty now—they'd been empty all week. But even without the storm, Doris wouldn't have been around at this time of day anyway. It was nearly six, and Doris never, *never* worked past two. The way she saw it, she didn't need eight hours to get eight hours of work done. Besides, bridge games at the San Marcos Retirement Center began at three o'clock sharp, and Doris never missed a bridge game. Next to pushing him around, there was nothing the sixty-two-year-old woman liked more than playing bridge.

Coop smiled, leafing through the mound of mail. It was all junk, flyers and advertisements—nothing of importance. If there had been anything important, Doris never would have left it for him to take care of, anyway.

He glanced at the phone. At least his electronic voice mail service was his own. Doris wanted no part of it, thank God. As far as she was concerned, if it didn't involve a pen and paper or her antiquated Royal typewriter, it was considered high tech, and Doris simply didn't do high tech.

Coop picked up the receiver, hearing the rapid clicking sounding along with the dial tone that indicated he had taped messages waiting. He punched in his code and waited while the computer retrieved his calls, wondering just what he had missed in the frenzy of the past several days.

Coop listened to the perky voice of Barbara Reynolds, the insurance agent who'd taken over his account last year. Hearing that the premium on his copter was coming due wasn't exactly news he was anxious to hear. Neither was Dale McCannon's message that followed. Coop understood when a property manager started talking about renegotiating anything, it meant only one thing—his rent was going up.

As he listened, Coop picked up a pencil from the cup by the phone and doodled absently on the year-old calendar that lay among the clutter on top of his desk. He blackened a tooth of Miss January, who was clad in a teeny bikini and stocking cap made from the colorful labels of a popular brand of motor oil. He'd finished one front tooth and had just begun sketching a mustache across the top of her smiling lips when the next message began to play.

It took a moment for it to register what it was he was listening to, to identify the voice and understand the words being spoken. However, when recognition finally sunk in, the pencil slipped from his hand, landing on the cluttered desk and rolling into oblivion.

It had been two years, and yet Coop recognized his former father-in-law's voice immediately. Morris Chandler had raised five kids on his own, and there wasn't much that could get him upset—but he sounded upset now. In fact, he sounded terrified.

As he listened to Mo's message, Coop felt a cold dampness settle over the room, a cold that seemed to seep into his bones and turn his blood to ice. Kelsey was in the hospital. Mo hadn't said how or why—just that she was in the hospital and needed him. It seemed impossible.

Coop stared at the defaced calendar, but he wasn't seeing the spoiled image of the model in the picture. He was seeing an image in his mind, seeing the face of the woman he had married, the face of the woman who had promised to love him forever. Only Kelsey had broken her promise—broken it and walked away. Two years ago she had decided their marriage was over, had decided what was broken couldn't be fixed, what they once had was over forever.

It had been a bad time for both of them, a time when they should have pulled together, when they should have helped each other heal. Except there had been nothing she had wanted from him—not his comfort, not his support and certainly not his love.

His hand flexed nervously around the telephone receiver, and he closed his eyes. Mo was telling him she needed him now, she was in the hospital and needed him. How could that be?

He heard the beeping that signaled the end of one message and the start of another, and before he could think or react, Mo Chandler's voice came on the line again. The second message was short and to the point, and the third shorter still, with Mo leaving the same cryptic message, the same succinct dispatch—Kelsey needed him. The only things different in each message was the tone of Mo's voice. It grew more urgent and a little more desperate in each.

When the line finally went dead, Coop quickly punched in a code and replayed the messages. Except there was nothing else to hear, no further information to procure, no hidden message he'd missed the first time around. Coop hung up the phone and slowly rose to his feet.

He stood there for a moment, not sure what he should do—stand, sit, walk or run as far away as he could. He felt stunned, a little like he'd been caught in a wind shear and was heading toward the ground in a tailspin.

Glancing at the phone, he snatched it and punched in Mo Chandler's number. He didn't have to look up the number. Mo's number, like everything else about Kelsey Chandler Reed, had been permanently burned into his memory a long time ago.

He felt a ripple of anxiety while he waited for the connection to go through. The blood rushed through his veins, and there was a bitter taste in his mouth he hadn't experienced in a long time—not since his days with the Navy SEALS. He'd feared for his life back then, and for the lives of those depending on him, and the fear was no less real now. He wasn't on a mission to save the world from disaster this time, but he did have to save himself from the past.

With a loud click, the call finally connected. Coop held his breath as the phone rang once, twice. His mind raced as he tried to decide what to say, practicing lines in his head. There were so many things he wanted to know, but he didn't want to just start blurting out one question after another.

The phone rang for a fifth, then a sixth time. He thought of Mo's words on the message. *If there isn't anyone at the house...* But there had always been someone at Mo's house, always one of Kelsey's brothers or sisters or nieces or nephews.

Eight, nine—Coop felt the muscles in his stomach tighten. Where was everyone?

Finally, he accepted the inevitable and dropped the phone to the cradle. No one was going to answer. The air left his lungs in one long sigh. He wasn't sure if he felt relieved or disappointed. What did he do now? Wait and try again? Go home?

He walked around the desk, stopped at the window and looked at the sky. It was dark, and the misty rain had made the runway wet. The landing lights reflected brightly off the slick surface, sending streaks of color in all directions. But Coop's thoughts were too far away, his mind too distracted to see anything at all. All he really could think about was Kelsey.

What had happened? Why would she need to see him? Was she sick? Had there been an accident?

A bolt of fear traveled through him like lights streaking across the wet pavement. He should be doing something, something more than just standing there staring out a window. He needed to call Mo, call the hospital—call out the National Guard!

But, for the moment, all he could do was stand there and stare. It had taken him two years to pull his life together, to bury the memories deep enough so he could cope with the pain. He couldn't afford to open up those wounds, couldn't afford to start hurting all over again.

And yet Mo said she needed him. There had been no mistake. How could that be? They had been leading separate lives for two years. There had been no communication, no contact between them. What could have happened to make her want to see him again? What did she need from him after all this time?

Coop closed his eyes, thinking of his ex-wife, picturing her laughing blue eyes and honey-colored hair. Emotion swelled in his chest, pressing tight against his heart and making it difficult to breathe. It had been a long time since he'd allowed himself to think of her. He'd had to work hard to bury the memories, had to search long and hard to find a hole in his soul deep enough to bury them in. Otherwise, he never would have survived. He drew them out now, spreading them in his head and letting himself remember everything.

He remembered waking up after surgery in the recovery room of the ICU. Her beautiful face had been the first thing he'd seen, and he thought he must have fallen in love right then. Somehow he had just known she was the one, the woman for him. She'd been his nurse then, tending to his injuries and nurturing him to health, but by the time the bullet wound in his back had healed and the stitches from the surgery were out, he'd made her his wife.

Kelsey had been strong and independent—two things the wife of a Navy SEAL had to be. His missions had been dangerous and had often taken him away for months at a time. Kelsey had worried, but she'd adjusted. She had handled the worry and the long separations like she handled everything in her life—smoothly and proficiently.

Coop opened his eyes, watching the moon peek through the thin cloud covering. He could still remember how it had felt to come home to her waiting arms after the long nights away. Nothing seemed to matter then—not the Navy, not even the commission he'd worked so hard to get. She'd meant everything to him, and even before she'd asked him, he'd begun to think about leaving the SEALs. He'd had enough of life on the edge. He'd wanted to settle down, lead a normal life—with kids and a house and Kelsey in his arms forever. When he'd resigned from the Navy and started Reed Helicopter four years ago, he'd thought he had everything he'd ever want.

Coop rubbed his tired eyes. Of course, that had been before it had all come crashing down, before anger and pain had eroded her love. Before Kelsey had demanded a divorce.

He turned from the window, went to the desk and picked up the phone again, then punched in the number for directory assistance. As he listened to the halting recorded voice on the line, he scribbled the number for Community General Hospital in Santa Ynez across the toothless smile of Miss January. Taking another deep breath, he punched the number into the dial, not wanting to stop for too long or give himself an opportunity to change his mind.

"Good evening, Community General. How may I direct your call?"

Coop hesitated, hearing the sound of his heart pounding in his ears. "Uh, I'm trying to get in touch with Morris Chandler."

"Is he a patient?"

"Uh, no—I mean, I don't think so."

"I'm sorry, sir, I don't understand." The disembodied

voice had a practiced patience. "Are you looking for a doctor?"

"No, actually, I got a message—" Coop stopped, feeling thick-tongued and stupid. "I think...I mean, Mr. Chandler is visiting a patient there."

"What's the patient's name?"

"Kelsey. Kelsey Reed."

He waited, recognizing the sound of fingers on a keyboard as the receptionist punched information into the computer. He heard the pounding of his heart become a roar.

"I'm sorry, sir, Mrs. Reed is allowed no visitors."

A wave of nausea washed over him. He knew Mo had said something had happened, that Kelsey was in the hospital, but hearing it confirmed by the bland, dispassionate voice on the phone made it real.

"Could—" His voice failed, and he cleared his throat loudly. "Could you connect me to her room?"

There was more tapping of computer keys before the voice came on the line. "I'm sorry, sir, there are no calls allowed through, either."

"Oh, God." Coop dropped the phone. It landed with a thud across Miss January's midriff. Somewhere in the back of his brain he heard the distant voice of the receptionist on the line and knew Doris would read him the riot act for leaving the phone off the hook, but he couldn't be bothered with that now. He was already making his way to the door.

If he got the chopper fueled up and left right away, he could be in Santa Ynez in about a half hour. He'd been fooling himself thinking there was ever any question whether he would go. Of course he would go. Kelsey was in the hospital. She needed him, and that was all that mattered.

* * *

"Kelsey, come on. We've got to get out of here now!"

Okay, okay, she was coming. Couldn't he see she was working as fast as she could? The bleeding had nearly stopped, and if she could get the bandage to hold just a little longer...

"Kelsey, there's no time. Come on."

His voice echoed in her ears, and she could almost see his face. But who was he? Why didn't he just leave her alone? She was hurrying, but she couldn't leave until her job was done. There was still one kid. Couldn't he see that there was one last kid?

"Kelsey, hurry."

She could see his face now, could see the hand extended toward her. It was such a kind face, and there was a vague air of familiarity about him, and yet she didn't know who he was. Why did he keep calling to her? Why did he look so frightened?

"Kelsey."

She heard his voice, but it was growing faint. He was saying something else, mouthing wild, frantic words, and she had to strain to listen. Her head hurt so much, the pain throbbed at her temples and across her eyes. And the noise. There was so much noise.

She closed her eyes, seeing the pallid, ashen faces of the children. Oh, God, there had been so many children, and they'd all been hurt, all been crying. She had to get them out. The children. The children.

The pain in her head grew unbearable, and the noise was deafening. The noise and the pain—they were killing her. She was going to die, she knew it, could feel the life draining out of her. She was going to die, and there was nothing she could do to stop it.

"Coop," she screamed. *It only seemed right that her*

*husband's name be the last on her lips—the husband she
had disappointed, the husband she had lost. She'd sent
him away, given up her claim and tried to deny her love,
but the time for truth had come. "Cooper, I love you. I
love you, Coop."*

"Kelsey."

Suddenly, like a plug being pulled on a television set,
everything went black. Images faded, and the roar died to
a quiet hum. There was no more screaming, no more children crying. There was just the quiet sound of her name
being called, and a terrible, painful throbbing in her head.

"Kelsey, come on, sweetheart. Wake up."

"Coop?" Her voice sounded raw and coarse in her
ears, and it pounded at her temples like an animal ramming the door of its cage.

"No, sweetheart, it's me. It's Dad."

"Daddy," she repeated breathlessly. Getting words
from her brain to her mouth seemed like such a complicated procedure, and she felt drained of energy. "Daddy.
Where's Coop? Why isn't he here?"

"Don't worry, he'll be here, don't get upset. Your dinner tray is here. Wake up now—you need to eat something, need to build up your strength."

Kelsey cracked her lids a fraction, but the shaft of light
that darted in and crashed against her naked eyeball felt
like an arrow.

Pain exploded in her head, sucking the air from her
lungs and leaving her breathless and weak. She brought a
hand up, rubbed her eyes and pushed the confused, disjointed remnants of the dream to the back of her brain
where she didn't have to think about them any longer.

"Daddy," she whispered, bracing herself against the
throbbing in her head. The dream was gone, but she
couldn't seem to clear the fog in her brain. "Did you talk

to him—does he know? Did you tell Coop what's happened?''

"Not yet," he said, reaching to the controls along the side of the bed and slowing raising the head. "But I'm working on it. We all are."

The aroma of food finally found its way to her olfactory nerves, and she cracked one lid again, bracing herself against the rush of light. It came and exploded inside her skull like a million tiny bits of lightning, but like fireworks in the sky, it quickly faded.

"Is your head bothering you tonight?"

"It hurts," she said, gingerly turning her head on the pillow and looking at her father. The dark circles beneath his eyes and his somber, drawn expression made her uneasy. "But at least it stops me from thinking about the aching in my leg."

Mo Chandler glanced at the molded vinyl cast on her leg and took his daughter's hand in his, stroking the top of it. "I wish I could do something. I feel so darned helpless."

Kelsey smiled, giving his hand a squeeze and slowly opening her other eye. "Don't worry so much. I'm fine."

"Maybe I could talk to the doctor. See if there's something he could give you—for the pain, I mean. Maybe an aspirin, or—"

"No, Dad, please, it's all right," Kelsey said, stopping him with another squeeze of the hand. She concentrated on keeping her voice low, her words deliberate. That way the throbbing didn't hurt so much. "I'm okay, really. And head injuries aren't given medication, not—" She stopped, wincing and rubbing her temple with her free hand. She was feeling a little better. The fog was lifting and the world was beginning to make sense again. "Not right away, anyway. The doctor will prescribe something when he can.''

Mo drew in a tired breath, giving her hand another pat. ''I guess you'd know, sweetheart.'' He turned and pulled the tray between them, slipping the lids off the plates.

''I'm worried about you,'' she said, watching him as he prepared her tray. ''You look so tired.''

He looked at her and breathed a small laugh. ''I am tired. You practically scared the life out of me, in case you don't know it.''

Kelsey felt a stinging in her eyes, and she blinked it quickly away. She reached a hand out. ''Why don't you go on home and get some rest. I'll be fine here.''

''I'm not going anywhere,'' Mo said in a voice that made it clear the subject wasn't up for debate. ''And you're going to eat your dinner.''

Kelsey knew better than to argue with him. Besides, she felt too weak and too tired to try.

She glanced at the tray in front of her. The food on the plates looked like usual hospital fare—lukewarm meat loaf and hard mashed potatoes. It probably would have looked more appetizing had she an appetite, but she didn't. Still, she knew she had to eat. She didn't like the heavy fatigue that seemed to settle over her at the slightest strain.

''Did you talk to Doris?'' she asked, spearing a cube of meat and popping it into her mouth.

Mo looked up, trying to picture the woman Kelsey had introduced to him years before. ''Uh, no. No, she wasn't in.''

''Doris wasn't at the office?'' Kelsey scooped up a forkful of mashed potatoes. ''That doesn't sound right.''

''You're forgetting about the storm,'' he said pointedly, shifting uneasily on the bed. ''It's thrown everyone off.''

"That's right, the storm," Kelsey mumbled, setting her fork on the tray. "I guess I did forget." She pushed the table away, struggling to sit up, but the effort sent a shooting pain down her leg. "He's…he's all right, though, isn't he? Coop, I mean. He's all right?"

"He's fine," Mo insisted, trying to sound optimistic. "Just fine. Just not easy to get a hold of. You know pilots are always the first needed during rescues—and the last ones finished."

She sank against the pillows, the heavy fatigue settling over her again. "Yeah, and of course Coop would be the first to volunteer, the first to want to help. I'm sure he must have told me. I must have…" Her words trailed off, and she shook her head. It was that fog again—clouding her brain and making everything seem surreal. "I guess I must have forgotten."

"Sweetheart," Mo said, reaching across the table and taking her hand again. "Remember what the doctors said. You need to give yourself a chance to get better, to heal." He gave her hand a little shake. "The memories will come back then. You'll see."

"Right," Kelsey mumbled, turning her head away. She felt like crying, felt like climbing out of bed and running away, trying to get as far away from the fog and the confusion as she could.

Only she couldn't run and she couldn't cry. The heavy cast on her leg was like an anchor, weighing her down, and tears were not something she'd ever allowed herself to give in to. Ever since she was eight years old and her mother had died, leaving her to be the "little Mommy" to her younger brothers and sisters, she'd been the strong one in the family, the one everyone looked to for advice and support, the one who could handle anything. Except it was different this time. This time she was scared. This time she wasn't sure she could handle it alone.

"And remember," Mo said quickly, troubled by the strain on her face. "The doctors said what you didn't need was to get upset about anything. You just need a little rest and relaxation."

"And Coop," she whispered.

Mo's frown deepened. "Well, yes, of course, and Coop."

"I just wish he'd get here," she murmured, staring through the miniblinds to the dark sky outside.

Despite how independent she'd always been, despite how strong, she needed Coop—she always had. Coop had a way of making everything better, and she knew he would make this better, too. She knew when he got here she'd feel right again, and the blanks in her past wouldn't frighten her so.

"Coop," she murmured, watching the light of a plane making its way across the night sky. "I can always depend on him—I always have."

Chapter 2

"Cooper. By God, I don't believe it—you're here."

Coop looked up at the sound of his name and saw Morris Chandler step off the crowded elevator and into the small hospital lobby. Mo headed across the polished tile entry toward him like a torpedo honing in on its target.

"You're here," he said again, catching Coop in a bear hug. "I—I can't believe it, I don't know what to say. Thank you. Thank you for coming."

"I got here as fast as I could," Coop said, embarrassed by the sudden lump of emotion that had formed in his throat.

He stepped back and looked at the man who had once been like a father to him. Mo had never been a muscular man, but his sharp features and tall, lanky frame had always had a strength in them. Which only made the sight of him now all the more disturbing. Only two years had passed since they'd stood face-to-face, but Mo looked ancient. His shoulders were bent, causing him to look shorter

than his five feet, ten inches, and dark circles caused his
eyes to look wide and deep.

"I tried to call—"

"You're here now," Mo interrupted. Emotion made his
voice waver, and his eyes grew moist with tears. "That's
all that's important."

"What is it, Mo? Where's Kelsey? What's happened?"

"Oh, Coop," Mo stammered, the waver in his voice
growing worse. "It…it was bad, Coop. Kelsey…we
thought there for a while…we—" He squeezed his eyes
tight and shook his head.

"Mo, tell me," Coop demanded, clutching Mo's thin
arm. "My God, what's happened?"

"She's okay, she's better now—better," Mo assured
him. The wave of emotion that had gripped at him at the
sight of Coop was ebbing, and he pulled in a deep breath.
"I'm sorry, it's just that when I saw you standing
there…" He stopped and shook his head again. "The
emotion—it got to me, the memories…"

"I know," Coop mumbled, clearing his throat and
dropping his gaze to the gleaming tile floor. Seeing Mo
had been difficult for him, too. "Tell me. What
happened?"

"It was the storm," Mo said simply. "You know what
it's been like everywhere—how much destruction, how
many people hurt. The first wave of rain moved through
here about a week ago—caught everyone by surprise, did
a lot of damage. The worst was to an elementary school
near Solvang. Damn rain came down so fast it collapsed
the roof, then the wind brought the whole building
down." He shook his head again. "It was terrible. The
place was full of kids—a real tragedy." He squeezed his
eyes tight. "Kelsey…she was with one of the emergency

medical teams that went up there to work with the victims and she...she got hurt bad, Coop. We nearly lost her.''

Coop felt like he'd taken a belly flop into the water from the deck of an aircraft carrier. The muscles in his stomach convulsed, pushing all the air from his lungs and making him feel light-headed.

''She had been working inside the building—or what was left of it,'' Mo continued. ''There was a kid trapped down in the rubble. He was hurt, bleeding, and—well, you know how Kelsey feels about kids.''

Coop felt like he'd taken another blow to the midsection. He knew better than anyone how Kelsey felt about children. She loved them, adored them, and discovering she could never have any of her own had not only destroyed their marriage, it had nearly killed her.

''Anyway,'' Mo went on with a tired sigh, ''with the wind and everything, the building became so unstable they were forced to halt the rescue efforts. Only Kelsey refused to leave the little boy. Somehow, she managed to pull him out of there.'' His voice became wistful. ''The boy's ankle was tangled in the straps of a backpack or something. They said she ripped through two thick nylon straps with her bare hands to pull him free, can you imagine that?''

Yeah, Coop thought, feeling a little wistful himself. He could imagine it. Kelsey had always been one of those people who let nothing stand in her way. She had a will of iron when it came to something she wanted. Only once had he seen her beaten down, only once had he seen her give up a fight and let despair and hopelessness get the best of her. He believed their marriage could have withstood anything—except knowing they could never have a family. Kelsey had wanted that more than anything—even more than him.

He felt a dull throbbing in his temples as he let his mind drift. If he lived to be a hundred, he would never forget the sight of her in that hospital bed the morning they had gotten the news. The doctors had tried to be optimistic, talking about alternatives, adoption, but Kelsey had heard none of it. All she knew was she would never conceive, and it was as if all the life had drained out of her, all the fight. It had been the beginning of the end for them, for their marriage, for their love. Things were never the same between them after that morning.

"She got the boy out," Mo continued, his voice strained as he struggled with another wave of emotion. "Only it was pretty shaky where they'd been working and..." He closed his eyes and shook his head. "They couldn't get to her in time, and the whole place came down on top of her."

"No," Coop gasped, feeling the floor beneath his feet begin to sway. He touched the wall for support. "God, no."

"It took almost two days of digging, but they finally managed to reach her. She was unconscious by that time, and remained in a coma for four more days." He stopped to collect himself again, rubbing his tired eyes. "I have to tell you, Coop, those were the longest six days of my life. I don't know which was worse—knowing she was under all that rubble or seeing her lying unconscious." He wiped at the moisture in his eyes. "But thank the Lord it's over. She's out of the coma, and the doctors say she's going to be fine."

"Can...can I see her?" Coop asked, hoping he had the courage to see her in a hospital bed again.

"Yes, of course, but...we should talk first. There's something else—"

"Coop!"

Coop and Mo looked up as Kelsey's brothers and sisters came rushing toward them. There was a blur of regards and introductions and a two-year gap to fill in. Everyone seemed to talk at once—new spouses, new children—and it all was peppered with a flurry of hugs and tears and cries of comfort.

Coop greeted the people who had once been his family with genuine affection. Having grown up an only child, he had envied Kelsey her siblings, and in the four years they'd been married, he'd come to think of them as his family, too. He'd missed them since the divorce—the closeness, the caring. He hadn't realized how much until this moment.

Still, his joy in being reunited was marred by the reason for it. The thought of Kelsey hurt, in a hospital bed, gnawed at him. He wanted to go to her, needed to see for himself that she was all right.

As soon as he was able, he pulled Mo to one side. "I want to see her, Mo," he said in a low voice. "I want to see her now."

"First we need to talk."

"We can talk later," Coop insisted, heading in the direction of the elevators.

"No," Mo said firmly, stopping him with a hand on his arm. "We have to talk now." He led Coop to a quiet spot away from the others. "There's something you have to know before you see her."

"What is it?" Coop asked uneasily, the hair at the nape of his neck starting to prick. "Mo, what is it? What haven't you told me?"

Mo drew in a deep breath. "The doctors say she has a type of amnesia—"

"What?" Coop felt the blood draining from his face. "What are you saying?"

"They say it was the head injuries, but they can't be sure. It could be the effects of the coma, too. There are things she can't remember—things about her life."

Coop could barely hear through the ringing in his ears. "Kelsey doesn't know who she is?"

"Not exactly."

Coop glared at him. "Then what, exactly?"

"There are only certain things she's forgotten. She knows me and her family. She remembers she's a nurse, that she worked in a hospital."

"That doesn't sound like amnesia to me."

"No, I know, but that's what the doctors are calling it. She hasn't forgotten everything—just some things."

"What things, Mo?" Had she forgotten him, forgotten what they once had shared? "What doesn't she remember?"

Mo's shoulders drooped as he looked up into Coop's blue eyes. "The divorce. She thinks you're still married."

Kelsey took a deep breath and tried again, pushing against the mattress with as much strength as she could muster. She might as well have been tied down with a grappling hook, for all the good it did. She hadn't moved an inch. The cast on her leg felt more like a block of cement than a state-of-the-art, formfitting vinyl mold, and all she'd succeeded in doing was exhausting herself.

With a sigh, she fell back against the pillows. She hated the weakness that robbed her of her strength, hated being flat on her back and relying on others to get her what she wanted—and what she wanted right now was to sit up, not propped against a bunch of pillows and an electronically aided mattress like a rag doll with no will of her own.

Except she was a rag doll, lying there staring at the

ceiling and lacking the energy to even feel frustrated. A heavy wave of fatigue washed over her—an insidious, repugnant fatigue that drained her of strength the way a vampire drained his victims of blood. Weariness moved through her system, permeating every inch of tissue, muscle, blood, bone, causing her eyelids to droop for want of sleep.

Except she didn't want to sleep—not yet, anyway. She didn't want to drift into that dark abyss where her dreams took her, that place where sounds and images dazed and confused her and where the things she couldn't see frightened her far more than those she could.

She brought a weak hand to her eyes and rubbed her heavy lids. Maybe if she gave in for a while, just closed her eyes and rested for a few moments, she'd have enough strength to try again, to sit up and act like a normal person. The last thing she wanted Coop to see when he walked through that door was a helpless woman.

Coop. How she wished he would come. She believed the doctors when they said she was going to be all right, believed everyone who had been telling her that since the moment she had come out of the coma. As a nurse, she'd seen cases like her own before—knew that with a little rest, a little time, her brain would heal, the fog would lift and her life would be back to normal again. She would just believe it a little more if she heard Coop say it.

Letting her eyes drift closed, she drew in a shaky breath. She thought of Coop, imagining his handsome smile and deep blue eyes. Only he wouldn't be smiling when he walked through that door. He'd be worried. She'd never been sick before, had never been the patient. It was going to bother him to see her like this. It bothered her, too.

Coop wouldn't want her to see that he was worried. He

would mask his concern by teasing and joking. He would find a way to make her laugh. And while she might be the nurse of the family, she knew he would insist on taking care of her, making them both feel better.

The slight sting of tears burned her eyes, and she quickly blinked it away. Where was this urge to cry coming from? Did it have something to do with her injuries? Was it something that would go away? She never cried, never, and yet it seemed she'd been on the verge of tears since she'd awakened from the coma. She didn't want Coop to see her all weepy and weak, or he really would think something was wrong.

"Coop, where are you?" she mumbled into the darkness. "Why aren't you here?"

Her voice sounded faint and helpless in her ears, and she hated the weakness in her that made her too tired to care. If only Coop was there, she'd feel better. She wouldn't have to explain things to him, wouldn't have to put up a brave front or try to put her feelings into words. He would understand how frightened she was, understand how awful it made her feel.

She turned her head, looking at the small clock on the stand beside the bed. Eight-fifteen. Visiting hours would be over soon—not that anything like that would stop Coop. When he got there, he'd find her, one way or another. It didn't matter how far he had to travel, or what time of day it was, Coop would find a way to get there. It was the thing she loved about him most—his tenacity, his determination. Coop was a man who would let nothing stop him from getting what he wanted, and she would forever be grateful he wanted her.

The drowsiness was becoming critical, and she felt the dreamy darkness beckoning to her. She hated the black holes in her memory, hated the fact that there were things in her life she no longer remembered—but she remembered Coop, and the love they shared, and that was all that was important. That was all she needed.

"I...I don't get it." Coop stared at the doctor sitting on the opposite side of the wide mahogany desk and shook his head. "It doesn't make sense."

Dr. Mannie Cohen closed the chart and slipped it onto the stack on the desk. "You're right, it doesn't. Head injuries and brain trauma aren't easy things to understand."

Coop leaned forward in his chair. "I thought when someone had amnesia they forgot everything."

"Sometimes they do, sometimes they don't," the doctor admitted. "These things don't follow a set pattern."

"What kind of damn answer is that?" Coop demanded. He was furious, and he wasn't sure where to direct it. He rose off his chair and leaned across the desk toward the doctor. "I thought you were supposed to be some sort of specialist. I thought you were supposed to know about this stuff."

"Look, Mr. Reed, there's nothing more I'd like to do than be able to answer all your questions, but the fact is I can't—no one can. I'm trying to be honest with you." He spoke in a calm voice, unfazed by Coop's anger. He understood the anger and the frustration, had experienced the same things himself. He leaned forward, resting his elbows on the desk. "I can tell you about the research being done, about advances that have been made. I can cite statistical projections and percentages on rates of recovery and long-term prognosis. But the fact is, when it comes to these kinds of injuries, we're basically feeling our way in the dark. Each one is different, unique. It's impossible to say what's normal and what isn't."

Coop pushed himself away from the desk and walked to the window. He stared across the dark parking lot, having a hard time believing what he was hearing. "So in other words what you're saying is Kelsey remembers everything about her life except that our marriage ended?"

"Well, it's not quite as simple as that," Dr. Cohen replied. He rose and walked to the coat stand by the door. He slipped off his white hospital-issue coat, tossed it over a hook and reached for a comfortable and well-worn tweed jacket. "In talking with Mo and the rest of her family, there appears to be a number of breaks in your wife's—"

"Ex-wife," Coop pointed out in a flat voice. He'd had two years, but he still found it hard to say.

"Right, sorry, ex-wife," Mannie conceded, slipping an arm into his jacket. "As I was saying, there seem to be other gaps in your ex-wife's memory, as well. Obviously the most significant is that particular segment dealing with the divorce. She has no recollection of it. There are some things that have occurred since the divorce she is aware of—even though there are some holes. For example, she doesn't remember moving to Santa Ynez or working here at the hospital, yet she knew me—knew my name, knew who I was, knew others on staff. She knows she's a nurse, but she doesn't remember working, doesn't remember having a job. She doesn't remember the apartment she's lived in for the past two years, but she remembers news events, election results. She has some recollection of how she was injured and about the children she tended, but she can't remember where she was or why she was there." He slipped the other arm into the jacket and looked across the office at Coop. "Gaps."

"Gaps," Coop repeated. He didn't know what to think.

He felt a little like he'd been buried beneath several tons of rubble himself, and nothing was making sense.

"And no doubt there are other inconsistencies, things she knows about, others she's forgotten. Things that just haven't come up yet." The doctor paused for a moment, studying Coop's reaction. "Like I said, these sorts of injuries don't follow a set pattern. There's no way to know what to expect."

Coop rubbed his tired eyes. It didn't surprise him that Kelsey would want to forget that period of her life. That last year they'd been together had been marred with tragedy and pain. He would block it out himself if he could.

"Okay," he said after a moment. "So basically what you're saying is that Kelsey still thinks we're married, still living in Santa Barbara together. Beyond that, it's anybody's guess?"

Dr. Cohen returned to his desk and sat down. "Basically, that's it."

Coop stepped back from the window, feeling restless and uneasy. "Will she get better? Will she get her memory back, or is this a permanent thing?"

"There's no way to know at this point if the memory loss will be permanent," Dr. Cohen confessed. "The good news is she suffered no brain damage, nothing physical that would make it impossible for her to remember. She could wake up tomorrow morning and have everything back."

"And the bad news?"

The doctor shrugged, looking at him. "It could take twenty years. There's no way to know."

Coop slowly sat down, suddenly feeling the fatigue of too many hours without sleep. "So what do we do? How do you treat this?"

"We don't," Dr. Cohen said simply. "The broken leg

and the cuts and bruises we can take care of. She needs rest so that the body and the mind have a chance to heal. There's a very high likelihood her memory will come back eventually. The overwhelming majority of amnesia victims make a complete recovery, despite how different each case is. If they have a common ground, that's it.''

Coop thought for a moment, then leaned back in the chair. ''So what do we do in the meantime?''

The doctor drew in a deep breath. ''That's the reason I asked Mo to let me talk to you before you saw her.'' He sat up, his fingers resting lightly on the desk. ''Kelsey's more than just a patient around here. She may not remember everyone on the staff, but they remember her. She's a terrific nurse, and a very special person.'' He stopped, glancing across the desk at Coop. ''But then, I guess I don't have to tell you that.''

''You're right, you don't,'' Coop said coolly. Mannie Cohen might have been a balding, middle-aged doctor with a decidedly settled appearance, but that didn't seem to make a difference. Coop didn't need another man to remind him how special Kelsey was.

''Yes, well,'' Dr. Cohen said, shifting uneasily in his chair. He reached for her chart from the stack and opened it again. ''I've consulted with all the doctors involved in her treatment. Vince Hamilton is the orthopedist who did the surgery on her leg. Brian Anderson's the consulting internist, and Gloria Crowell is a psychiatrist we brought in who specializes in amnesia cases. We all feel given the right circumstances, and enough time, Kelsey's chances for a complete recovery are very good.''

Coop's gaze narrowed. He suddenly began to feel uneasy. ''The right circumstances?''

The older man lowered the open chart to the desk and pushed it to one side. ''Memory loss, the kind that Kelsey has suffered, isn't something we see very often. Her loss deals to a large extent with those memories connected in one way or another with your divorce.'' He leaned back in his chair, tenting his hands together. ''Granted, there are gaps concerning other facets of her life, but those could simply be her way of explaining why things in her life don't make sense, and—''

''Wait, wait,'' Coop said, raising a hand and cutting him off. ''You've lost me here. What do you mean, her way of explaining things?''

''Well,'' Dr. Cohen said, taking a deep breath. ''Take for example her job here at the hospital. It's not the job she had when she was married to you—different place, different people. There is no way she can explain why she has a different job in a different place, why she works in Santa Ynez when she lives in Santa Barbara.''

''Right,'' Coop said, trying to see the logic. ''It doesn't make sense.''

''Exactly. So how does she explain it?'' He gestured, making his point with palms to the ceiling. ''She forgets it—even though she knows she had a job, knows a lot about this particular hospital and recognizes me and others on the staff, she has no memory of where she'd been working. He paused, sitting back in his chair. ''No memory, no need to explain.''

''I guess that makes sense.'' Coop sighed, considering what the doctor had said. ''As much as any of this does.''

''Which gets us back to circumstances,'' Dr. Cohen continued. ''I think you'll see when you talk to her that Kelsey finds these gaps in her memory very stressful, very frustrating. It's understandable. The problem is, she's still very weak. She needs time to heal, to build up her strength, get healthy again. My colleagues and I have some concerns as to the effect the shock of discovering the truth could have on her.''

''You think it could interfere with her recovery?''

''It's difficult to say exactly what would happen, but I don't see it doing her any good—not right now, anyway.'' He paused, searching for the right words. ''She needs to be ready to remember, needs to be strong enough to handle the truth. We go to her now, tell her everything, there's a chance the shock would push those memories so far back she'd never be able to retrieve them.''

Coop was quiet, trying to understand and absorb. ''So what are you suggesting?''

''We're suggesting she be given the chance to remember on her own.''

''You don't want me to see her, then?''

''Oh, no, on the contrary.''

Coop felt the hair on the back of his neck start to tingle again. ''You mean, you want me to lie to her? Let her believe we're still married?''

''I don't see it as lying, exactly.''

''No? You're asking me to keep the truth from her. If that's not lying, what would you call it?''

''I'd call it giving her a chance—the best chance she has to get better.'' Dr. Cohen leaned forward in his chair, staring at the man who sat opposite him. ''Look, I know this is a lot to take in right now. It's unusual, to say the least, but if it could help Kelsey, isn't it worth a chance?''

Coop sat back, feeling a little like he'd taken a wrong turn somewhere and had ended up in the Twilight Zone. Maybe he was suffering from a lack of sleep. The whole situation sounded so fantastic, surreal.

''I'm suppose to pretend?'' he asked slowly, feeling strangely winded, as if oxygen was no longer finding its way into his lungs. "You want me to go in there and playact at being her husband, is that it?"

"You were her husband once," Dr. Cohen pointed out dryly. "I wouldn't think it would be such a difficult thing to do."

"No?"

"No," he said firmly. "She's going to have to stay in the hospital for at least another week, probably longer. We'll be able to monitor her closely, and she'll have sessions with Dr. Crowell, who will help her deal with the amnesia." He raised a shoulder. "And who knows? A lot can happen in a week. The two of you spend some time together, you start helping her fill in the blanks here and there—it might trigger something. It could start a domino effect—she remembers one thing, then another and so on." Dr. Cohen rested his palms flat on the desk and spread his fingers wide. "Or you could walk in that room right now, she could take one look at you and bam!— everything could come back, just like that."

"Okay," Coop said, conceding that point but ready to counter with one of his own. "That sounds just dandy, but what if her memory doesn't come back just like that? What if there is no domino effect? What do we do then? What do we do if the time comes for her to be released and she still doesn't remember?"

Dr. Cohen sank back in his chair, giving Coop a frank look. "Then we reevaluate things."

Coop stood, walked to the window and stared out into the night. Reevaluate. It was one of those words like renegotiate, just another way of saying he was screwed. He turned to the doctor. "You talked to Mo about this?"

The older man arched a brow. "He seemed to think you'd be willing." He slowly brought his hands up, tenting them together, and regarded Coop carefully. "You know, there's a possibility she's blocked out that part of her life for a reason. Aren't you a little curious? Don't you think you should find out why that is?''

Coop turned to the window again, pulling in a shaky breath. He already knew why, and knew the kindest thing would be if she never had to remember again.

He closed his eyes, picturing her in his mind. Until today, he wasn't sure he'd ever see her again, let alone have another chance to be her husband. Only this time it wouldn't be real. It would only be pretense, and he wasn't sure he could do it.

Being with Kelsey meant getting involved again. He'd had two years to try to put his life back together, but he wasn't sure it had been long enough. He wasn't sure he was strong enough to get involved only to watch her walk out of his life a second time.

Slowly, Coop turned and made his way silently to the door.

''What did you decide?'' Mannie Cohen asked.

Coop paused, his hand on the door, and gave the doctor a sidelong glance. ''Decide? You make it sound as though I have a choice.''

''Of course you have a choice,'' Dr. Cohen insisted, rising to his feet. ''There are always choices.''

''You've never had a woman get under your skin before, have you, Doc?''

The other man straightened his shoulders. ''There have been women in my life—my wife, my ex—if that's what you mean.''

Coop laughed, a raw, sad sound that echoed through the small office. ''None of these women of yours has ever gotten to you, though—none of them has ever gotten a hold of you good, have they?''

''Why do you say that?''

Coop opened the door. ''Because if they had, you never could have asked me to do this.''

Chapter 3

"Coop, sweetie, I can hardly believe this."

Coop leaned his forehead against the hard plastic molding that enclosed the pay phone in the lobby and pictured Doris DeAngelo on the other end of the line. "I know, I can hardly believe it myself."

"But she's...she's out of danger now, isn't she? I mean, she's going to be all right?"

"Oh, yeah, the doctors seem confident she'll make a full recovery," Coop assured her. He'd neglected to mention anything about memory loss to Doris. It was just too confusing and too complicated to get into on the phone. "But it may take some time. Anyway, I'm going to be up here for..." His voice trailed off, and he brought a hand up and rubbed his eyes. "Well, I'll be up here—I'm not sure for how long. Hold down the fort for me, will you?"

"Don't I always?" Doris asked affectionately. "I'll

line up someone to take the flights, don't worry—but Coop, honey, would you like me to come up?''

Coop closed his eyes, taking the offer for what it was—a show of affection. A part of him would have liked nothing more than to have Doris's broad, understanding shoulder to cry on. They might rib each other, sparring and scrapping, but the fondness between them was real.

''No,'' he said with a tired sigh. ''I'm okay, but I appreciate the offer.'' He opened his eyes and saw Mo Chandler step off the elevator and start across the lobby toward him. ''Besides, I need you to make sure I've still got a business to come back to.''

''Don't worry about that,'' Doris assured him. ''I can't afford to let this place go under. Where else would I find a cushy job like this and a boss I could push around as easily as you?''

Her words were full of humor, but Coop heard and understood the emotion behind them. ''Thanks, Doris.''

''Take care of her, Coop,'' Doris said, serious. ''Kelsey's one of the special ones.''

Coop drew in a deep breath. ''You won't get an argument from me on that. Talk to you later.''

Coop slipped the receiver onto the hook and turned to Mo. ''Doris DeAngelo,'' he said, by way of explanation. ''I don't know if you remember her.''

''Sure I do,'' Mo said, nodding and remembering Kelsey mentioning the name earlier. ''Works for you, right?''

''Right,'' Coop agreed.

Mo hesitated. ''Dr. Cohen said he talked to you, that you agreed to…well, that you agreed to help.''

Coop gave him a deliberate look. ''You didn't really doubt that I would, did you?''

''No, not really,'' Mo admitted, dropping his gaze to the shiny tiled floor. ''But I realize it's a lot to ask, getting you up here, asking you to—to go along with this. Especially after…''

Coop put a hand up, stopping him. ''This is for Kelsey. You know I'd do anything if it meant helping her get better.''

Mo blinked. ''You know, I don't know if I ever told you…I mean about before, about what happened. I don't know if I ever said how sorry I was. Kelsey was in such bad shape, took everything so hard. I know you were hurting, too, though.''

Coop struggled, not wanting to think about the unhappiness that had touched so many of their lives.

Swallowing the hard lump of emotion in his throat, he gave Mo a gentle pat on the shoulder. ''It was a long time ago. Water under the bridge.'' He took a deep breath, forcing the memories beneath the surface, and nodded toward the open elevator door. ''Come on, show me where her room is.''

Mo hesitated. ''You know, it's late. She might be asleep by now. You could probably wait, if you wanted, until morning. Give yourself a chance to…to rest up a bit.''

Coop looked into Mo's tired eyes and smiled. He understood and appreciated the reprieve his former father-in-law was offering, but he also knew it would only be putting off the inevitable. Awake or asleep, he had to see Kelsey now—tonight. He could talk all he wanted about water under the bridge, about things being over and done with, but the fact was, the bridge had collapsed and she was back in his life for real.

''No,'' Coop said, shaking his head. ''I want to see her for a little while, anyway, even if she is asleep.'' He stopped, the hand on Mo's shoulder pressing firm. ''You understand.''

"Yeah," Mo mumbled, stepping inside the elevator and pressing the button for the eighth floor.

They made the ride in silence, both staring at the row of numbers above the door. When number eight glowed bright, a loud ping sounded, and the elevator eased to a stop.

"It's this way," Mo said, pointing to his left as they stepped out of the elevator and into the corridor. "In the isolation ward."

Coop turned and gave him a puzzled look. "Isolation?"

"Her doctors thought it would be better this way," Mo explained. "With her being so hazy about everything— the hospital and all the people. They just thought the fewer visitors she had, the less confusing it would be." As they passed the nurse's station, he nodded to the woman sitting behind the desk. "It's pretty much just me and the other kids who visit."

"I see," Coop said quietly.

They came to a stop outside her room. Coop stared at the door, wondering for a moment if he had enough courage to walk inside. He'd been handed some rough assignments as a SEAL, but he couldn't remember one as tough as this.

"I'll, uh, I'll be down the hall in the waiting room," Mo said awkwardly. "I've, uh, been spending the nights there, so if you need me..."

Coop nodded, reaching for the handle of the door. He felt a little like a prisoner about to face the firing squad rather than a husband about to see his wife.

He could have waited, could have walked away and put this off until the morning, but that only would have delayed the inevitable. Besides, when it came to Kelsey, he'd never been able to walk away, never been able to put a hold on his feelings. He'd promised to play a part from his past for the sake of her future, and once it was over, it would be Kelsey doing the walking—away from him again.

The door quietly drifted closed behind him. The room was dark—too dark after the bright lights of the hall— and it took a few moments for his eyes to adjust. Coop stood in the darkness, listening to the quiet hum of equipment and machinery from somewhere in the shadows, feeling apprehension grow thick and dry in his throat.

Objects in the room began to slowly take shape, transforming out of the gloom like an image in a photographer's darkroom emerging on a print in a chemical tray. He could see two hospital beds, one empty, one partially obscured by a curtain that had been drawn around it. A small light showed from inside the curtain, creating a delicate radiance that glowed in a soft circle along the cloth.

Coop felt the apprehension in his throat growing as he stared at that faint, dim light, knowing Kelsey lay just on the other side. He'd spent the last two years trying to forget her, trying to stop himself from thinking of her as his wife. Yet now all that would have to change. He would have to ignore the years that had passed, overlook all that had been said and done and pretend it was the way it used to be—at least until she remembered.

He moved silently across the room, but his legs felt leaden and numb. The hard rubber soles of his boots sounded bleak and hollow against the floor's slick surface.

What would she see when she looked at him? What reaction would he trigger? Would those sleeping memories suddenly be awakened? Would she remember everything and send him on his way, or would she look at him and see her husband?

He thought of their life together, of the hundreds of

little details and half-forgotten customs and patterns that had made up their four years of marriage. Would he remember enough? Did he remember what it felt like to be her husband?

He tried to ready himself, tried to get into the right frame of mind, to psyche himself up. He was going to see her again, and he had to be prepared—but when he stepped around the curtain and looked into the face of the woman who once had been his wife, he realized he hadn't prepared himself enough.

Surrounded by pillows, Kelsey lay sleeping peacefully to the quiet drone of the monitors and machines that were positioned around her bed like sentries on guard. Her long, blond hair splayed out across the pillows like a golden halo around the face of an angel. And that's how she looked—angelic. She looked as he remembered her, like Kelsey, *his* Kelsey, beautiful and familiar.

She looked like his wife.

He stood at the foot of the bed, watching her sleep and feeling life returning to those parts of him that had been dead for two long years. Memories assailed him from all sides, spanning the spectrum of human emotion from hurt to healing, happy to sad. A million tiny snippets traveled through his brain like pictures in a photo album, bringing back a life and a love he'd thought were lost to him forever. She was like an oasis in the desert, like the sun after a long winter night, and for the first time in two years, he felt he was where he was meant to be.

He slowly moved around the bed, weaving his way through the monitors, taking care not to wake her. He reached for a chair beside the bed, slid it close and sat down. He welcomed the quiet moment, welcomed the opportunity to study her.

He could see the evidence of injury along her forehead

and cheek, could see the outline of the heavy cast that encircled her leg. A large bruise marred the delicate skin above her brow, and a number of small cuts and scrapes had left her cheek and arms marked and discolored. His heart twisted tight in his chest as he thought of the trauma she'd been through, of the tons of concrete and rubble that had buried her alive.

Children. Mo had told her she'd been in that collapsed building trying to help children. There wasn't a doubt in Coop's mind she would have given her life that day if it meant a child would have lived—no doubt at all.

"Kelsey," he whispered. He reached for her hand, slipping it into his. "Oh, sweetheart, I'm so sorry."

And he was sorry—sorry about so much. He wasn't a man given to tears, and the stinging sensation in his eyes felt strange and unfamiliar. He felt like crying for all the hurt and the pain he'd been unable to protect her from.

"Coop? Cooper?"

At the sound of her voice, his heart lurched in his chest, ramming violently against his rib cage. "Right here," he whispered, squeezing her hand tight. "I'm right here."

But there was no response. She'd only been mumbling in her sleep, calling out from a dream, unaware he was there.

He settled back in the chair, slowly stroking her hand and giving his heart a chance to find its normal rhythm again. There would be time later to talk, to start the play-acting. For now, it was enough to sit there, to watch her chest rise and fall with life and to know she was all right.

She stirred. Her head shifted back and forth on the pillows, and her nose twitched. Before Coop could react, before his heart could beat or his pulse jump, he found himself looking into her sleepy blue eyes.

"Coop?" she murmured, her voice barely a whisper.

"Hi, babe," he said, reaching out and running a finger along her cheek.

Babe. He'd forgotten he used to call her that.

"Oh, Coop," she whispered, her voice trembling with emotion. She reached up, slipping a hand around his finger, and her eyes glistened bright with tears. "Coop, tell me it's really you, tell me I'm not just dreaming again."

"It's me," he whispered, watching as his fingers naturally interlocked with hers. Seeing the emotion in her sweet face, hearing it in her voice had tears smarting in his eyes.

"Oh, Coop." She reached out, pulling on his sleeve and causing him to shift from the chair to the side of the bed. "I'm so glad you're here."

"I'm glad, too," he whispered, finding it a little unsettling how easy it was to slip into the role of her husband. "You gave me quite a scare."

"Oh, Coop." She sighed, pulling him close. "I love you so much."

Her declaration had been as honest as it had been sudden, and it made him feel sick inside. If her doctors had thought the mere sight of him would jolt her memory into place, they'd been sorely mistaken. This was a woman in love with her husband, and she had no qualms about telling him so.

"Kelsey," he said, feeling more like a traitor than a friend trying to help. She looked so soft, so vulnerable, and the lie felt so ugly inside him.

"Hold me, Coop," she murmured, brushing her lips against his. "Hold me tight."

"Kelsey," he mumbled again, his pulse throbbing hard and fierce in his neck. She was so close he could feel the softness of her breath along his cheek. He felt himself catapulted back in time, to when she was his wife and the most natural thing in the world had been to comfort and to hold her.

"I missed you so much," she murmured against his mouth. "I love you."

Almost instinctively, he found himself responding as she pushed her mouth to his. The kiss was warm and sweet—almost chaste, but it sent a jolt of emotion through him that had every nerve in his body reacting.

"God, Kelsey," he said with a raw voice. Her lips were warm and wet, and the taste of her moved through his system like a rocket to the heart. He had agreed to pretend, agreed to go through the motions of being a devoted husband again, but a part of him had never let go, a part of him had never been able to sever the bond they once had shared. "I...I love you, too."

He kissed her this time—a long, tender kiss fraught with all the emotion churning around inside him. He'd known the charade would be difficult, but he realized now it was not for the reasons he thought. Playing the part of her husband was surprisingly easy. The hard part was remembering he was acting.

"Let me look at you," she said finally, pushing him away. She surveyed his face carefully.

Coop felt every muscle in his body grow tense as she cupped his cheeks with her hands and slowly perused his face. Would she notice something different? Would she realize he didn't look quite the same?

"You look exhausted," she murmured, her thumbs brushing the tender area beneath his eyes. "I'll bet you haven't slept in days."

Coop released a long sigh, his body relaxing. "It's been a while," he admitted. "But you're the one who needs rest." He settled her against the pillows again. "Go back to sleep."

"I don't want to sleep, all I do is sleep," she murmured. "Besides, I don't want you disappearing on me again."

"I'm not going anywhere," he promised, brushing her hair from her face. "You're stuck with me."

She breathed out a sigh, smiling at him. "And I feel better already."

Coop closed his eyes, drawing in a shaky breath. He felt dazed, as if reality had taken a holiday and left him scrambling. "Good. Now tell me how you *really* feel."

Her smile stiffened a little. She really didn't want to tell him her head throbbed and the ache in her leg was slowly driving her crazy. "I'm fine," she lied. "Really. Especially now that you're here." Uncomfortable, she changed the subject. "Tell me, how did they finally track you down?"

Coop sat up. "Track me down?"

"Yeah, I told Dad if Doris didn't know where to find you, no one would know."

"Oh, right," Coop said with a nod. "I got tied up with the rescue teams out on the rigs. They took some big hits during the storm. Things were a real mess for a while. I, uh, didn't have a chance to check in."

Kelsey laid her head against the pillows and stared at the ceiling. "Oh, right, the storm."

Coop saw the tiny line between her brows deepen. He remembered that tiny line. It had always been a sure sign something was bothering her.

"It kind of shut everything down for a while," he explained, doing what he could to keep his tone conversational. "Communications have been a real problem. I came as soon as I heard."

She turned her head, giving him a sad smile, making the tiny line deepen. "You knew I'd be waiting."

He nodded, giving her hand a gentle squeeze. "Yeah, I knew."

Her smile slowly faded. "Have you had a chance to talk to the doctor?"

Coop nodded. "I talked with Dr. Cohen before I came in."

"He told you, then?" she asked hesitantly, glancing away. "About the memory loss? How mixed up I get?"

She didn't have to tell him how frightened she was—it was there in her eyes and in her voice. He found himself leaning close, gathering both her hands in his. "We talked about it, yes."

"You know, it's nothing to worry about," she said, struggling to sound convincing. "This sort of thing happens all the time." She pulled against his hold and struggled to sit up. "I'm going to be all right, though. Dr. Cohen said I would, so you don't have to worry. I'm going to get better and remember."

"Hold on, hold on," Coop insisted in a soft voice, hearing the panic in her voice. He guided her head carefully onto the pillows. "What Dr. Cohen said was that you needed rest. We can talk about all this in the morning. Right now, I want you to close your eyes and get some sleep. You look exhausted."

Kelsey sank back, her eyes filling with tears. She was exhausted—her small burst of energy was gone, and suddenly she felt drained and weak.

"I...I hate this," she confessed, her bottom lip quivering. "I hate feeling useless and weak all the time."

He leaned down and gathered her close. "You're not useless, and you're weak because you need rest. Give yourself some time, give yourself a chance to get your strength back."

She was quiet for a long time, but Coop could feel the

tension in her body, felt the force with which she held him. She was terrified, and struggling desperately against it.

"You know," he whispered, responding as a husband comforting his wife, "we're going to get through this. It's going to be all right."

"But, Coop, it's…it's so awful." Like water bursting through a levee break, she collapsed against his shoulder and allowed herself to cry for the first time since she woke up and discovered her whole world had changed. "I—I get so scared, so mixed up. Some things don't seem to make sense. There are details I can't remember. I feel so alone, so scared." She clutched at the worn leather of his flight jacket. "What am I so afraid of?"

It seemed natural to hold her, to stroke her long, silky hair from her face and to soothe her with soft words in her ear. She needed support, needed reassurance, needed soft, soothing words. It didn't matter at the moment what was real and what wasn't. What mattered was that she needed comfort, and he could give it to her.

"You're frightened because you're tired," he whispered, feeling her body tremble beneath him and wanting nothing more than to take away the fear. "You need to go to sleep, and I promise you will feel better in the morning." His arms tightened around her. "We're going to get through this, I promise. I'm right here with you, and everything's going to be all right now."

Gradually, bit by bit, the trembling stopped. He could feel her body relax, could feel the tension slip from her muscles.

"Don't leave me, Coop," she mumbled sleepily against his shoulder. "Don't leave me alone."

"I won't."

"Promise?"

He hesitated for only an instant. "I promise."

She was quiet for a long time—so long he began to think she'd fallen asleep. Suddenly she lifted her head.

"Don't tell anyone, promise me?" she pleaded. "Dad, or the family—don't tell them I cried, that I was afraid."

Coop smiled, stroking her long hair. It was so like her to be worried about everyone but herself, for her to be the little mommy again.

"It'll be our secret," he whispered, emotion making it difficult to get the words out.

She drifted to sleep then, her body growing limp and relaxed in his arms. He didn't want to think too hard about how natural it felt to soothe and comfort her—not now, with the darkness surrounding them and her sleeping so peacefully in his arms. He couldn't afford to, couldn't risk reflecting on why there had never been another woman, why he hadn't remarried and started a new life with someone else. This wasn't the time for him to speculate on how he could live in a separate world from hers, lead a separate life and yet still feel a bond.

He'd given his word, had promised to do what he could to help her get better. There would be time later to debate the wisdom of that decision, to argue the pros and cons, to contemplate his misgivings. Right now he was content to be where he was—holding her, giving her comfort where he could.

He sat in the darkness, listening to her steady, even breathing and the quiet purr of the monitors around the bed. She might have been the one suffering from amnesia, but he was discovering there were gaps in his memory, as well. He'd forgotten what it was like to feel needed by her. He'd forgotten he could bring her comfort and solace by his mere presence.

She stirred against him, murmuring his name in her

sleep. It had been a long time since he'd held her, since they'd touched and kissed and behaved like a married couple.

His hand paused as he stroked her hair. Except they weren't a married couple any longer, and it was important he remind himself of that. He was going through the motions, doing and saying the things he had to in order to keep up the pretense, to prevent reality from crashing down on her and destroying any chance she would have of getting better.

He shifted, feeling the hard metal frame of the bed cutting into his back. He suddenly felt restless and uneasy. He didn't want to think about what would happen when she regained her memory, didn't want to think about what her reaction to him might be. How would she feel when that door in her brain finally opened, when the memories came flooding back? Would she think of this night? Would she remember how he'd held her and kissed her and acted out a lie?

She murmured his name again, and he pressed a gentle kiss into her satiny hair, whispering soft, soothing words. Would she be willing to listen, would she appreciate and understand? Or would she want him out of her life forever—again.

"It's no big deal."

"No big deal?" Kelsey folded her arms across her chest and gave him a killing look. "You tell me I sold my Bug and I don't have even the vaguest recollection of any of it. You don't call that a big deal?"

Coop slowly lowered his coffee cup to the narrow table that separated them, wishing there was some way to start the morning all over again. He'd stayed in her room until she was soundly asleep, then joined Mo in the waiting room where they'd spent the night talking and trying to get some sleep. Just before dawn, after Mo had left for home to get a quick shower and shave, he'd returned to Kelsey's room to be there when she woke up and to share a breakfast tray.

It was obvious she was feeling better. Her color was good, and she looked rested and beautiful as they sat on the bed together and talked. Things had been going fine until the subject of her VW came up.

He still remembered when the men from the junkyard had arrived to tow the thing away—Kelsey had cried all morning. She'd had the car since college and had stubbornly refused to let him replace it. When the car finally gave out about six months before the divorce, he'd almost been grateful. He'd hoped the new luxury car he'd bought her to replace it would boost her sagging spirits, maybe start some good feelings between them—but it had been too late.

"I didn't mean it that way," he insisted, pushing the table to one side.

"No?" she said stiffly. "Then how did you mean it?"

"I just meant I don't think you should let it upset you."

"Well, it does upset me. I loved that car. How could I have just sold my car and not even remember?"

"You didn't just sell it," he insisted. "It was old, it died. We had to replace it—there was no other choice."

She knew she was overreacting, knew she was making too much of it, but she couldn't seem to help herself. "Maybe it could have been fixed."

The feeling of déjà vu was hard to ignore. He'd had this conversation before. "Kelsey," he said in a carefully controlled voice. "It wouldn't run, it couldn't be fixed. There was nothing else to do but tow it to the junkyard."

The moment the words were out, he regretted them.

"The junkyard?" She gasped. "I sold my Bug for junk?"

He scooted closer. She was so upset, so agitated, and it made him feel helpless and awkward. This had happened so long ago, it felt strange rehashing it now. He had to keep reminding himself the past was her present, that what he'd had two years to come to terms with was all new to her.

"If it's any consolation, it was my idea," he said, pushing a strand of hair from her forehead. She tried hard to mask her fear with anger, but it was there in her eyes— the same fear he'd seen last night—and it touched at something deep in him. "You didn't want to do it."

She looked at him, feeling like an emotional wreck and hating it. "I don't even remember. How could I not remember something like that?"

A hard knot of emotion twisted tight against his heart. There was so much she had to remember, so much she would have to face and learn to deal with all over again.

"The doctor said there would be gaps. He told us both to expect them," he reminded her, pulling her arms loose from across her chest and gathering a soft hand in his. "This just happens to be one of them."

"*One* of them?" she snapped, struggling to pull her hand free. She didn't want to be comforted, didn't want to be treated with kid gloves. She wanted out of the bed and out of the hospital. "You make it sound like I forgot to jot something down on my shopping list. Coop, huge portions of my life are gone, and damn it, I want them back. *I want them back.*"

"I know you do," he said, ignoring her protests. "I do, too. But getting angry and upset isn't going to bring them back."

"No? Then what, Coop? Tell me, what will make me remember? Tell me and I'll do it—I'll do anything."

As elusive as her memories were, his were flying at him with breakneck speed. He remembered her temper, her flashes of anger and how she could come out fighting when she felt herself backed into a corner. It was part of what had made them such a good balance for one another—her fire a complement to his steady, more sedate disposition.

"Filling in the blanks," he said, bringing her hand slowly to his lips and pressing a soft kiss on each fingertip.

"You make it sound so easy." She sighed.

The brilliant flash of anger had died as quickly as it had flared, and the fear was once more evident in her eyes.

"What's so hard?" he asked simply. "We come across something you've forgotten, I'll fill in the blanks—and I'll keep filling in the blanks until you know everything." It shouldn't have pleased him so much to see the tension slip from her body, but it did. It made him feel better knowing he could comfort her, that he could make a difference in how she felt. It made the deception more palatable somehow, made it seem less like lying and more like helping. "And one of these days, we're going to fill in a blank, and it's going to bring all of it back."

She looked at him with such large, hopeful eyes, it made him want to believe, too.

"You think so?"

"I really do," he said, wishing he felt as confident as he sounded.

Kelsey slumped against her pillows, giving his hand a squeeze. "I've been such a pain. I'm sorry."

"Stop it," he insisted. The thought of her apologizing to him made him uncomfortable. He quickly released her hand, reaching for the table and sliding it in place. "What have you got to be sorry for?"

"For brooding about everything," she said with a tired sigh. "For fussing and whining like a baby."

Coop picked up her fork from the breakfast tray and handed it to her. "Well, you have been kind of whiny," he conceded, hoping to tease her out of the mood.

"No, I mean it," she insisted, taking the fork from him and dropping it on the tray next to her plate. "You're tired, and you've been through a rough time yourself, and yet you rush up here to be with me—and what do I do? First I cry all over you like some kind of emotional basket case, and then I bite your head off."

"Yeah," Coop agreed, grabbing a slice of toast from the tray and taking a bite. Crying had always embarrassed her. To a little girl who had convinced herself at the age of eight that she had to be strong for the sake of everyone else, tears were a cardinal no-no, a sure sign of weakness. "You know, now that I think about it, you have been kind of a pain in the neck." He took another bite of toast. "I take it back. *You* should apologize. I mean, you'd think you were flat on your back in a hospital or something."

Kelsey laughed at his teasing, giving him a playful swat over the table. "You're not supposed to agree with me."

Coop popped the last of the toast into his mouth and gave her an innocent look. "No?"

"No. You're supposed to object and tell me I'm all wrong, that I've been nothing but charming and could never be a pain in the neck."

He considered this. "In other words, you want me to lie to you, is that it?"

In a move that seemed to defy her impaired condition, she reached across the table and grabbed his shirt, pulling him toward her. "Actually, I just want you."

Coop looked into her clear blue eyes and swallowed hard. Suddenly everything had changed. The light banter, the teasing, the easy conversation were gone, and the border between past and present blurred. "Is—is that right?"

"Yeah, that's right. And when it comes right down to it, what are a few gaps, a few blank spots? I remember you, that's all that's important. The rest is mere details." She pushed her mouth to his in a kiss that was as passionate as it was sudden. "Coop," she whispered against his lips. "Let's make love."

Chapter 4

Emotion tightened thick and hot in Coop's throat, and he experienced one moment of sheer, absolute, unadulterated panic.

This wasn't what they'd agreed on, wasn't part of the bargain he had made with Mo and Dr. Cohen. It was a far cry from helping a sick friend. This was real-life husband and wife material, too personal and too intimate for playacting.

There was such love in her eyes—*real* love—and it tore at his soul. He had to look away, knowing one day she was going to wake up and remember the love she was feeling didn't exist any longer. Holding her in the darkness had been one thing, but it was daylight now, and there were no dark corners to hide his feelings.

"H-here?" he stammered, feeling a little like he did when he was fifteen and the college coed who lived across the street had invited him in for a soda. "In a hospital bed?"

Kelsey laughed, arching a brow. "We've done it in a lot stranger places than this."

Coop closed his eyes, not even wanting to think about that right now. "Yeah, but not with you recuperating from major injuries."

"Worried I won't be able to keep up?" she asked with a small laugh, brushing her lips against his.

His mind scrambled, like a computer sorting through a million bytes of information, searching for a reasonable explanation, some kind of believable excuse.

"You're not very nice to tempt me like this—especially since I can't accept," he said, but nerves robbed his words of any teasing affect, leaving him feeling awkward and embarrassed. Clearing his throat, he pulled away a little. "But you're going to be out of commission for a while, I'm afraid. Doctor's orders."

Her smile faded. "Dr. Cohen said that?"

"Yeah, last night," he lied.

Kelsey's blue eyes narrowed. "What else did Dr. Cohen say that you haven't told me?"

He looked at her, startled. "Nothing."

"Cooper, is there something you're not telling me?"

There were a million things he wasn't telling her, and guilt beamed across his face like the beacon of a lighthouse. In a feeble effort to distract her, he picked up the fork and offered it to her again.

"Why would you say something like that?"

"Because of that—" she knocked his hand away and gestured to his face "—that look on your face."

"Look?" he asked, awareness causing his already stiff expression to become even more rigid. "What look?"

"*That* look," she said, gesturing again. "That hand-in-the-cookie-jar look." She leaned forward and grabbed him by the arm. "What are you keeping from me, Coop?

Did the doctors tell you something? Is there something I don't know? Because if there is, I want you to tell me. I want to know—right now.''

Coop tossed the fork on the tray and drew in a deep breath. In the four years they'd been married, he'd never lied to her—not ever, not once. Yet he'd been back in her life less than twelve hours, and the lies and half-truths were piling up faster than he could count. He could tell himself he was just trying to do the right thing, but it didn't make it any easier. A lie was still a lie, no matter how noble the cause.

He looked at her across the narrow table, seeing the tension in her shoulders, the anger in her eyes, and seeing past all that. As much as he hated the lies, as much as he hated avoiding the truth, he would do whatever it took to give her back her life. The void in her past terrified her, and he knew she'd never have a true moment of peace until she'd gotten her memory back—no matter how painful it was.

He reached across the table, slipped a finger beneath her chin and tilted her head to look at him. ''If there was something else, I'd tell you,'' he said in an uncompromising voice, ignoring the cold, empty feeling in the pit of his stomach. ''If I seem awkward or uncomfortable, it's just because...'' He paused, letting his thumb trace the outline of her lips, searching for the words. ''I nearly lost you,'' he whispered, not having to lie about the emotion that suddenly swelled in his heart. ''I don't want to do anything to put you at risk again, and if that means we have to wait before we can...well, you know, before we *can,* then I want to wait.''

She looked at him, slipped a hand around his wrist and released a heavy sigh of relief. ''I'm sorry,'' she moaned, shaking her head. ''I...I don't know what's the matter with me. It's just that ever since the coma, things have felt so…so different. It's made me suspicious of everything. I'm really sorry.''

It seemed only natural to lean down and brush her cheek with a kiss, something a husband would do for his wife. Still, having her apologize to him made the empty feeling in his stomach even worse. In an effort to assuage his guilt, he fell back to teasing, hoping to lighten the mood.

''If you don't stop apologizing, I'm going to be the one getting suspicious,'' he joked, reaching down and picking up her fork. Pushing it into her hand, he pointed at the tray. ''Now finish your breakfast, or I'll take my chopper and go home.''

Kelsey smiled, taking the fork. ''Home. God, I can't wait to get home.'' She scooped up a forkful of eggs and popped it into her mouth. ''Did I happen to mention I hate being stuck here?''

''Once or twice,'' he said dryly. He sipped at his coffee and watched her while she chatted and ate. It wasn't even nine yet, but he was already exhausted. It had been one hell of a morning— a roller coaster of emotion.

He would have to be a lot more careful if he was going to avoid the kinds of mistakes he'd made this morning. He still wasn't exactly sure how the whole subject of her car had come up. She'd mentioned something about the helicopter, he'd mentioned something about the car, and before he knew it, they were knee-deep in an argument he'd had with her years before.

He finished the cup, set it on the tray and reached for the coffee carafe to pour them both more. He needed the caffeine, as much as he could get this morning, but what he really wanted was Dr. Cohen's head on a plate.

The good doctor had suggested he help Kelsey fill in

the blanks. He just hadn't mentioned how difficult it was going to be. Kelsey had been terribly upset to learn about her car, which only made him dread all the other things she would have to rediscover.

Still, the morning hadn't been a complete wash. He'd learned one very important thing—he was going to have to be a lot more careful or he was never going to be able to make it work.

"Cooper said you got a little upset this morning."

Kelsey glanced away from the window to the woman sitting in the chair beside the bed. She wasn't in the mood to talk, wasn't in the mood to lie there and do nothing, either, but she had little choice. "I wasn't upset."

Dr. Gloria Crowell paused as she wrote in the notebook on her lap, then peered at Kelsey over the top of her glasses. "Oh?"

Kelsey took a deep breath, hearing the skepticism in the doctor's voice and hating it. Hadn't she been poked and prodded enough for one day? "All right, all right, I got a little upset. What's the big deal?"

Dr. Crowell slowly closed the notebook and leaned back in the chair. "Would you like to tell me about it?"

"No."

"Why not?"

Kelsey groaned loudly and covered her face with her hands. "Psychiatrists. You people drive me nuts—*crazy.*"

"Is that right? A little like having a difficult patient?"

Kelsey stopped and peeked through her hands. "Okay, Doctor, point made."

"Good. So, why don't we talk about it—this morning, I mean. What got you so upset?"

"You mean other than the fact that I junked my car and couldn't remember doing it?"

"Think that would do it?"

Kelsey turned and glared at the woman beside her. "Don't you?"

Dr. Crowell smiled. "I'm the shrink, remember? I'm the one who gets to answer questions with other questions."

Kelsey couldn't help smiling, too, liking the woman in spite of herself. "And you're so good at it."

"You think so?"

Kelsey rolled her eyes. "You know, if I wasn't crazy before, I would be, listening to you ask questions."

"Oh? Is that why you work so hard to avoid answering them?"

The smile on Kelsey's face faded. Maybe she didn't like her so much, after all. "I'm not avoiding anything."

"No?"

"No!" Kelsey insisted, turning away. The move was too quick, too careless, and it sent an arrow of pain shooting up her leg from somewhere beneath the cast. She fell back against the pillows and pounded the mattress with her fist. "Look, I know you had to drive up here from Santa Barbara, but couldn't we do this some other time? I told you yesterday I wasn't ready for this. I don't feel like talking." She turned her head. "I don't feel like having my psyche probed at the moment."

"Sure," Dr. Crowell said, making no move to leave. "We can do this any time you want. Just have the nurse give me a call. I thought since I was here and—"

"And I was so upset?" Kelsey snapped sarcastically.

Dr. Crowell leaned forward in the chair. "You seem a little upset now."

Tears stung Kelsey's eyes. She impatiently blinked them away. "Okay, maybe I am upset, but why does everyone keep making such a big deal about it? Why can't all of you just leave me alone?'' The tears became too much, despite her efforts to push them aside, and they streamed down her cheeks. ''I feel lousy, I'm snapping everyone's head off, and I can't stop crying. Why can't I stop crying? Ever since I woke up from that stupid coma, I want to cry.''

''And that's a problem?''

She shook her head. ''You don't understand. I don't cry. I never cry.'' She turned and looked at the doctor again. ''Never.''

''Maybe you need to now,'' Dr. Crowell pointed out simply. ''Why not just let yourself go, get it all out?''

Kelsey lifted her head off the pillows and glared at the woman. ''Because that's not what I do. I don't cry.'' She sniffed loudly, swiping at the tears on her cheek. ''It's just that everything is so…so *different* now.''

''Different? From what?''

Kelsey steeled herself, trying to will away the emotion, will away the fear. ''From before.''

''Before the accident?''

Kelsey pounded her fist against the mattress again. ''Yes, before the accident, before I woke up and found out I couldn't remember everything, that huge parts of my life were missing.''

''So that's what you want. The way things were before?''

Kelsey looked at the psychiatrist, feeling herself start to tremble. She felt like screaming at the woman, felt like ordering her out of her room and out of her life, and yet a part of her wanted to run sobbing into her arms.

''I—I don't know what I want, Dr. Crowell,'' she confessed, weary of trying to put up a front, of pretending nothing was wrong. ''I don't know what's the matter with me. Nothing seems right anymore, nothing makes sense—

nothing except Coop. Being with him is the only thing that feels real. No one else realizes what it's like, no one else understands there is this big hole in my life—this big, black, ugly hole that—that..."

Dr. Crowell waited, watching Kelsey struggle. A trained eye wasn't needed to see the words were difficult for her and the emotions almost impossible. "It frightens you, doesn't it?"

Kelsey felt the fear like an entity within her, and her bottom lip trembled. "It scares me to death."

"I'd like to try to understand," Dr. Crowell said, leaning forward in the chair and slipping a hand over Kelsey's. "I think I can help, if you'd let me."

Kelsey turned to her. "How?"

"Talk to me," she said, leaning back in the chair again. "Tell me what it was like, your life before the accident."

Kelsey looked at the woman who had come so highly recommended, the specialist all her doctors had said would help her get her memories back. She was a rather formidable-looking individual, with her short-cropped hair and wire-rimmed glasses—not the kind of person with broad, motherly shoulders to cry on. Still, there was something about the woman Kelsey found herself responding to, something that made her want to open up and talk.

She wasn't sure where it all came from—the words, the emotions—but before she knew what was happening, they were pouring out of her like sand through an hourglass. For the next hour and a half she talked about her childhood, her brothers and sisters, the loss of her mother. She talked about nursing and helping people, and about the bad dreams she'd been having. And she talked about Coop—a lot about Coop.

It would take her a while to decide what kind of an expert Gloria Crowell was on memory loss, but when it came to listening, the woman was a master. By the time the doctor had finished making the last of her notations in the tablet on her lap, Kelsey felt drained of energy— and eons better.

"For someone who didn't feel like talking, I guess I did pretty good," she said with a wry laugh. The smile faded from her lips. "Look, Dr. Crowell, about earlier...I was in a bad mood and —"

The doctor stopped her with a hand on the arm. "Hey, no explanations needed." She bent, opened her briefcase beside the chair and slipped the notebook inside. "Besides, I've got a pretty tough hide—and there's nothing I like better than a challenge." She slid a glance at Kelsey and winked. "And I want you to notice I didn't say a tough nut to crack!"

Kelsey laughed, appreciating the joke, but as she watched Gloria pack up her case, her laughter died and she nervously began to twist the end of the sheet between her fingers. "So? What do you think?"

"About?"

"About me," Kelsey said with a nervous laugh. "Is it hopeless? Am I crazy—a tough nut to crack? Or do you think I'll get my memories back?"

Dr. Crowell straightened, running a hand through her short hair. "You want them back?"

"More questions." Kelsey groaned, rolling her eyes. "For once, please, just a straight answer. What do you think?"

The doctor zipped her briefcase closed and stood up, stepping close to the bed. "Kelsey, there are never any guarantees in my line of work, but if there's one thing I've learned in twenty years of psychiatry, it's that a person can do just about anything they want, if they want it bad enough. If you want to remember bad enough, you will—when the time's right, when you're ready.''

Kelsey breathed out a long sigh and smiled. ''Thanks, Doctor.''

She watched the doctor open the door and disappear down the hall. Then she reached for the buttons on the control panel mounted on the railing beside her and lowered the bed until she was lying flat. She stared at the ceiling, thinking about Dr. Crowell and the things they had talked about.

Actually she'd done most of the talking, but the doctor had been skillful in steering her in the direction she wanted. She wasn't sure if the session had done much about the amnesia—the gaping holes in her memory were still there. But she couldn't deny she felt better, and that counted for something.

She closed her eyes, feeling fatigue heavy on her lids, and let her thoughts drift to Coop. Having him with her was better than any pill or therapy session the doctors could offer. When they were together, it was as if nothing bad could ever happen. There was nothing they couldn't get through together.

Still, a sense of loss nagged at her. Something major was missing in her life, something hidden in those lost memories, and she had to get it back, had to remember.

She let herself drift toward the darkness, too weary to sort it out now. She surrendered to the warmth and the security of sleep, telling herself once she got her memories back, the sadness would go away, the sense of loss would disappear. In the meantime, she had her life and the man she loved—and that was all she needed.

''It's only been four days,'' Coop snapped, feeling his blood pressure start to climb like mercury in a thermometer. "You said she'd have to stay for at least a week, probably longer."

"I know what I said, and believe me, all of us here wish she would," Dr. Cohen insisted, gesturing to the other two doctors sitting at the conference table with them. "But you've talked to her, you know how she feels. She's doing great, and she is determined to go home."

"You're her doctors. Can't you insist? Tell her there are tests you need to run or something?" Coop pushed his chair away from the table and stood up. "For God's sake, make something up."

"The fact is, Mr. Reed," Vince Hamilton, the doctor of orthopedics, said, leaning forward and resting his elbows on the table, "we have no reason to keep her. And as a nurse, Kelsey's aware of that. There's nothing she's doing here that she couldn't be doing at home—bed rest, relaxation." He stopped and gestured to the woman sitting beside him. "It's not necessary that she be hospitalized to continue her sessions with Dr. Crowell, and as tending orthopedist, I can tell you she won't be ready for physical therapy on her leg until the cast comes off, and that won't happen for at least another five weeks."

Coop turned to Mo, who sat at the table with them. "You couldn't talk her out of this?"

Mo shook his head slowly. "You know what it's like trying to talk Kelsey out of something once her mind's made up—and believe me, she's got her mind made up to go home."

Coop ran a hand through his hair. He'd only returned to Santa Ynez this morning and wasn't ready for this. He'd flown the chopper back to Santa Barbara yesterday to tie up loose ends with Doris, make arrangements for another pilot to handle his flights while he was gone and check on things at his house. The break had felt good after three emotionally packed days. He'd arrived at the hospital this morning feeling refreshed and renewed—until now.

"Okay," he said after a moment, glaring across the table at the team of doctors. He was furious with them, and anger made him strike out, hate everything about this—the charade, the doctors, and most of all his part in it. "So have any of you brain surgeons thought about what we're suppose to do now?" He zeroed his gaze on Dr. Cohen. "Isn't it time to *reevaluate* treatment?"

"I was hoping we could do that now," Dr. Cohen said stiffly. He drew in a deep breath, pushing his glasses against the bridge of his nose. "And I don't think we're going to get anything accomplished hurling accusations back and forth."

"Hurling accusations." Coop snorted, shaking his head. "I love it. Anyone with the audacity to question your judgment is suddenly hurling accusations."

"I think we all need to pull together here," Dr. Cohen said. "For Kelsey's sake."

"Oh, yes, by all means, for Kelsey's sake," he scoffed. He leaned over the table toward the doctor. "It's easy looking out for Kelsey's interests as long as you're not the one in there lying to her, isn't it, Doc?"

"Mr. Reed," Dr. Cohen said in a reasonable voice. "The pretense hasn't been easy on any of us, but the fact is she's made remarkable headway. She's up and around much sooner than we'd expected. She's alert and gaining strength every day. Her physical progress has been nothing short of extraordinary."

"Except her physical progress isn't what we're lying to her about, is it?"

Mannie Cohen sat back in his chair, rubbing his eyes.

"Sit down, Cooper," he said in a tired voice. "Let's try and figure out where we go from here."

Pushing himself away from the table, Coop grabbed his chair and sank into it. He felt the eyes of the three doctors boring into him, scrutinizing and inspecting every move he made. He knew he was acting like a jerk, overreacting, spouting off, but he couldn't seem to help it. It hadn't been easy posing as Kelsey's husband, opening up the memories of what they'd once had and lost, making believe the last two years had never happened. Three days at her bedside had left him drained and exhausted. What was he suppose to do if they released her?

Dr. Cohen opened the chart in front of him. "Dr. Crowell," he said, swiveling his chair in her direction. "You've had a chance to speak with Kelsey a number of times in the past three days. Give us your thoughts on how she's progressing."

Gloria Crowell flipped open the notebook on the table in front of her and looked over her notes. "Well, I agree Kelsey's progress has been encouraging. She's stronger, certainly less fragile emotionally than she was during our first session." She paused, flipped the notebook closed and drew in a deep breath. "But I won't lie to you, she's got a ways to go."

"Physically or emotionally?" Mo asked.

Dr. Crowell shifted in her chair. "Of course, this is just my opinion, and Dr. Cohen and Dr. Hamilton might be in a better position to judge, but I don't see much right now that is going to interfere with Kelsey's physical recovery. You just have to look at her to see she is definitely on the mend as far as that goes. Emotionally, however, I think there are still some obstacles we have to get over."

"You make it sound as though she's emotionally unstable," Coop snapped angrily, tired of doctors and their theories. "I've been with the woman almost constantly in the last three days. Kelsey is one of the most stable people in this place."

"Oh, I agree. Believe me, I wouldn't characterize Kelsey's condition as unstable at all," Dr. Crowell insisted, overlooking his anger. "However, she is still quite sensitive emotionally."

"What would be your thoughts on making her aware of the situation?" Mannie Cohen asked. "Is she strong enough to handle it?"

Gloria Crowell leaned back in her chair, resting her elbows on the arms. "If you want to know if I think she can take the truth right now, I'd have to say, of course. We could all get up right now and walk into her room and tell her everything, and I would bet she would still continue to get stronger, and her leg would still continue to mend. But if you're asking me if we'd be doing her psyche any good—I'm afraid I'd have my doubts."

"But if she's better, and she's strong enough, doesn't she deserve to know?" Coop insisted.

Dr. Crowell shrugged. "Maybe we better decide right now exactly what it is we're aiming for. I mean, do we want Kelsey to *know* her past, or do we want her to *remember* it? There's a big difference."

Coop's frown deepened. "You make it sound like telling Kelsey the truth would prevent her from remembering at all."

Gloria Crowell leaned forward, choosing her words carefully. "My opinion is as it's always been—in the long run, I think it would be better for Kelsey to be allowed to remember on her own, and I think given enough time she will. As far as I'm concerned, simply sitting her down and reading off a list of things she doesn't remember would only add to her anxiety and wouldn't bring those memories back any faster. In fact, I think we run the risk of pushing them so deeply into her subconscious she might never be able to recover them.''

"Then what do we do?" Mo asked, sounding discouraged. "Go on pretending forever?"

"No, of course not," she said, resting an assuring hand on his arm. "And it's not a matter of forever. I'm just talking about giving her a real chance. It's only been a few days. We're just getting started here. It's going to take more than a few days to convince her it's okay to remember.''

"Okay to remember?" Coop shook his head and laughed sadly. "I'm sorry, Doc, that's sounding real close to psychobabble. Why wouldn't Kelsey feel it was *okay* to remember?"

Gloria Crowell had to smile. "Think of it this way, Mr. Reed. Selective amnesia is just that—*selective*. Patients tend to pick and choose what they don't want to remember. Most of the time they hang onto the good and block out the rest." She paused, her smile fading and her voice turning thoughtful. "Kelsey found a place in her past where she could feel safe. We all know her history, we all know what she's blocked out, and it's not difficult to understand why. It's how she survived the fear of being buried alive, how she survived the trauma of being trapped, of being severely injured. She went to a place in her mind where she felt safe and blocked out everything else. And it's my feeling she's not going to remember until she feels it's safe to do so."

Coop felt a dull throb start to pulsate at his temples. He would have liked nothing more than to stand up and start ranting again, to vent some of the frustration building in his chest and accuse them all of not knowing what they were talking about. Unfortunately, what Gloria Crowell said made sense. As painful as those memories would be for her, Kelsey deserved a chance to remember, a chance to feel whole again.

"So where does that leave us?" he asked, looking at each of the doctors facing him. "I take her home? Continue to act like we're married?" He tossed his hands up, giving them all a deliberate look. "I don't know about the rest of you, but I can see some obvious complications arising from a situation like that. Kelsey may have forgotten we're divorced, but I haven't."

Mannie Cohen leaned back in his chair, tapping a thoughtful finger along his lips. "Perhaps it wouldn't be as difficult as you think. After all, it wouldn't be as though you'd be assuming, uh, well..." He cleared his throat awkwardly. "I mean, she still has a lot of recuperating to do. She's going to need bed rest, special care that will limit her physical activity considerably."

"Not to mention that she has a heavy cast on her leg," Vince Hamilton added. "That could be reason enough for you to suggest sleeping in a guest room."

Coop listened as they discussed the possibilities, feeling tense and overwhelmed. How had things gotten so out of hand? How could they expect him to do this? It had been one thing to sit at her bedside, to hold her hand and share a meal tray with her. But to live together?

He thought of the house they had bought together, the house high in the hills overlooking Santa Barbara and the blue Pacific, the house they had shared as husband and wife. Stepping into a life that had been over for two long years seemed unthinkable. In the past three days, the lines between reality and fantasy, between marriage and divorce had blurred. They would be in danger of disappearing completely if he and Kelsey started living together.

"I want to help," he murmured after a moment. "I really do, I just don't know if I can—"

"No," Mo said firmly, cutting him off and slowly rising to his feet. "This isn't right, this isn't what we agreed on." He turned and looked at Coop. "I never meant for this to happen. When I asked for your help, I never dreamed it would go this far. It isn't fair to you, and it isn't fair to Kelsey." He turned to the three doctors. "I think we should tell her everything, tell her the truth."

Gloria Crowell's gaze darted from Mo to Coop, then back again. "Of course, it's up to you," she conceded reluctantly. "And I don't mind admitting I'm disappointed. I certainly understand your reluctance, and if it's your decision not to continue, I think we should go to Kelsey as soon as possible and—"

"No." Coop stood up, turning to Mo. "Look, Mo, I appreciate you giving me the option, I really do, but I can't let you do it."

"But, Coop, I can't ask you to—"

"You're not asking," Coop insisted. "It's my choice, my decision." He stopped, drawing in a deep breath, knowing he'd never really had a choice. He would never be able to live with himself if he walked out on her now. "Dr. Crowell is right. We're not talking forever, we're just talking about giving Kelsey a chance."

"Coop," Mo said, his tired eyes bright with tears. "I don't think you realize... I mean, after everything that happened, I don't think you know—"

"What I'm getting myself into?" Coop finished for him with a sad laugh. "I think I have a pretty good idea." He turned and faced his former father-in-law. "Mo, we're talking about Kelsey here, and giving her back her life.

There's no decision about it, it's what has to be done.''
He sat down, and gestured to the chair beside him. ''Now,
sit down and let's figure out how we're going to do this.''

Chapter 5

"There, how does that feel?"

Kelsey tested the seat belt and shoulder harness that anchored her in the seat. "Feels good."

"Sure they're not too tight?" Coop asked, wedging an extra pillow between the door panel and her cast. "Because I can loosen them a little."

Kelsey watched as he fidgeted over her, tucking and adjusting, moving the seat and repositioning her heavy cast. She stopped him with a hand on his shoulder. "I'm fine, really. Quit fussing."

Coop leaned back. He was fussing, too much, probably, but he was edgy and uneasy. It had taken a small miracle to prepare for her homecoming, but with the help of Mo and Kelsey's two sisters, they'd managed to get things done. Her clothes hung in the closet next to his, and her toothbrush was in his medicine cabinet. Yet despite their efforts, the house looked a far cry from the way it had when she'd lived there. She'd no doubt have questions, but he'd cross that bridge when they got to it.

"Sorry," he said, releasing a deep sigh. "Just want you to be comfortable."

"It's a twenty-five minute flight—thirty tops. I'll be fine," she insisted, settling in the seat. "I still don't know why you didn't just let me ride to Santa Barbara with you yesterday."

"I told you, because I wanted to fly you in the copter." He turned and gave the hard cast on her leg a small rap with his knuckles. "You wouldn't have been very comfortable in the car with this thing."

"I wanted out of this place so badly," she mumbled, peering at the towering hospital building, "I would have been willing to walk."

"Well, you're not going to be walking anywhere for a while," he said, taking a blanket and tossing it over her lap. "You're going to rest. Otherwise I'll haul your cute bottom right back here."

She laughed, reaching up and pushing his long hair from his forehead. "You'd have to catch me first."

He saw the sparkle in her eyes and felt emotion swell in his heart. He was almost used to being around her again, of her wanting to touch and tease and kiss him again—*almost*. "Feeling a little feisty this morning, are we?"

She started to laugh again, but something distracted her. As he watched, the smile on her lips faded, and her expression grew thoughtful.

"What is it?" he asked, wondering if a memory had been triggered, if something had come back.

"Your hair," she murmured absently.

"What about it?"

Her fingers drifted to his sideburn. "There's a little

gray in it.'' She lifted her gaze to his. ''In the sunlight, I can see it. You've got gray in your hair.''

He smiled, but the look in her eyes concerned him. ''How nice of you to point that out.''

''No,'' she said, ignoring the humor in his voice. ''I...I never noticed before.''

''Just be grateful it isn't stark white after the scare you gave me,'' he said dryly, hoping to coax her out of the somber mood.

But his teasing couldn't budge her. Instead, her hand went to her own hair. She pulled a long strand from behind her shoulder and examined it. ''Is there a mirror in here?''

''What are you doing?'' He knew exactly what she was doing. He gently pulled her hand away. ''You don't have any gray hair.''

''I want to look,'' she insisted, grabbing her hair again.

''Kelsey, stop,'' he said, taking her by the shoulders and giving her a shake. ''What is it? What's the matter? You're getting upset. Why?''

She looked at him, her eyes filled with emotion. ''I...I hadn't thought to notice before. I mean, I looked in the mirror this morning—I brushed my hair, brushed my teeth, but I didn't even pay attention. There are so many things I never paid any attention to before....''

Her voice drifted off, and she gave her head a shake. She was upset, and it had to stop. Time had passed, time she didn't remember. But that was hardly news to her now. She would remember someday, but until then she had to find a way to live with the gaps, to live with the little surprises she was bound to encounter. She had to stop breaking down at the slightest provocation, had to stop allowing emotion and fear to interrupt and interfere. This was a great day—she was going home! The memory loss had cost her enough already. She didn't want it to cost her the joy of this day, as well.

"Tell me," he prompted. "Why the sad face?"

"It's nothing," she insisted, pulling away just a little. She hated the fear that nibbled at the edge of her consciousness, hated feeling emotional and out of control. "It's just... It still throws me, I guess, coming face-to-face with something I've forgotten. I mean, it's been almost a week, you'd think I'd be used to it by now. Yet it still gets to me. There is part of my life—" She stopped, searching his face. "Parts of *our* life that are missing. A million little things. Like whether I have gray in my hair or not. Just little things that are gone, and it unnerves me when I come across them."

"You know, it's not going to be that way forever," he reminded her, all too aware of what it was going to cost them both when she finally did fill in all those blanks. "There's every reason to believe those memories will come back."

"Oh, I know," she said, running her palm along his cheek. "And I do believe that, I really do. It's just a little unnerving when you assume things are one way, and then you find out they're not that way at all. I just don't know what to expect anymore."

Coop felt her words like a blow. She believed they were married, and someday she was going to realize the truth. That realization was going to do more than unnerve her, and he just hoped he would be given a chance to explain.

"Maybe the best thing would be to try to take things as they come," he suggested.

"Like gray hair?"

He heard the teasing tone and sagged with relief. "You don't have gray hair," he stated flatly, slowly releasing his hold on her arm and helping her settle in the seat again. He didn't want to think about the risks that lay ahead. It was enough to get through one emotional hurdle at a time, and taking her to the house they'd once shared as man and wife was going to be a high one. "I'm the only one getting old around here."

"Well, that's a relief." Kelsey laughed, glancing down at the long strand of her hair lying across the front of her robe. "But when I get home I'm getting in front of the mirror and taking a good look—see if I really look the way I think I do."

He reached out suddenly, catching her chin in his hand. "If it means anything, I think you're more beautiful now than you've ever been."

The passion in his voice took her by surprise, and the smile slowly faded from her lips. "Coop," she murmured. "I love you."

"You two ready to go?"

They both looked up as Dr. Mannie Cohen came across the hospital helipad toward them, his white coat flapping against the wind.

"Just about," Coop said, stepping out of the passenger compartment of the helicopter as the doctor approached. "Just have to get the engine warmed up, then we'll be out of here."

Dr. Cohen nodded, turned to Kelsey and ducked his head inside the aircraft. "How are you feeling?"

"Like a million bucks," Kelsey said, smiling as she leaned forward to greet him. The move was a little too sudden, though, and sent a shooting pain down her leg, a not-so-subtle reminder of just how much recuperating she had left to do. She groaned, her smile cracking and slowly fading to a grimace. "Well, maybe a few dollars short of a million."

Dr. Cohen smiled. "So it isn't necessary for me to remind you to take it easy?"

"No," Kelsey said, rubbing the muscle along her thigh. "I think I get the message."

"You'll need these," he said, holding up the manila folder he carried in his hand. "They're your release papers. I wanted to bring them personally." He handed the folder to her. "You're officially sprung."

Kelsey looked at the papers, and then into Mannie Cohen's round, smooth face. "Thank you," she said, her throat tight with emotion. "You've been great—about everything. I really appreciate it."

"Thank me by taking care of yourself," he said, giving her arm a comforting pat. "And remember, bed rest for the first week, keep your activities at an absolute minimum, then just slow and easy after that. Got it?"

Kelsey smiled. "I've got it, I've got it."

"And I'll be monitoring your progress with Dr. Crowell, so if you don't keep your appointments, you'll have me to contend with."

"Anything but that," she teased dryly.

"Regular meals, plenty of sleep," he continued. "And I want you here in three weeks for a checkup."

"All right, all right," Kelsey said, rolling her eyes. "You know I got all this when we went over it the first time."

He arched a brow and gave her a deliberate look. "Yes, and we all know how quickly patients tend to forget the promises they make before being checked out."

"Don't worry," she assured him. "I won't forget." She glanced at Coop. "I've got too many people around to remind me."

Dr. Cohen followed her gaze. "Yeah, I guess you do." He turned to Kelsey. "He's a good man."

"I know," Kelsey mused, watching Coop as he walked around the helicopter, making small adjustments here and there. "Sometimes I think I've got to be the luckiest woman alive."

"And the other times?"

Kelsey looked at Dr. Cohen. "Other times, I know it."

Dr. Cohen leaned close, his hand covering hers, and he gave it a gentle squeeze. "Good luck, and promise you'll call me if you need anything. Promise?"

Kelsey covered his hand with her free one. "I promise. And thanks again."

Dr. Cohen walked to the front of the aircraft, where Coop stood waiting.

"She looks good," he commented. "You've been good for her."

Coop drew in a deep breath and shook his head. "Let's see if you feel the same way when you see her in three weeks. I'm not sure I can pull this thing off."

"Look," Dr. Cohen said hesitantly. He shifted his weight awkwardly from one foot to the other. "I don't pretend to know what went on with the two of you, what happened with the divorce and everything, but I've had time to watch you together, to see they way you are together—"

"You're right, Doc," Coop said, cutting him off. He didn't want to talk about what he had lost, what once had been there, but disappeared. "You don't know what happened."

"The kind of love I see in Kelsey's eyes when she looks at you isn't something that changes."

Coop's hands balled into fists and he walked several steps from the helicopter. "Damn it, Doc, don't do this," he said in a low voice. "I've got to walk away from this thing. She's going to remember, and everything's going to be back the way it was before the accident. Nothing's going to change.''

"Maybe," Dr. Cohen said thoughtfully, following him across the pavement. "But maybe something could come out of all this. Maybe the two of you..." He stopped, looking into Coop's angry eyes. "Maybe it's not too late for a second chance."

Coop stared at Mannie Cohen's full cheeks and round blue eyes. He didn't want to hear about what if or maybe. He'd had two years to think about what had happened and the choices he'd been forced to make.

The good doctor might mean well, but he hadn't been there. He hadn't seen the hope drain out of her and the love die in her eyes. She might have forgotten the past for a while, but there would be no going back. Soon they would be face-to-face with the truth—she no longer loved him.

"Look, Doc, I know you mean well, but I just don't see it happening for us again." He turned, faced him and extended a hand. "I, uh, I know I got hotheaded at times, said a lot of stupid things, but you saved her life, and I appreciate everything you did."

Dr. Cohen nodded, taking Coop's hand. "For what it's worth, I think you're doing the right thing—for Kelsey, I mean. Turning your life upside down, putting your feelings aside—it takes guts."

"Guts?" Coop laughed sadly, shaking his head. "I don't think so. You see, Doc, when it comes to Kelsey, I've always been a pushover."

Dr. Cohen nodded solemnly. He gave Kelsey a wave, turned and headed across the helipad toward the hospital. Coop watched for a moment, thinking about the flight to Santa Barbara and what the next few weeks would hold.

It was too dangerous to think this grand drama they

were acting out was anything more than a scheme, a program, a plan to enable Kelsey to get better. He couldn't afford to start fooling himself.

"He's a good doctor," Kelsey said as Coop stepped inside the helicopter and checked her harness again. "I was lucky."

"Yeah, well, I guess we all get lucky once in a while," he mumbled, securing the hatch on the overhead storage bin.

"I know we've worked together before," Kelsey mused thoughtfully. "I just wish I could remember where or when." She shook her head, then gave Coop a determined smile. "But I'll just take it as it comes. I'll remember when the time's right."

He glanced at her and smiled, too. "See? Now was that so hard?" He made another quick scan of the compartment, then looked at her again. "Things look okay in here. Ready to go?"

"What do you think?" She laughed, catching the edge of his leather jacket and pulling him close. "I seem to remember we were working pretty hard at starting a family when all this happened. We both wanted kids." She smiled, bringing her mouth to his for a gentle kiss. "I take it that hasn't changed."

The smile on Coop's face stiffened, and he felt the steady rhythm of his pulse stumble and become erratic. Some lies were harder to tell than others, and this was a killer.

"No," he whispered against her lips. "Wanting kids hasn't changed."

He let her lips find his again, but he took no joy in the tender kiss. Sadness and guilt weighed too heavily in his heart. He tried to tell himself he hadn't really lied, that the *desire* to have a child had never changed. But a sin of omission was a sin nonetheless. Someday she would know the truth again, would know a child of her own was just not in the cards.

"Take me home," she murmured.

He slowly nodded, stepped out of the passenger compartment and secured the hatch tight. He climbed into the pilot's seat and began flipping switches and pushing buttons. He pulled on the headset, then brought the huge turbines above them to life. They were going home—home to the house they had hoped to fill with children. The rooms sat empty now, dark, cold, and lifeless, like his hope for the future.

He signaled to Kelsey they were about to take off. She waved, smiling and excited, and for a moment he wished he could forget all those painful memories, too. Her eyes were alive with the promise of what could be. He felt old and tired with the knowledge of what was.

"Some redecorating?"

"Yeah," he said, shoving the key into the dead bolt lock and twisting it. "We, uh, started a while back."

"A while back?" she repeated in disbelief. "How far back?"

"I don't know," he mumbled vaguely as he pushed her wheelchair through the open doorway and into the tiled entry hall. "A while—I don't remember."

"You never mentioned anything about redecorating," she mumbled, peering through the foyer into the living room. This was not the house she remembered, not the home she and Coop had made for themselves. "My God," she gasped, her eyes growing wide. "Why...why didn't you say something?"

"I don't know," he said irritably. Defensiveness made him snap. The words had a hard edge. "I didn't think about it, I guess. I did have a few other things on my mind, you know.''

"You just assumed I'd remember?'' she snapped back, matching his sharp tone with sarcasm.

He closed his eyes, hating everything about the situation at that moment. They had never redecorated. It had been another lie, another excuse to pile on top of the ones he'd told her already. But he hadn't exactly been given much choice. He'd had to explain the empty house some way, and the truth wasn't exactly available to him at the moment.

"You're right,'' he said with a tired sigh. He set the brake on the wheelchair. "I should have said something. I guess I just wasn't thinking. I'm sorry.''

"No,'' Kelsey said quietly, covering his hand with hers. She drew in a deep breath and shook her head. "It's not your fault. It caught me by surprise, that's all, and I overreacted. Just something else I wasn't expecting.''

Coop quickly turned away, heading for the door. He didn't want to see the emotion in her eyes, didn't want to see the remorse or regret. He hated it even more when she put the blame on herself, when she apologized as though she was the one telling lies.

"I'll, uh, bring in the other stuff,'' he mumbled.

"The place is so…so empty,'' she said after a moment, glancing through the archway to the vacant formal dining room. She turned back just as he made his way inside with a heavy suitcase in one hand and a pair of crutches in the other. "What happened to all our stuff?''

"It's not empty,'' Coop insisted, as though saying it with force and conviction would somehow make it true. "We still have a lot of stuff.''

"We do?'' she asked skeptically.

"Sure we do—in the family room and the bedroom.''

He deposited everything inside, then closed the door behind him. "It's just the whole project is taking longer than we expected, you know, to get at the painting and papering."

"And all the other furniture?" she insisted, curiosity getting the best of her. "The couch, the sofa? And..." She turned and stared at the dining room again, then gasped loudly. "My mother's hutch! My God, Coop, where's my mother's hutch? Don't tell me I got rid of that. It was all I had of hers."

"The hutch," Coop said, remembering the cherry wood china closet Kelsey had cherished so much. "No, no, God, no. It's just...well, it's out..." His heart raced, leaving him light-headed. "Being...refinished."

"Refinished?"

Coop shot her a dubious look, uncertain she would buy the explanation. "Yeah."

"Well, thank God for that," Kelsey said, letting out a deep sigh. "The car was bad enough, but if I'd gotten rid of my mother's hutch, too—well, I really would have had to be crazy."

"Yeah, well," Coop said again. He felt almost giddy with relief. "You should know you'd never do anything like that. And you're not crazy."

"No?" she asked dryly. "Well, I'm glad one of us doesn't think so." She drew in a deep breath, gesturing to the empty rooms. "So, what about the rest of the stuff?"

"The rest," Coop repeated, his momentary burst of elation suddenly deflated. "Well, let's see...the rest of it. Uh, what we kept we put in storage." He released the brake, then pushed her down the hall toward the family room and bedrooms. "What we didn't we sold in a garage sale and will replace."

"Wow," she murmured, looking at the sparse furnishings. "This is really quite a project. Whose idea was it—yours or mine?"

"I don't know," Coop said, stopping at the counter that divided the family room and the spacious kitchen. "It was just sort of a mutual thing, I guess. You hungry?"

Kelsey shook her head. "No, as much as I hate to admit it, I'm actually feeling a little tired."

"No problem," he assured her, thinking that was about the best news he'd had all morning. Scrambling for excuses and explanations had left him exhausted, and he wouldn't mind some time alone to collect himself and get focused. He pushed the wheelchair into the hallway toward the master bedroom. "You take a nap, and I'll bring you a tray later."

"Hmm," she mused, turning and smiling at him. "You waiting on me. I think I could get to like this."

He pushed her past the bedrooms that sat empty, grateful he'd at least had the foresight to close the doors. She didn't need to know right now that those rooms would never be occupied by their children—and he didn't need any reminders of that right now, either.

"Here we go," he said, wheeling her through the open double doors of the bedroom suite. "All ready for you."

Kelsey leaned forward, her jaw dropping. "What's all this?"

"What's what?" Coop asked innocently as he quickly crossed the room, pulling open the drapes over the French doors to reveal a breathtaking view of Santa Barbara and the Pacific Ocean.

"*This,*" she said, pointing to the elaborate hospital bed in the middle of the room.

"The bed? What about it?"

She glared at him. "A *hospital* bed?"

"Dr. Hamilton recommended it," he offered meekly. "I, uh, I thought you'd be…happy."

"Where's our bed?"

He thought of the king-size white enameled iron bed they had shared during four years of marriage. Kelsey had left it when she'd moved out, and he'd given it away soon after that. He hardly could have offered her the lumpy futon he'd been sleeping on ever since.

"Oh, I, uh, moved it," he said evasively, making a vague gesture toward the garage.

"Then move it back," she insisted. "I want to sleep in my own bed—with you."

This was the moment he had been dreading, the moment that had kept him awake all night. Just how was he going to convince her they couldn't share a bed and make it sound not only believable, but plausible?

"This will be much better for you," he insisted, starting the speech he'd rehearsed a million times. He walked across the room and picked up the remote control device, moving the bed into various positions. "See how great it is? You can fall asleep looking out at the ocean." He pushed a few more buttons, elevating the foot of the bed. "I know how hard it is for you to get comfortable with that thing on your leg. This will be great for that. You'll rest much better in this than our old bed."

"It's so…so *ugly*."

Coop turned and gave her a stern look. "Of course it's ugly, it's a hospital bed. What did you expect?"

"I expected my own bed."

"Well, aesthetics aren't what I'm concerned about right now," he said. "I'm concerned about you being able to rest comfortably."

Kelsey watched as he turned to the controls and manipulated the bed. "Where will you sleep, then?"

Coop's hands froze. He could feel her eyes boring into his back, but he didn't dare turn around. She'd always been able to read his expression, and one look was all it would take.

"In one of the spare rooms," he said in a flat voice.

"What?"

Coop steeled himself, carefully schooling his expression, and turned. "Just for a while," he insisted. "What's the big deal?"

"The big deal is if I'd wanted to sleep alone in a hospital bed, I would have stayed in the hospital."

Coop tossed the remote control on the mattress. "Look," he said, walking to the wheelchair and kneeling in front of her. "You're exhausted. Let's talk about this later, okay?"

Kelsey closed her eyes. She was exhausted—exhausted, disappointed, confused and annoyed. And damn it, she felt like crying again.

"I just want my life back," she whispered, hating the tears in her eyes.

"I know," he said, slipping a hand under her chin. "And you'll have it back, too—just not in one day."

"You're right, I know," she said, leaning her head back and looking at him. "Was I always such a pill, or is this a new thing for me?"

He smiled, stood and wheeled her to the side of the bed, then gathered her in his arms. "To be as big a pain as you are, years of practice are necessary."

"Thanks a lot," she said, giving him a swat and smiling despite how lousy she felt. "Like I'd believe anything you said, anyway."

His smile threatened to crack just a little. If she only knew how fast and loose he'd played with the truth in the past several days.

He carefully settled her on the bed, adjusting the cast on the mattress. "How does that feel?"

"Okay, I guess," she admitted reluctantly, lying back against the pillow. Actually, it felt wonderful, and she wanted nothing more than to sink under the covers and sleep for about a week. "I still don't see why we have to sleep in separate rooms."

"It's just easier this way," he said as casually as he could. He wanted to move the conversation away from their sleeping arrangements. "We'll both rest better, and if you need anything…" He reached for the nightstand beside the bed. "Just ring."

Kelsey laughed when she saw the small brass bell he held up. "You'll be my butler?"

"Why not?" He laughed, handing her the bell. He lowered himself to the edge of the bed, tucking the covers around her. "I'm already your slave."

Kelsey reached over and ran a hand up his arm. "I really am sorry about all this. I guess I just expected too much. I thought if I was home, things would start to feel normal again."

"I know you hate hearing this, but it's—"

"I know, I know," she said with a tired laugh, cutting him off. "You don't have to say it. It's going to take time. I understand that." Her smile faded, and she raised her head. "I just get impatient, that's all. Impatient and frustrated."

"Well," he said in a soft voice. "If it's any consolation, I get impatient, too."

She settled against the pillows again. "I just want things to be the way they were, instead of all mixed up and confused."

"Things seem confusing now because you're exhausted," he whispered, catching her hand in his. "It's been a big morning for both of us. Why don't you try to get some rest? I'll check out the fridge and see what I can rustle us up for lunch.''

''Coop?'' she said when he moved to leave.

''Yeah?''

''I'm really glad to be home.''

Coop watched as she drifted to sleep, feeling his chest constrict. He envied the peace he saw in her face, the tranquillity that came with not remembering the pain and the sorrow of the past few years.

A safe place. That's what Gloria Crowell had said Kelsey had wanted—a safe place to hide from the pain and the fear.

He leaned down and kissed her gently on the cheek. She'd come back to him—for a while, anyway—because he made her feel safe, and as much as he wanted her to heal and get better, a part of him wished it could stay this way forever.

Chapter 6

"Finish it up."

Kelsey glanced at her half-eaten ravioli on the plate in front of her and shook her head. "I can't."

"You promised you'd clean your plate," Coop reminded her.

"I'm too stuffed."

His glared at her, his gaze narrowing. "You don't like my home cooking?"

She looked at him, imitating his expression.

"It's not going to work. These are Vince's ravioli, I'd recognize them anywhere."

He laughed. He should have known better than to try to fool her. The small Italian deli had been a favorite of theirs, and Kelsey had particularly loved the ravioli. "I heated them in the microwave, I put them on the plate. That classifies as home cooking."

"That classifies as take-out," she corrected, pushing the tray to the mattress. "And you put a mountain of them on that plate in the first place.'' She patted her abdomen. ''I ate so much it hurts.''

He smiled as he rose from his chair beside the bed and reached for the tray. He had given her a generous portion, and she'd done better than he'd expected.

''Dr. Cohen says you need to gain weight,'' he said, setting the tray on the nightstand.

''Well, I'm not going to do it in one night,'' she insisted, reaching for the remote control and adjusting the position of the bed. ''Besides, you mark my words. If I do put on a few pounds, Dr. Cohen will be after me to lose weight.'' She sank back against the pillows. ''It's a sick little joke doctors like—lulling you into a false sense of insecurity. They're never going to tell you you're fine. They're afraid it will put them out of business.''

''Want some more wine before I take these out?''

''Now *that*,'' she said with a broad smile, holding up her glass, ''I've got room for.''

He filled her glass. ''This will help you sleep.''

''Like I need help. All I do is sleep,'' she mumbled, taking the glass from him. ''I practically slept all day.''

''You needed the rest,'' he said, gathering the remaining dishes and stacking them on the tray. So had he. The day had been an emotional drain on them both—for different reasons. ''I'll take these out,'' he said, carefully lifting the tray. ''Want anything else before I leave?'' He nodded in the direction of the open French doors. ''Is it getting too cool?''

She shook her head. ''No, it's great.''

''You're warm enough? Want another blanket?''

''I'm fine,'' she insisted, lifting her wineglass. ''And this will help keep the chill off.''

''There's cheesecake in the fridge,'' he said as he started for the door.

Her eyes widened. "Vince's cheesecake?"

He glanced at her. "Want a piece?"

She thought for a minute, then shook her head. "I'm tempted, but I just can't right now. Maybe later."

"I'm going to clean up," he said, heading for the door. "Ring if you need anything, okay?"

"Okay," she said, watching as he disappeared around the corner.

She leaned back, gazing through the French doors to the panoramic view. It had turned dark, and the lights from the city glittered like jewels in a treasure box. The ocean had turned a dark gray, and a heavy fog rested just above the surface.

Kelsey sipped her wine and watched the fog make its slow journey toward the shore. It would soon move over the city, dimming the lights to a cryptic glow and making the world seem eerie and strange.

Her mind drifted, thinking of the nights she and Coop had lain together in their bed and watched the fog swallow up the world around them. It hadn't felt eerie to her then, it had felt cozy and safe—like the world had whittled down to just the two of them, and they were a million miles away from everyone else.

She heard the faint rattle of dishes in the distance and pictured Coop at work in the kitchen. This wasn't their bed, and he wasn't with her, but it still felt cozy and safe. She was home where she belonged, and just knowing he was close was enough.

He had been so sweet, so attentive today—waiting on her hand and foot, seeing to and anticipating her every need. She wished she could have handled things better, wished she'd been more thoughtful of his feelings.

First she'd made that idiotic comment about gray hair, then she'd reacted so badly about the redecorating thing.

Why couldn't she have just chilled out a little and not gotten so upset? Why had she made such an issue of everything?

She squeezed her eyes tight, trying not to think about how unbalanced and frightened those things had made her feel, trying to push aside the fear she couldn't explain. Maybe everyone was right. Maybe she was pushing too hard, expecting too much too soon. She thought she'd prepared herself for changes, thought she'd been ready for those things that were different. But knowing there would be changes and actually coming face-to-face with them had proved to be very different.

Kelsey opened her eyes, took another sip of wine and watched small halos begin to form around the lights as the fog drifted closer.

"Forward," she murmured before taking another drink of wine.

That's where she wanted to look—forward, because she didn't dare look back. There were too many holes there, too many blank spaces and glaring inconsistences for anything to make sense. If she had made some mistakes today, if she'd let things sneak up on her and take her by surprise, she'd do better tomorrow.

She finished her wine, feeling its warmth infiltrate her system, making her muscles relax and her lids grow heavy. This time the drowsiness felt good—a result of too much food and wine and darkness.

"Forward," she said again, feeling more content and relaxed than she had since the morning she'd awaken from the coma. "Take it as it comes, and look forward."

"Did you say something?"

She looked up as Coop walked through the door. "Not really."

"It's awfully dark in here," he said, gesturing to the

lone lamp burning on the nightstand. "Want me to turn on some lights?"

Kelsey shook her head. "It's nice in the dark. I've just been enjoying the view."

Coop peered through the open doors, then shot her a dubious look. "I think maybe you've been dreaming. There isn't a view tonight, it's too foggy."

Kelsey smiled, too relaxed to muster a laugh. The fog had indeed moved in, shrouding the sky and causing the lights, the city and the ocean to all but disappear. "So I'm enjoying the view of the fog."

"Whatever you say," he conceded, making a play of raising his brow in disbelief. He sat on the edge of the bed, serious now. "You do look sleepy, though. Why don't I close the doors, then if you drift off—"

She stopped him as he started to stand. "No, don't, please. I'm not tired—not really. It just feels good to lie here and relax." She slipped a hand around his arm. "It feels good to be home."

He started to settle on the bed, but moved again. "Then let me fix you a cup of tea. I got some herbal raspberry—"

"Coop, stop," she insisted, cutting him off. "I don't want a cup of tea. I don't want anything else to eat or drink." She tugged on the sleeve of his shirt, forcing him to sit on the bed. "I just want you to sit with me for a while." She scooted to one side. "Come on, there's room for both of us."

Coop gingerly lowered himself to the mattress. He'd hoped she would just drift off to sleep—no fuss, no muss. It would have made things so much easier for him.

"Come on," she urged, inching over a little more. "You can squeeze in."

Everything in him wanted to get up and start running,

as hard and as fast as he could—away from the narrow bed, away from the whole situation, and especially away from her. This was more than biting the bullet, this was torture—plain and simple.

He eased himself against the pillows, feeling stiff and clumsy. His feet dangled stubbornly over the side, forcing him into an awkward half-reclining, half-sitting position.

"I don't think this will be very comfortable for you," he mumbled, feeling anything but comfortable himself.

"It'll be fine," she assured him. "Scoot a little closer, come on."

He looked at her, aware of the mixture of emotions churning inside him—a witch's brew of feelings bubbling and boiling just below the surface. He was making too much of this, making it harder for himself than was necessary, but he couldn't seem to help it. This had once been their bedroom, and she had once been his wife. If they'd still been married, if the charade he was acting out had been truth, it would have been perfectly natural for them to share this quiet moment together.

Only it wasn't the truth, it was a lie. A noble lie, maybe, but a lie nonetheless. And because he knew, because he understood, it made the familiarity, the intimacy seem just plain wrong.

"Come on," she urged again, reaching for his arm and slipping it around her neck. "I'm not made of glass."

"I—I just don't want to hurt you," he lied. What he didn't want was to hurt himself. Except at the moment there was no way to protect himself, no way to hold her at arm's length.

"There," she murmured, as he slowly settled his weight against her. "I told you we would fit."

Fit. Coop slipped his arm around her, pillowed her head with his shoulder and pulled her close. Air seeped from his lungs in one long, slow sigh, and warily his body began to relax. They did fit—like pieces of a puzzle, their bodies molded together with ease and familiarity.

He thought of all the complaints he'd heard men make about marriage, about couples becoming too content with each other, too comfortable. But holding her in the darkness in the room they once had shared, he realized there was a lot to be said for comfort and contentment. There was something that felt so right about holding her. It was as though he really had stepped back in time, as though they really were still man and wife.

"Comfortable?"

Coop glanced into her upturned face. He wouldn't have used that exact adjective to describe how he was feeling at that moment, but surprisingly he found it would do. "Yeah. How about you?"

She smiled, hugging him close. "Very."

"You got enough room?" He lifted his head off the pillow, glancing at her cast. "Your leg feel okay?"

"Actually it feels pretty good." She rose just a little, shifting the heavy cast several inches back and forth beneath the covers. "See? I can move it now without that shooting pain up my side."

"Maybe you're just getting the hang of that thing," he suggested.

"I hope not," she said, looking at him. "I don't want the hang of it. I want it off as soon as possible. Then maybe I can get back to some seriously 'normal' living." She smiled at him, moving her body against his. "Having an anchor around my ankle sort of slows me down, if you know what I mean."

He knew she was teasing, but the boldness of her actions sent a shaft of desire rocketing through him. It nearly took his breath.

"Slow down, tiger," he said, struggling to keep his voice light and teasing. "One thing at a time."

"Party pooper," she said, giving him a quick peck on the cheek. Glancing over his shoulder to the nightstand, she nodded her head. "Okay, since you won't let me have any fun, grab the TV remote and let's see what's on the tube."

Coop reached for the remote and flipped on the small set in the armoire in the corner. The blank rectangle roared to life, flooding the room with sound and an eerie white glow.

Coop settled back and watched the images on the screen, but his mind was too crowded to concentrate on any of them. It was such a mundane act, lying there watching television together—something they had done countless times when they'd been married. He'd thought nothing of it then, but tonight it was having a profound effect on him.

As they surfed through the channels, catching bits and pieces of news broadcasts, entertainment magazines and sitcoms, he was aware of Kelsey beside him—aware of how her warmth had slowly mingled with his, how their breathing had become synchronized and even and how their bodies had molded together to fashion one form on the bed. It was as if they had created their own private cocoon, a place immune to everything else, even the passage of time.

"Hey, look, just like my car," Kelsey said, pointing to the commercial playing. She turned and looked at him. "You know, I remember when you first drove up out front and started honking. I was so shocked to see you sitting behind the wheel. I mean, I had no idea that you—"

She stopped suddenly and sat straight up.

"Kelsey, what is it? What's the matter?"

"My God," she gasped, covering her mouth with both hands. "Oh, my God, Coop."

"Kelsey," he said, sitting up. He grabbed her by the upper arms, the look on her face causing his heart to race wildly. "What is it?"

"Coop," she said, looking at him with wide, round eyes. "Coop—my car. My *car.* Not the Bug, the new one—it's a Volvo."

"I know it's a Volvo," he said, hearing the panic in his voice. "What about it?"

"I remember," she said in a whispery voice, her eyes bright with wonder. "Coop. My God, Coop, don't you see? I remembered!"

"It was just there," Kelsey said. She reached down, pushed on the wheel and turned the chair away from the window that overlooked the small tiled courtyard. She looked at Gloria Crowell, sitting in the large wing chair in the corner, and made a helpless gesture with her hands. "Just like that. I mean I was talking about it, picturing it in my head before I even realized I was remembering. I guess I don't know what I expected—sirens maybe, flashing lights. Maybe the earth moving. But it wasn't like that at all. It was just there, like it had never left. Just…*there.*"

"How'd that make you feel?"

Kelsey frowned and sighed heavily. "Could you forget the psychiatrist questions for just one minute and enjoy this with me?"

Dr. Crowell looked up from her notes and tossed the pencil she was holding over one shoulder. Kelsey's good-natured grappling and grousing had come to be an integral part of their sessions, and as a doctor, she was finding it a good barometer in judging those areas Kelsey found particularly troubling.

"Good idea," she said. She leaned back in her chair, smiling broadly. "Let's enjoy it. Tell me again."

Kelsey laughed and recounted everything she'd remembered—in detail—one more time. Despite the fact that she found her incessant questions irritating at times—and difficult to answer almost all the time—Kelsey had come to like Gloria Crowell very much. She almost looked forward to their weekly sessions, even though the idea of someone rummaging around her subconscious made her uneasy.

Yet she knew it was all part of her treatment, all part of her road to recovery. For reasons she still couldn't understand, she felt the need to resist, to shield and protect herself from those dark holes in her memory. However, Dr. Crowell seemed to understand her reluctance. She would push, but not too hard.

"You realize," Dr. Crowell said after Kelsey had finished the story again, "we've got our crack."

Kelsey's brow wrinkled. "Excuse me?"

"Our crack," the doctor repeated, coming forward in her chair. "In the door. You've cracked that door in your brain. You've started to remember." She opened a drawer in the end table next to her chair and pulled out another pencil. "Now all we have to do is get you to push it the rest of the way open. Sounds like being home has helped. What you do think?"

"Oh, yeah," Kelsey said, swiveling her wheelchair and staring into the courtyard again. She was thoughtful for a moment, staring out at the people milling about, ducking in and out of the other offices in the small professional complex. "I know everyone told me things would start to come back," she said after a while. "You, Dr. Cohen, Coop—you all kept telling me I just needed to give it some time, that I needed to be patient, that I'd get better."

She looked at the doctor behind the desk. "But you know, until now, I'm not sure I ever thought that could happen."

"Oh, it'll happen, Kelsey," Gloria assured her. "If you let it."

"Surprise."

"What the—" Coop jumped, his voice cracking at the sight of Kelsey standing beneath the arched entry of the breakfast nook, precariously balanced between two crutches. He scrambled to his feet, the bulky Sunday newspaper in his lap spilling to the floor, and rushed around the breakfast table toward her. "What the hell do you think you're doing?"

"I've decided to join you for breakfast," she said, smiling at the look of shocked surprise on his face. She took a few wobbly hops forward, clumsily moving the crutches. "I wanted to surprise you."

"You did that," he said dryly, carefully maneuvering her into one of the Windsor-style chairs at the table. "And you nearly gave me a heart attack in the process. What the hell are you doing up, anyway?"

"Saving my sanity," she said, sliding the crutches together and gingerly balancing them against the wall. "Another day in that bedroom and I would have gone stark, raving mad."

"Don't you think you're rushing things a little?" He pulled out a chair and helped her lift her cast to rest it on the seat. "The doctor didn't give his okay for this. He said bed rest."

"Bed rest, not prison," she said. "That's what the bedroom was beginning to feel like. I haven't done anything but rest since I got home, anyway. I deserve a break."

Coop shook his head. "Well, you should have called me. I would have helped you if you'd wanted to come out. I could make a bed for you on the sofa in the family room.''

"I don't want a bed on the sofa. I want to sit at the table like a real person," she said sweetly. "Besides, if I'd called you, it would have spoiled the surprise."

"Some surprise," he snorted, giving her a stern look. "What if you'd fallen? You could have hurt yourself, ended up in the hospital again."

"Oh, quit being such a spoilsport," she complained, making a face. "I didn't fall and I didn't get hurt. I'm fine. As a matter of fact—" she settled in the chair and smiled "—I feel great. Hand me some of that paper. You through with the funnies?" She stopped and blinked her eyes coyly. "I'll take a cup of coffee, too, if it's not too much trouble."

"I still don't know about this," Coop mumbled, snatching the newspaper from the floor. He slid it across the table toward her. "Cream and sugar?"

Kelsey glanced up from the paper, crinkling her nose. "You know just how I like it."

He snatched his empty mug off the table and walked into the kitchen. He took a clean mug from the cupboard and he reached for the coffee carafe, then poured her a mug and filled his own.

"Maybe you should call Dr. Cohen," he said, spooning two sugars into her cup.

"Mannie?" she asked absently, perusing the front section of the paper. "What for? I'll be seeing him next week, anyway."

He picked up the mugs and carried them into the nook. "I know, but you should check to see if it's all right for you to be up and about on those things." He pointed to the crutches. "Or at least call Dr. Hamilton."

She peered over the paper. "Why shouldn't it be all

right for me to use my crutches? It's what they gave them to me for.''

He sat down across from her. "They gave them to you to use when you're strong enough. I'm not sure you're strong enough. You promised you wouldn't push it."

"I'm fine," she insisted, lowering the paper a fraction. "I've been out of the hospital for two weeks, and I've been out of that bedroom exactly twice—and that was only to make my appointments with Dr. Crowell. I hardly think that could be considered pushing it."

"I wheel you on the patio in your chair," he reminded her.

She have him a dark look. "That hardly counts." She glanced at the crutches, gesturing with a nod. "Besides, I want to get the hang of those things. Then I'll be able to get around on my own steam and not have to be so dependent on you all the time."

"I want you to be dependent on me."

The words were out before he'd had a chance to stop them—not that he could have anyway. They were the truth. If he'd learned one thing in the two weeks since her release from the hospital, it was what it felt like to be needed again, to matter in someone's life, and he couldn't deny he'd missed it.

She smiled across the table at him. "You're sweet, but I know this can't be much fun for you." She rested her elbows on the table and leaned forward. "And I know what Mannie would say—he'd tell me to take it slow and easy, and that's exactly what I'm going to do. Slow and easy. Believe me, I don't want to do anything that would put me flat on my back again, either."

Coop let out a long sigh. She was like a little bird learning to fly, and there was nothing that was going to stop her. "You sure you feel strong enough?"

She leaned back in the chair, reaching for the paper again. "Well, if I do feel a little weak now, I'm sure it's nothing a little breakfast wouldn't cure."

Coop rolled his eyes. "If you'd stayed in bed, I'd have brought it to you."

She peered over the paper again. "You've got a thing for that little brass bell, don't you?"

He laughed, picked up his coffee mug and pushed himself away from the table. "Yeah, it makes me feel a little like your boy toy." He headed for the kitchen. "Omelet and toast all right with you?"

"With jalapeño peppers and salsa?" she asked hopefully, her eyes wide.

He cringed and shook his head. Her ability to eat fiery chilies and the spiciest of salsas never ceased to amaze him. "As long as I don't have to watch," he muttered. "How you can ruin perfectly good eggs with that stuff I'll never understand."

He set to work, pulling out eggs from the refrigerator and unhooking pans from the rack above the stove. He tried not to think about how much he'd missed their lazy Sunday mornings together—perusing the paper, lingering over breakfast. In the past fourteen days he'd been forced to remember a lot of things he really hadn't wanted to— things he missed, things he had lost.

It seemed hard to believe that two weeks had passed since her release from the hospital. The days had flown by in a blur of emotion and strain—difficult days despite their speed. He'd had to field telephone calls, explain away changes and answer about a million questions she had about one thing or another. And even though he'd all but turned over the day-to-day operation of Reed Helicopter Service to Doris and a substitute pilot, there were still things that had come up, things he'd had to see to personally. However, regardless of the physical and emotional strain of the past two weeks, he'd managed to survive—and that wasn't something he'd been sure he could do two weeks ago.

He glanced into the nook, watching as she scanned the newspaper, sipping her coffee. He shouldn't have been surprised to find her up and about on her own. Her progress had been nothing short of miraculous. Each day she seemed to improve and grow stronger. The bumps and bruises that had once marred her beautiful skin had healed and disappeared, and she no longer complained about the pain in her leg. Sunny afternoons on the patio had obliterated any trace of hospital pallor, leaving her skin with a rich, lush glow. She was not only getting better, she was thriving.

Yet even more amazing than the healing of her tangible wounds were the improvements to those injuries that were harder to see. Each day it was becoming more evident that she was remembering, that their elaborate charade was working. Her memory was coming back.

Coop thought back to that first night in her bed, her first night home from the hospital. Him driving her new car up the front drive hadn't exactly been a major event in their lives, but the mere fact that she'd remembered at all made it seem momentous.

Except recovering that one memory had been just the beginning. There had been other things since then—dozens of small, seemingly insignificant incidents that by themselves weren't pivotal, but when blended together painted a very clear picture that her mind was being stimulated and memories were coming back.

He cracked the eggs, dropped them into a bowl and whisked them together. It was only a matter of time, he knew that now. Just a matter of time before it all came back, before she remembered everything.

He poured the eggs into the pan, glancing at her. She looked up, giving him a smile and blowing him a kiss. He felt a pressure build around his rib cage, a tight band of tension that made it difficult to draw in a breath. Would she still be smiling at him when she remembered, when she learned the truth? Would she understand and accept before kicking him out of her life again?

Chapter 7

"It's remarkable, really," Mannie Cohen mused, scanning the chart in front of him. He looked up, slipped off his horn-rimmed glasses and turned to Coop. "Except I don't know why I'm surprised. Kelsey is a remarkable woman."

Coop nodded, gazing at the crowded parking lot of Community General Hospital. He wasn't thinking about Mannie Cohen and his reflections on Kelsey and her progress. Instead, he was remembering that night over a month ago when he'd first stood here and stared at the parking lot below. It had been almost deserted back then, not bustling with cars and people as it was now, but that wasn't the only thing that had changed in the past four weeks. His entire life had been transformed since then.

"And the reports from Dr. Crowell seem to be just as encouraging," Dr. Cohen continued. He flipped the chart closed, tossing it on his desk and sitting up. "No doubt about it, she's remembering more and more."

"Yeah," Coop mumbled. "More and more."

He watched a young mother with two small children in tow and an infant in her arms make her way across the lot, carefully herding the children through the parked cars. He admired the careful, nurturing way she protected her children, despite the fact her arms were filled with the baby she was holding. Kelsey would have been that kind of mother. She would have protected her children no matter what the situation.

He turned from the window, feeling an ache in his chest. Except there would be no children for Kelsey, and one day soon she was going to remember that.

"How are things going between the two of you?"

Coop looked up, shrugging casually. "Okay—given the situation." He pushed himself away from the window and walked to the desk. "Of course that was with her stuck in bed most of the time. All that's changing pretty quick." He sat in the chair opposite the doctor. "Who knows what it's going to be like with her up and around more. She's already talking about getting rid of the hospital bed."

Dr. Cohen picked up a pencil, and wove it absently between his fingers. "For what it's worth, I advised her it would be a good idea to hold off on any...*activity* for a while longer."

"Activity?" Coop laughed, shaking his head. "And what do you advise for me, Doc?"

Dr. Cohen dropped the pencil and leaned back in his seat. Resting his elbows on the arms of the chair, he tented his fingers together, peering at Coop over the top.

"Something you want to talk about, Coop?"

Coop snorted, leaning against the hard back of the chair. "I thought you were an internist, Doc, not a shrink."

"I don't have to be a shrink to see you've got something eating at you."

"You mean other than the fact that I'm living with my ex-wife and pretending the last two years of our lives never happened?"

"Is that it? Is that what's got you tied up in knots?"

"You don't think that's enough?"

Mannie Cohen smiled. "I think maybe you're more worried about her getting her memory back than a little subterfuge, am I right?"

"A little subterfuge?" Coop laughed—a harsh, mocking sound. "Oh, that's good. Is that a little like saying World War Two was a small altercation?"

"Not really," Dr. Cohen replied, unaffected by Coop's jeering laughter. "And you haven't answered my question."

Coop's smile faded. "If you think I don't want Kelsey to get better—then no, you're not right."

"Oh, I don't have a doubt you want Kelsey to get better," Dr. Cohen insisted, pausing for a moment. "I'm just not so sure you're anxious for her to remember."

"You think I should be?" Coop charged, coming forward in his chair. "Do you have any idea how she's going to feel when she remembers, when she realizes we've been lying to her all this time?"

"It also means she won't be your wife, and the two of you won't be playing house any longer."

Anger flashed red-hot, and Coop was on his feet in a heartbeat. "What the hell is that supposed to mean?"

"It means I think it's time you started being honest with yourself."

Coop glared into Mannie Cohen's face, hating him at that moment. He wanted to crawl across the desk and grab the guy by the throat and deny everything. Only it wouldn't do any good. Mannie Cohen had seen right through him, and there was no argument he could make, no denial he could offer in the face of the truth.

"If it had been my call," Coop said, the anger dying in his veins, "there would be no need to pretend. We would still be married—she'd still be my wife." He rubbed a tired hand over his eyes and looked at the doctor. "How's that for honesty?"

"I suspected as much," Mannie Cohen replied. "You're still in love with her."

Coop felt the doctor's words penetrate to the very core of his soul, that deep, dark place where he'd stowed all those forbidden feelings the divorce decree declared he didn't feel any longer.

He laughed, feeling more tired and weary than he did after seventy-two hours in the air. "Is it that obvious?"

Dr. Cohen shrugged. "If you're looking—and I have been for a while." He hesitated, tapping the pencil against his palm. "You know, you're not the only man who wanted a woman he couldn't have." He paused again, his voice lowering. "It happens to the best of us—even out-of-shape bald guys like me."

Coop looked at the man behind the desk, feeling a little as though he was seeing him for the first time. A moment ago he'd hated the doctor with his platitudes and medical double-talk, and would have liked nothing more than to vent a little of his well-deserved anger and frustration against the good doctor's square jaw. Now he felt a kinship, an alliance that stemmed from understanding—man to man.

"I'm living with the woman, Doc," Coop said. "I'm with her day and night." He drew in a shaky breath, relieved to talk about what he hadn't been able to talk about to anyone else. "I know the score, I know this isn't real—

nothing she says to me is real. I know that just because she doesn't remember we're not married any longer it doesn't mean I've been given the green light to take her to bed." He ran a hand through his shaggy hair and shook his head. "I'm not interested in taking advantage of her. It's just...damn, I'm not made of stone, either."

Mannie Cohen reached for the pencil that had rolled down the length of the desk blotter and rested against the leather-trimmed edge. "If it's any consolation, there's a good chance it won't be much longer. Everything points to her making a full recovery. I believe she will remember everything."

"Yeah." Coop slowly walked to the window and stared out. "And once she remembers, she'll want me gone again."

"You don't know that."

Coop turned and looked at him. "You forget, Doc, I've been through this before." He paused, growing thoughtful. "It's just a matter of time. I know it, I accept it."

"Do you?"

He laughed. "What choice do I have?"

"Maybe not any," Dr. Cohen conceded, jabbing the pencil onto the blotter and snapping the lead. "But things are different now. A lot has happened in the past two years. You've both had time to think, to be alone, and...feelings can change."

"That's just it," Coop said, walking to the desk. "Her feelings did change. It's what broke us up two years ago and it's what will break us up again." He extended a hand over the desk. "Look, Doc, I appreciate the try, I really do. But it's over."

"What is it?"
"A walking cast."

Coop frowned, staring at the narrow blue cast that covered her foot and calf. "It looks like a boot."

"It's supposed to," she said, turning it from side to side to give him a better view. "So you can walk on it."

Coop moved her jacket from across his lap to the vinyl cushion beside him. He slowly rose to his feet. His frown deepened. "It looks so small."

Kelsey looked at him and grinned. "I know, isn't it great?" She took a few quick steps with her crutches. "And see how much better? It's so light compared to the other one."

"Yeah," he muttered, watching as she made her way across the narrow waiting area off the corridor outside Vince Hamilton's office. "I can see that."

"I almost feel like I could run in it. Let's see."

"Kelsey!"

She giggled at his reaction, stopping him with a hand on his chest. "Calm down, calm down, I'm just kidding. No running, I promise." She took a step closer. "Not yet, anyway."

He looked at her. Even in the glaring white light of the hospital corridor that made the healthiest people look sick, she looked great, the very picture of life and vitality. Her blue eyes were clear and sparkled with excitement, and her long, golden hair shone with platinum highlights.

He reached out, brushing his fingers along her cheek. Her skin felt like satin against his hand and glowed warm and rich like honey. He heard Mannie Cohen's words in his head, words that were like a clock ticking in his brain. *It won't be much longer. Everything points to a full recovery. She'll remember everything…*

"Kelsey," he murmured, slipping his free hand around her waist and pulling her close. He wanted to hold on to the moment, wanted to stretch it and pull at it, make it last forever. "Kelsey."

Something in his expression, in his voice, the intensity in his eyes made the smile on her face fade. "Coop, what is it?"

He brought his mouth to hers. "Tell me," he whispered against her lips. "Tell me you're mine. Let me hear the words. Tell me you're mine."

"Yes," she said, her breath coming in quick, short pants. "Yes, yours. Always yours."

Coop closed his eyes. "Mine," he growled, crushing his mouth against hers. "Remember that."

The kiss was hard and fierce and filled with all the turbulence inside him. He wanted her to remember, wanted her to mark the moment in her heart and not forget when the memories came back. He wanted her to know what she had felt, what it was they had together before she sent him away again.

"I love you, Coop," she whispered, looking at him.

And at that moment, he could see the love in her eyes. She had loved him once, deeply and completely, the way he had loved her. Love had been in her heart and in her soul before it had deteriorated and disappeared.

Pain twisted in his chest. He'd spent two years thinking about it, two years trying to find a reason things had happened the way they did. If only she could have turned to him. If only she'd taken his comfort and strength. But she hadn't. Instead, she'd allowed the pain and the bitterness to ravage her love, to destroy everything they'd had.

He pulled away from her, squeezing his eyes shut. Looking at her was like looking through a window into the past. She had loved him. How could feelings just disappear? Were pain and disappointment powerful enough to destroy love? Even after two years, he still didn't know. Where did love go when it died?

"Coop?"

Coop jumped, startled, and opened his eyes. "Yeah?"

"What is it? What's the matter?"

He saw the concern in her eyes, and the ache in his heart intensified. "Nothing. Everything's fine."

"You look upset."

"Me?" He shook his head, feeling embarrassed. "No, I'm fine."

"Are you sure?" she asked, lifting her hand to his cheek. "If it's that crack I made about running, I wasn't serious—"

"No," he said, cutting her off by pressing a kiss into her palm. "No, it's…it's not that." He looked at her. If only he could tell her. If only he could explain the clutch of emotion that gripped him like a vise—the regret, the sorrow, the sadness of what they had lost—but he couldn't. There was no way he could make her understand all the feelings in his heart without telling her everything—and she would know everything soon enough. "I'm…I'm just glad you're here with me now—right now."

"I'm glad, too," she murmured.

He saw the line between her brows deepen, and drew in a deep breath. He had to lighten things up and push aside the memories. It was too dangerous getting her suspicious, and he was far too vulnerable.

"What say we get out of here?" he asked, plastering a smile on his face and sweeping his emotions aside like dust under a rug.

"No, wait a minute," she said, stopping him with a hand on his sleeve. "I wish you'd talk to me."

"About what?"

"I'm worried about you."

"Me? What for?" He leaned close, lowering his voice. "I'm not the one who had a building fall down on me, remember?"

Kelsey's frown deepened. "What was all that about?"

"All what?" He walked to the elevator and punched the button.

"Damn it, Coop," she said, coming straight at him and backing him against the wall. "Don't play dumb with me. What happened back there?"

The elevator door opened, but they both ignored it. After a moment, the door slid closed, leaving the hall silent and empty.

"I kissed you," he said, but his voice sounded defensive and guarded even to his own ears. "What's the big deal? A man can't kiss his wife anymore?"

"That wasn't just a kiss."

"No?"

"No."

Coop stared at her. He wanted to joke, wanted to play dumb and mock her concern, but it would do no good. She would see through the act as easily as she'd seen through his joking denials.

"Okay," he said after a moment, pushing away from her. "Okay, maybe it just scares me a little, that's all. Maybe it bothers me when I think about losing you."

"You haven't lost me," she whispered, slipping a hand on his arm. "And you never will."

Coop steeled himself against the truth. Just hearing her say the words meant something, even though he knew they weren't true. She believed them, and for now, that was enough.

"Come on," she said, smiling at him and pressing the button again. "Let's go home."

"Yeah, home," he mumbled absently, turning at the sound of the elevator door sliding open. He reached out to help her, but she stopped him.

"No," she said, shaking her head. "I can do it myself."

He gave her a tired smile, stepping to one side and making a gallant sweeping gesture with his hands. "After you, madame."

"You see," she said, taking a few wobbly steps forward. "I've been thinking."

"Oh?" he said dryly, following behind her.

There were several people in the elevator, and as she moved forward, they all stepped back, giving her a wide berth.

"Yeah," she continued, making her way inside the elevator. Despite the new cast, it took considerable effort to maneuver in the cramped enclosure. "You've been the one doing all the work the last few weeks—taking care of me."

"I'm not complaining."

"I know," she said, smiling at him as the door slid closed. Leaning close, she lowered her voice. "I think it's time I started taking care of you a little, too."

Coop felt a lump of emotion form in his throat. "You just concentrate on getting better."

"I am better," she insisted, with a boastful shrug. "I'm up, I'm around and..." She wiggled her crutches. "And these things are a piece of cake."

Just then the elevator jostled slowly to a stop. The movement was leisurely, but enough to throw her off balance. To catch herself, she shifted her left crutch. Unfortunately, instead of the smooth tile of the elevator's floor, she planted the rubber end of the crutch squarely on the toe of the orderly standing beside her.

"I'm terribly sorry," she said, turning quickly.

However, the move made her more unstable. Flustered, she quickly tried to compensate, shifting directions and moving back, only to slap the older gentleman to her left on the backside with the end of her other crutch.

"Oh—oh, my," she gasped, seeing his shocked expression. "I am so sorry. Please, excuse me. I'm very sorry."

Coop watched, trying hard not to let the laughter that bubbled just below the surface escape.

"A piece of cake, huh?" he said, offering her a steady arm out of the elevator.

"Just remember," she warned, seeing his bemused expression and shooting him a killing look. "I've got a crutch in my hand, and I know how to use it."

Kelsey hobbled closer to the living room window, peering out through the darkness to the car that had just pulled into the drive across the street. She knew the couple who emerged from the minivan with their two young children were her neighbors. She knew because Coop had told her, not because she remembered.

She watched as the family made their way up the walk, the little boy running ahead playfully while his baby sister rested a sleepy head on her father's shoulder as he carried her to the house.

Kelsey searched for something familiar about the picture playing out before her, and the people in it, something that would trigger a memory, bring some recognition, but there was nothing. As hard as she tried, she couldn't seem to force the memories, couldn't demand recall. Like it or not, the people disappearing into the house were strangers to her.

"Get used to it," she mumbled in the darkness, closing

her eyes and rubbing them. But she knew she never would. She'd never get used to the black holes and the blank spots, never accept the empty cavities in her past that made strangers out of neighbors.

She opened her eyes, turned from the window and stared at the blackness of the barren living room. There was a lot she would never get used to—like living in a house she had loved, a home she remembered and wondering why it felt so different to her now.

Her eyes followed the stark expanse of carpet that spread unchecked and unused through the room. What could have ever possessed her to get rid of all their things? What had she been thinking?

She thought of the things she'd recovered, the small bits and pieces of the past that were slowly coming back. Someday she would remember, and everything would make sense again. She believed that, trusted it was going to happen. Her memory was coming back, and when it did all the questions would be answered, all the holes filled in, and the blank spots wouldn't frighten her ever again.

She turned to the window, watching the family inside the house across the street, seeing mother, father and children moving from room to room. She thought of her own house, one empty room after another. The empty rooms bothered her, bothered her the way the empty spaces in her memory did. She wanted all those empty spaces in her life filled in—wanted to fill them with hope, and happiness, and love.

In the distance she heard the sound of the shower, heard the water running, and she felt herself smiling.

Coop. She loved him for so many reasons, but it had been his strength and his caring that had sustained her in the weeks since the accident. It was his love that kept her sane, that kept her focused on the future so the fears from the past didn't take hold. He made her want to look ahead, made her want to think of the life they had in front of them rather than concentrating on a past she had yet to discover.

She caught a glimpse of movement from across the street and watched as the crazy shadows of father and child danced wildly over a closed drape. She thought of Coop, imagining what a wonderful father he would make. How many times had they dreamed the dream together, talking about the family they would have and the things they would do as parents?

As she watched the figures moving along the window, the smile slowly faded from her lips. Starting a family had been at the top of their agenda before the accident. If she hadn't gotten hurt, she might have been pregnant by now, might have been carrying Coop's child inside her at this moment.

She wanted it to happen, didn't want anything else to get in their way of starting a family. She couldn't remember the last time she'd taken a birth control pill—memory loss or no memory loss. It was just a matter of time.

She glanced at the cast on her leg. Unfortunately, there was just one small hitch. Mannie Cohen had been properly tactful and delicate, but his message had come in loud and clear—she should put any "marital activities" on hold for a while longer. He'd told her in no uncertain terms that she needed to give herself a chance to heal completely, and not risk her recovery by adding any extra stress to her life.

Kelsey had almost laughed at that. She'd never thought of her love life as stressful, exactly, but she knew Dr. Cohen was simply being cautious. She'd also been a nurse long enough to know that the link between mind and body wasn't something to be ignored. She was getting better—she was remembering more and more every day, and Dr. Hamilton had said there was a possibility she would have the cast off her leg completely in as early as a couple of weeks.

She thought of Coop and the hospital bed he'd had delivered to their room. She might have been the one injured, the one who had the broken bones and the scrapes and bruises, but the accident had been a difficult ordeal for him, as well.

She knew better than most people how difficult it was to sit on the sidelines while the person you loved was in danger. Coop's missions as a SEAL had often been hazardous, and she had laid awake more than one night wondering if he would return to her alive and in one piece. She understood his need for caution. She knew his desire to follow the doctor's orders to the letter came out of his fear and concern for her safety.

She listened to the water running, picturing him standing beneath the hot, steamy spray. His care and consideration during the past weeks had been sweet and endearing, a true act of love. He'd been careful not to push or press her to do more than she should. But nights alone on a lumpy futon two rooms away were beginning to take their toll on him.

She remembered the look in his eyes today in the hospital corridor and couldn't deny it pleased her that he found it difficult to keep his distance. She knew his secret now, understood his frustration—because despite his caution and concern, despite doctors' orders and his best intentions, he wanted her. She could see it in his eyes, on his face, in every move that he made.

She turned from the window and started through the living room toward the hall. Her crutches were silent on the plush carpet, and she moved through the darkness like a woman with a mission.

She did have a mission. She was going to have her life back, going to restore her past, heal her body and grab at the future. It might be too early to be thinking about throwing away crutches and removing casts, about making babies and planning a family, but she was still a woman, still a wife, and she could show her husband how much she loved him.

Chapter 8

Coop let the water wash over him, the fine spray stinging hot against his skin. It had been a long day—long and emotionally draining. He'd realized today he was still in love with his ex-wife. He'd not only admitted that to himself for the first time, but to Mannie Cohen, as well.

It had been a gut-wrenching realization because he knew how hopeless it was.

He raised his face to the water, wishing he could wash away the heavy layer of sorrow from his soul as easily as he could the day's dirt and grime from his skin. Except nothing was going to purge him of that particular affliction, not even time. He'd had two years to get her out of his system, to forget and go on with his life, only it hadn't been long enough.

The only thing he'd accomplished in the past two years had been to fool himself into going through the motions, dupe himself into putting up a front and pretending he didn't care. But it had been just a front, a ruse, like pretending to be her husband now. The cold, hard fact remained that he did care, he was still in love with Kelsey, and it didn't matter if he had two years or twenty, that was never going to change.

He reached for the soap, rubbing it between his palms until a rich lather formed. He felt bone weary, the kind of deep-down energy-depleting weariness that happens when the heart and the soul are strained to the limit.

Mannie Cohen's prediction that Kelsey would recover her memory soon was little consolation at the moment—not when the night stretched out in front of him like a long, lonely road. He needed strength to finish the job he'd started, to stick it out until she had recovered completely. But the way he felt right now, he wasn't sure from where he was going to summon that kind of energy.

She believed them to be man and wife, believed them to be in love and committed to building a life together. And sometimes, when they were together, when she would look into his eyes and talk about children and a family, he found himself wanting to believe, too. If only he could wipe out the last two years—erase them from his mind and start all over again. If only he could look down the road of his future and see her in it. But that would be wishing on a star, and he had stopped wishing when the love had faded from her eyes.

He spread the lather over his chest, its crisp scent mingling with the steam and filling the shower with a fragrant, misty cloud of mint. He breathed deep, not wanting to think about the heavy scene he'd pulled in the hospital corridor today, not wanting to think what an awkward situation he'd created.

It had been stupid to want her to declare her devotion—stupid and sophomoric. The kind of stunt an insecure kid would pull in school with his first steady girlfriend. Except that's the way he'd felt just then—like a vulnerable, defenseless, insecure kid. The words she had said, the emotion with which she had said them would mean nothing when her memory returned. They were as fleeting and ineffectual as their charade now.

And yet, for some reason, for some pathetic, inane, ridiculous reason, he'd needed to hear her say the words—despite how temporary, despite how untrue they would soon prove to be.

He closed his eyes again, stepped beneath the spray and let it wash the soap from his skin. He wished he could just shut off his mind, wished he could go to sleep and not lay in the darkness and think about how empty and barren his life would be without her. He didn't want to think about her alone in that ridiculous bed he'd had delivered, that bed he'd hoped would act like a shield, warning him off, that bed in which she slept each night alone.

He turned the faucet. The water instantly crashed cold against his skin. He needed it cold, as cold and as icy as he could get it to cool the heat gnawing at his insides. Dr. Cohen had cautioned Kelsey against sex in an effort to dissuade her from doing something he knew she would later regret. Only Dr. Cohen should have cautioned *him*, should have issued him the warning, because he was finding it more and more difficult to stay away from her.

She was the woman he loved, and for the moment, she loved him, too. She was the woman he had married, the woman he would spend his whole life wanting. She looked at him with the eyes of a wife—with love and passion and need. She touched him with the ease and the intimacy of a lover. In her mind he was her husband, her lover, but he was saddled with the truth—and truth placed the burden of restraint squarely on his shoulders.

The icy water did little to dull the ache in him. It just

battered against him, drowning his spirits and making the night ahead seem that much longer.

Maybe that was why he didn't hear the door open, why he didn't hear the footsteps cross the tiled floor. It was only when the shower curtain was moved slowly to one side, and he felt the rush of air against his wet skin, that he realized she was standing there.

"K-Kelsey," he stammered, his voice sounding hoarse and thick. "What are you—"

"Your towel," she murmured, cutting him off. She lifted the plush terry towel she held in one hand, and with the other she reached inside the stall and turned the water off. "I'll help you dry off."

She wasn't smiling. There was nothing playful or co-quettish in her demeanor, no teasing or kidding around. Her beautiful face was rigid and intense, and her eyes moved over him with a raw, salacious look. He wasn't thinking about modesty, about what should or shouldn't be done. He wasn't concerned about his nakedness or making any moves to dissuade her. He was too over-whelmed at the sight of her, too caught up in his reaction to make sense of anything else.

Her hands were on him, dragging the towel up his arms, over his chest, around his shoulders. Her touch was bold and uninhibited, and he felt coherent thought abandon his brain like the beads of water flowing down the shower wall.

Despite the freezing water that had drenched his body only moments before, he was burning up. Her slow, de-liberate movements had every nerve in his body alive and quivering. This wasn't supposed to be happening, wasn't part of the plan. This was real life—a wife with her hus-band, spontaneous and genuine. He had no idea how he was supposed to act. What was he supposed to do? How could he respond as a husband when he knew the truth?

"I've missed you," she murmured, dropping the towel as her hands moved over his body. Her arms linked around his waist and pulled him close, forcing him to step from the stall. Pressing her body close, she brought her lips to his. "Missed being with you like this."

"Kelsey," he whispered, his voice raspy and dry. The thin, wispy silk of her nightgown hid nothing, and he could feel every soft curve, every swell of her beautiful body. Her hands were massaging circles along his bottom, and his thoughts became scattered and confused. He wasn't sure any longer what was real and what was make-believe, what was the truth and what he'd made up.

However, one fact remained clear amid the clouds of confusion in his brain. One reality cut through the darkness like a beacon through the fog. Forever and for always, this was the woman he loved, the woman he would want until his last dying breath. Regardless of divorce papers and legal decrees, Kelsey Chandler Reed was his wife.

"Kelsey, please," he whispered, his words sounding more like a plea. The sweet scent of her hair was mingling with the crispy mint of the shower and creating a seductive aroma of desire and need. "W-we can't. We shouldn't."

She brushed her lips against his—a feathery kiss that barely made contact. "We won't." She pressed another light kiss against his lips. "That doesn't mean we can't touch." One hand slipped between them, and she found him hard and waiting. "That doesn't mean we can't be close."

Coop closed his eyes at the surge of raw pleasure that radiated from her touch and sent a spear of fire soaring through him. Close. It was a laughable way to describe what was happening to him at that moment. His legs began to tremble, and his lungs felt depleted and in need of air. The trembling in his legs spread to the rest of his body and made it difficult for him to speak. Somehow his hands found their way to her waist, and then up her sides and to her breasts. "Kelsey, I—"

The blaze within him exploded into a fire storm, consuming everything in its path, and he caught her up in his arms. Her mouth against his was soft and sweet, and he devoured her lips with a kiss as hungry and brutal as the need within him.

He'd kissed her many times in the weeks since the accident. It had made it difficult to keep perspective, had often played havoc with his emotions and with his peace of mind, but it had also been part and parcel of his role as her husband. But this kiss was different. This was a man kissing a woman, a husband kissing his wife, a need that threatened to rage out of control.

Kelsey surrendered to the kiss, surrendered to the passion and the need. His hands were wild on her, pressing her close—touching and caressing until she felt weak with desire. He'd been so careful since the accident, so reserved and restrained, handling her with kid gloves as though she would break. She had appreciated his care, understood his reserve, but she wanted the gloves off now, wanted to feel his fire and his passion, wanted to feel like his woman again.

"Coop," she whispered, as he pressed hot, wet kisses along her neck and shoulder. "Oh, Coop, I want you so much."

His breath came in deep, heavy pants, making coherent thought difficult. With a strength that rivaled Atlas, he swept her up in his arms, mindless of the cast on her leg.

Desire burned so hot and so potent in his veins, he could easily have moved the heavens to have her.

He wasn't aware of moving, of passing through the bath and into the hallway to what had been their room. He was only aware of her lips moving on his and the feel of her soft, supple body against his own. It didn't matter that the hospital bed was narrow, or that her walking cast grazed the metal railings. She was moving beneath him, her delicate breath sounding like a soft chant in his ear, and that was all that was important.

"Kelsey," he whispered in a harsh, raspy voice. In his whole life he never thought it could be like this again, never dared dream she would ever be in his arms again. "If...if we don't stop soon, I...I won't be able to."

"Coop," she murmured, her voice breathless and weak. She knew what she'd promised herself, knew what she'd vowed, but she hadn't expected to feel like this, hadn't expected to be so hungry. "I want you. I don't want to stop."

Catching the hem of her gown, he slowly inched it upward. He wanted nothing between them—not even a thin barrier of silk.

"Kelsey," he groaned, moonlight through the windows making her skin look as smooth and as flawless as the delicate silk that moved over it. "My Kelsey, my wife—"

The quiet warble of the telephone was as startling in the stillness of the house as an air-raid siren blasting into the night. Coop was thrown back to reality so fast, his heart almost stopped in his chest.

For a moment he could do nothing. He felt dazed and confused, as though he'd just been awakened from a dream.

He looked at Kelsey, seeing the soft, exquisite look of longing in her eyes, and truth hit him in the face with the force of a Mac truck. He hadn't been dreaming. He'd been about to screw up—big-time. There was no excuse he could offer, no justification for what he'd almost done. He started to reach for the phone.

"No," she moaned, stopping him with a hand on his arm. "Don't answer it. Let it ring."

He stared at her, feeling desire pulsate hot and defiant through his veins. He wanted nothing more than to let it ring, wanted nothing more than to give in to the hunger gnawing at him and let nature take its course. Would it be so wrong? Was it such a crime to want the woman he loved, to want to be with her, to pleasure her, to show her his love? Was it really taking advantage when she wanted him too?

The phone warbled again, and he felt the cold wave of reality began to cool the blood in his veins. He no longer had the right to be with her like this, no longer had the right to touch her or to want her. He reached for the telephone and picked it up.

Mo Chandler's voice was apologetic and sincere, and when Coop heard it, he felt the cold seep through him clear to his soul.

"It's your father," Coop said, handing her the phone.

He rose off the bed, not wanting to look at her, not wanting to see the disappointment in her face. Listening as she greeted her father with a soft, halting voice, he started for the door. He suddenly felt naked—unmasked and exposed for the fraud he was. They weren't married, they weren't even lovers, and he had no right to her bed or her body.

It was a long time before he heard her enter the family room where he sat in the pajama bottoms he had hastily donned, mindlessly watching the big-screen television.

"Everything okay with your dad?" he asked, reaching for the remote control and muting the audio controls.

"Everything's fine," she said in a quiet voice, stopping at the end of the hall. She hesitated, awkwardly shifting her crutches to one side. "Are you…coming back to bed?"

He punched the power button on the remote, and the television screen went black. He walked to where she stood.

"You go on ahead," he said as casually as he could. "I'm going to sit up for a while."

He reached out, lightly touching her on the arms. He would have preferred not to touch her at all, would have preferred not to chance that a touch would lead to an embrace, and an embrace to a kiss, and he would find himself lost again. As it was, he felt so stirred up it was going to take hours for him to recover. But she looked so lost standing there, so confused and uncertain it tore at his heart.

"I can wait for you," she offered, her voice barely audible in the silent house.

There was such sadness in her eyes he could barely look. "No, you're tired. You need your sleep. Do you need some help?"

"No, I don't need help," she snapped, finding her voice and jerking her arms away. "I want you to come with me."

"I…" He stopped, drawing in a shaky breath. "I don't think that's such a good idea."

"You didn't feel that way a little while ago."

"That was a mistake, and you know it."

"A mistake? For a man and wife to want to be together?"

Some of the pain in her voice had been replaced by

anger, and selfishly he felt relieved. It made her seem less vulnerable and made him feel less of a heel.

"You know what the doctor's orders are. You know you're still recuperating, still not ready yet."

"I think I know better than Mannie Cohen what I'm ready for."

"And I think maybe you should let the doctor do his job," he said, his voice booming.

"Is that the only reason, Coop?"

Her grim, bleak voice made a chill move through him. "What are you talking about?"

She hobbled a step closer. "There are a lot of things I've forgotten since the accident. Is there something about us I've forgotten?"

The chill traveled through his veins, and the ringing in his head became so loud he wasn't sure he'd heard her right. "Why—" His throat was raw with emotion, making it difficult to speak. "Why would you think something like that?"

"It's obvious you don't want to sleep with me."

"Is it?" he demanded, seeing the hurt and humiliation in her eyes and dying just a little. "You think I was pretending back there?"

"All I know is I...I had to come to you."

The look on her face was too much for him. Nothing was worth this, and surely the truth couldn't hurt anymore than she was hurting now.

"Kelsey, there's...there's something we need to talk about, something I have to tell you—"

"We don't have to talk for me to know you don't want me anymore."

Anger and frustration soared in him like molten lava. Reaching out, he grabbed her to him, sending her crutches crashing to the floor. He crushed his mouth against hers, but the kiss was not gentle. It was harsh and filled with all the emotions and desires he'd held in check for two long years.

"You little fool," he growled, his breath coming in huge, heavy gasps. "Don't you understand? I want you too much, that's the problem."

Where he found the strength to set her away from him and walk away, he'd never know—but he did. He had to. It was the only thing he could do.

He stalked into his lonely room and slammed the door behind him. The sound echoed thunderously through the empty house like the clang of a cell door. Another night on the futon—long, endless and uncomfortable. Only it wouldn't be a lumpy futon that would keep him awake tonight. The desire that pounded in his brain and pulled at his heart promised to make this the longest night of his life.

Kelsey reached for the spade and scooped a small indentation in the soft soil. She carefully lifted the last clump of ground cover from the plastic nursery tray and slipped it into the depression in the flower bed, packing it gently into place.

Sitting back, she took a swipe at the perspiration along her forehead and surveyed the progress she'd made so far. She'd been working all afternoon, ever since Coop had left to take care of some business at the airport, and the bright swatches of lavender and white alyssum that lined half the front walk proved instantly gratifying.

She turned and glanced at the empty expanse of bed leading toward the porch she still had left to do. Gardening wasn't exactly easy with the cast on her leg, even a scaled-down one. The weeks spent in a hospital bed had taken their toll on her physical strength. Her sore, aching muscles were beginning to protest every move she made.

Only she wasn't ready to stop yet. The job was only half finished, and she hated to leave a job half finished. She wanted to have it all done by the time Coop got back, wanted to show him she was hardly an invalid any longer.

Coop. Things had been strained between them the last several days—ever since *that night.* That's how she'd come to think of it. That night she had gone to him, that night he had kissed her, that night he had carried her to their bedroom.

That night he had walked away from her.

She closed her eyes. She didn't like thinking about it because ever since *that night,* nothing had been the same. There had been no harsh words between them, no confrontation or flares of temper—but she almost would have preferred that. Anything would have been better than the plastic, manufactured armistice they had now.

She looked at the house. Was that the reason she didn't want to go inside? Was that what made the tension build in the pit of her stomach?

She turned and stabbed the spade angrily into the ground. What was going on in her head? Why was she suddenly feeling uneasy about being home alone? She'd never been afraid before, at least not that she remembered. The whole thing didn't make sense.

She studied the house with its red Spanish tiled roof and gleaming white stucco walls and remembered the first time the realtor had brought them to see the place. They'd been ready to make an offer right then. She had always loved this house, she'd always been happy here, so why was she suddenly uncomfortable about being alone in it? Did it have something to do with the strain between Coop and her? She couldn't deny that his rejection the other night had hurt, because it had—very much—but what did that have to do with the house, and why was she avoiding going inside?

She scooted a few more inches up the walk, dragging the cast. She began working the soil again. Maybe it was just as well she was seeing a psychiatrist, because this whole thing sounded a little crazy. Except she wasn't sure her session with Gloria Crowell this morning had helped or made her feel worse.

Dr. Crowell's questions had been particularly annoying today, probing and disturbing, and not about anything Kelsey wanted to talk about. She'd wanted Gloria to give her some insight and understanding about Coop, about the strain between them and how she could correct it. But Dr. Crowell hadn't asked her questions about that. Instead, the dear doctor had assailed her with questions about the uneasiness she felt, about the discomfort she'd experienced at being alone in the house.

With the spade, Kelsey stabbed furiously at the soft dirt in the flower bed, but her hands were trembling, making her movements clumsy and uncoordinated. Carelessly, she pushed the spade against the solid edge of the walk, causing it to turn and twist her wrist painfully.

"Ouch!" She winced, pain shooting up her right arm.

Discouraged, she dropped the spade in the dirt and sank against the wheelbarrow. Maybe Dr. Crowell was right— maybe it was significant. Maybe she should try to figure out why she felt like shaking at the thought of her empty house and all its empty rooms. Was there something in her past that caused these feelings, something she'd forgotten that would explain how she felt?

She'd remembered a lot in the past several weeks, recovered many details about people and places, possessions and situations—but not all the blanks had been filled in.

There was still something in the blackness that frightened her, something that caused that awful knot to form in the pit of her stomach.

She rubbed at the tension building between her eyes, thinking about Dr. Crowell's questions. The doctor had pushed her today, had urged her to scrutinize her fear—and maybe she had been right. Maybe it was important that she face her fear, discover its roots. Except right now she didn't feel like examining anything, she just felt like trying to forget.

She sat up and reached for the spade again. Shrinks, she thought, punching at the ground. They were so good at asking questions and so bad at providing any answers.

She hollowed out several small cavities in the soil, then transferred plants to them. She worked quickly and with purpose, slipping one flowering cluster into the ground after another, as though the faster she worked the further she could push the fears away. She didn't want to think or speculate, didn't want to question or presume, she just wanted her life back.

"Pretty."

Kelsey jumped at the voice behind her. Twisting around, she recognized the little boy from across the street standing at the end of the walk.

"You think so?"

He nodded, skipping a few steps closer. "Looks like the colors on your shirt."

Kelsey slipped off her sunglasses and looked at the purple and white checked border that lined the collar of her camp shirt, comparing it to the colors of the ground cover. "Hey, you know, I think you're right."

The little boy took another few hesitant steps up the walk and pointed at the cast on her leg. "What's that?"

"I hurt my leg," she explained simply. Working pediatrics, she'd had to answer a lot of kids' questions over the years, and knew it was only natural for them to be curious about things that were different. She reached down and gave the plastic a tap. "This is called a cast, and will help it get better."

"Oh," he said, pulling a cookie from his pocket and taking a quick bite before dropping it inside again. "I hurt my leg once, too."

"Oh, yeah?"

"Yeah," he said, as he reached down and pulled up his pant leg. "Right here." He pointed to his knee. "Mommy put a bandage on it."

"Looks all better now."

"Yeah," he said, letting his pant leg fall. "My mommy planted flowers at our house, too."

Kelsey glanced across the street, noting the colorful abundance of flowers that swelled from the planters. "They look beautiful."

"I helped," he announced proudly.

Kelsey smiled, thinking how nice it would be to have a little boy of her own to help her with the gardening some day. "I'll bet you were a lot of help."

"Yeah," he said, hopping on one foot, then the other. He stopped abruptly and held up four fingers. "I'm this many years old."

"Really? Four years old?" Her brow knitted slightly. "Are you sure it's okay with your mom that you cross the street?"

He quickly nodded. "She says it's okay 'cause we live on a colleysack. I can walk around."

"A cul de sac," she corrected, nodding as he pointed to the curve at the end of the street. "I see."

"Yeah, but I'm still not supposed to cross," he explained, pointing to the blacktop. "'Cause that's where the cars are.'' He jumped back and forth between two concrete squares on the walk. ''Me and Jimmy Donaldson are the tallest at preschool.''

''No fooling?'' Kelsey's eyes widened. ''Well, I'll bet your mom and dad sure like having a big guy like you around.''

''Uh-huh,'' he said, nodding again. ''Daddy says our house looks like a flower shop now.''

Kelsey made a point of looking at his house again. ''Oh, I don't know, I think it looks pretty.'' She shifted her gaze to him. ''What do you think?''

He spun around and scrutinized his house for about a half a second, then looked at her. ''I think it looks pretty, too.'' He made his way up the walk toward her in little hops. ''But Daddy doesn't like flowers anyway. He's got damallagees.''

Kelsey blinked. ''Damallagees?''

He nodded. ''Yeah, when the flowers make him sneeze he says they bother his damallagees.''

''I see,'' Kelsey said, trying very hard to swallow the burst of laughter that swelled in her throat. She imagined flowers would bother anyone's damn allergies.

''My name's Jonathan.''

''Hi, Jonathan,'' she said with a soft chuckle, slipping her gardening glove off and offering him her hand. ''I'm Kelsey.''

''Hi, Kelsey,'' he said, giving her hand a shake. ''Mommy says you're the new lady who lives here.''

Kelsey laughed. ''The new lady?''

''Uh-huh,'' Jonathan said, picking up the spade and stirring the soil. ''Mommy says you must be Coop's new girlfriend.''

Kelsey's smile stiffened. ''Uh, actually, I'm Coop's wife.''

Chapter 9

Kelsey reached for the towel, watching through the kitchen window as a car pulled into the drive across the street. As she dried her hands, she saw Jonathan run from the house and tear across the lawn toward the car.

"Daddy's home."

She could hear his muted voice through the window and felt a ball of emotion form in her throat. He lunged at his father with arms wide open, and his dad swallowed him up in a big bear hug.

Kelsey turned away, slipping the towel onto the rack. She grabbed the crutches propped against the counter, then carefully made her way across the tiled kitchen floor and into the family room.

"How long have the people across the street lived there?"

Coop shrugged, his eyes fixed on the television screen. "A year maybe, year and a half," he said, leaning forward and reaching for the soft drink can on the coffee table in front of him. "I'm not sure."

"Did I know them?"

The soda can halted halfway to his mouth. He turned slowly and looked at her. "I...I don't know," he lied, lowering the can to the table. There was no way she could have known them. Holly and Christian Harding had moved into the neighborhood six months after Kelsey had moved out. "I don't think so. Why?"

"No reason," she said with a shrug, moving the crutches silently over the plush carpet and around the sofa. "Jonathan was over this afternoon."

Coop pictured the four-year-old in his head. "The little boy?"

"Yeah," she said, smiling as she remembered Jonathan's impish brown eyes and endless energy. "He helped me in the yard." She slid her crutches to one side and sat next to him on the sofa. "I just wondered if he'd ever done that before."

Coop forgot about the news broadcast he'd been watching and shifted his body toward hers. The last several days hadn't been easy ones—in fact, they'd been tense and uneasy.

How he wished he could go back to that night in the shower. How he wished he'd handled things better, had shown more control. Instead, he'd hurt her, and the whole situation had left them both so awkward and uncomfortable with each other they hadn't even been able to talk about it and clear the air. They'd gone back to their daily routines, being overly polite and artificially courteous and trying to pretend nothing had happened. But the peace was phony, and that only seemed to make matters worse.

"Did Jonathan say something?" he asked, kicking himself for having left her alone. It hadn't been easy keeping her away from friends and neighbors who might let something slip, but it was essential to make the pretense work.

"No," Kelsey said, shaking her head. "As a matter of fact, he told me his name and how old he was, so I assumed he didn't know me." She turned and looked at him. "He knows you, though."

"Oh, yeah?" Coop thought of the times he'd waved to the children across the street, of the holidays when they'd delivered homemade goodies to his door, and last Halloween when Jonathan and his baby sister were dressed as Snoopy and Woodstock.

"Yes, and apparently so does his mother."

Coop turned on the sofa and looked at her. "Oh, really."

"Really," Kelsey said, one brow arching. "As a matter of fact, it seems his mother is under the impression I'm your new girlfriend."

"Girlfriend?" The skin on the back of his neck tingled. He couldn't exactly blame the neighbors for having noticed her coming in and out with him. They weren't exactly accustomed to seeing a woman around the place. Despite the divorce, it had never seemed right to bring a woman home with him—not here. This had always been Kelsey's house, their home together. To have brought another woman here would have felt like cheating.

"The other night you mentioned there was something you needed to tell me," she said, steeling herself with a deep breath and looking at him. "Maybe you should tell me now."

Her face was calm and expressionless, but Coop saw the apprehension in her eyes, sensed the dread and the tension. She'd given him an opening to tell her the truth, given it to him on a silver platter. He had only to say it, had only to open his mouth and let it all come tumbling out. Only he needed time to prepare, time to find the words, to separate the truth from the lies and try and figure out how to explain the pretense from what he felt in his heart. How did he know if she was ready or not, how did he decide if it was right?

He dreaded the truth. The truth wasn't going to set him free, it was going to sink him. It was how he was going to lose her again.

"Kelsey," he said, drawing in a shaky breath. "I'm…I'm not sure this is the time for all this—"

"Don't lie to me, Coop," she said, cutting him off. Breathing deep, she looked him square in the face. "Be honest with me. Is there another woman?"

The question hit him like a glass of ice water in the face, only more startling. Of all the things he'd been concerned about, of all the things he'd thought she might question, that was about the last thing he'd expected her to ask.

"Another—" He cleared his throat and shook his head. "You think I'm involved with another woman?"

"If you're waiting until I'm strong enough to tell me, I'm strong enough now," she said, squaring her shoulders. "I want to know."

"Why would you think there was someone else? Because of what Jonathan said?"

"That," she admitted, her resolve showing signs of weakening. "And because…" Her voice started to quiver, and she struggled to clear it. "Because since the accident things have been *different* between us."

Coop felt a knot in his stomach. Of course things had been different, they were divorced. They hadn't been together as man and wife in over two years. If she was sensing anything, she was sensing that.

So how did he tell her that? How did he assure her

without telling her everything? He needed time to think, to consult with her doctors, to decide if he should confess everything or lose himself again in a sea of lies.

"Of course things have been different," he said with more force than he'd intended. "Have you forgotten about the accident?"

"I get the feeling I've forgotten a lot," she said, her blue eyes narrow and suspicious.

"Well, let me remind you," he snapped. "You nearly died. You were unconscious for four days, and you've had some pretty devastating injuries to recover from. Things are bound to be a little different for a while."

"For a while? Or forever?"

The hard knot was still in the pit of his stomach. "Is that what you think?"

"I don't know," she said, struggling. "I don't know what to think. I just know that ever since the accident you've been pulling away."

"If this is about the other night—"

"Of course this is about the other night."

He saw the same hurt and confusion in her eyes that had been there on that night. He drew in a tired breath. "Kelsey, sweetheart, you're making too much of that."

"Am I?"

"Yes," he insisted. "The other night meant nothing."

"I don't remember you ever walking away from me before."

"And you think it's because of another woman?"

She looked away. "It would explain a lot."

"No," he said quietly. "It would explain nothing, because it isn't true." He reached out, put a finger under her chin and tilted her head so she had to look at him. "Look, I know I handled things badly the other night. I hurt you, and I never meant for that to happen." He reached for her hand, bringing it to his lips and brushing a feathery kiss along her fingertips. "It's just, you touched me, and I lost control."

"But...you stopped," she whispered.

"Because the time wasn't right."

"And that really is the only reason?"

He turned her palm to his lips. "How could you think there was anyone else?"

"I've forgotten so much—"

Coop stopped her with a finger to her lips. It was only then he realized just how fragile she was. She looked strong, and her physical wounds had all but disappeared, but emotionally she was only beginning to heal.

"I love you," he murmured. The time would come when she would be strong enough to know everything, but not now, not tonight. "*You.* There could never be anyone else."

He pressed a kiss on her palm and looked into her clear blue eyes. She needed time to gain strength and confidence. Maybe they both did. He was still in love with her, and he wasn't sure he was strong enough to let her go again, wasn't sure he had the strength to face a future without her.

"Forget about the other night," he murmured, gathering her into his arms. "Just know that I love you, and I always will."

He pressed a kiss against her lips, feeling her body relax against his. She was warm and soft, and he wished at that moment he could hold her like this forever.

"Oh, Coop," she sighed, pulling away and looking at him. "I feel so stupid."

"Stupid? What do you have to feel stupid about? I'm the one who was slamming doors and acting like a two-year-old."

"You were upset," she said, pushing a lock of hair from his forehead. "It's just after the other night—I don't know, I had this awful sad feeling, a lost, lonely feeling— it's hard to explain. Anyway, I started thinking about all the blanks in my past, imagining the things I might have forgotten." She looked at him, giving her head a shake. "I started wondering what there was about us I'd forgotten. Were we as happy as I remember? Were we the same people? And then Jonathan started talking about your girlfriend, and I thought maybe…"

"I might have a girlfriend stashed somewhere?" he said, finishing for her.

She looked at him and grimaced. "I'm embarrassed now."

He didn't have the energy for any more lies, didn't have the stamina to think of another excuse. "Kelsey, there's never been anyone else, I swear. I love you—only you— and nothing that's happened between us could ever change that."

"Is it your feeling that you should tell her?"

Coop's grip on the telephone receiver tightened, and he mentally counted to ten. He'd had a long night, and his patience was at an end. He wasn't in the mood to deal with doctor doublespeak and question after question.

"It's my *feeling,* Dr. Crowell," he said in a tightly controlled voice, "that I don't know what the hell to do. I want help, not to sit here and talk about my feelings." He knew he was losing control, and forced several calming breaths into his lungs. "Dr. Cohen thought since you see Kelsey regularly, you'd be in a better position to advise me. So advise me. Do I tell her or don't I?"

"Well," Gloria Crowell said thoughtfully, "from what you're telling me…" She paused, and Coop heard her flipping through some papers. "From some of the things we've discussed in our last session, I think it's safe to say something's going on. She does seem to be sensing something—but she's not having actual memories."

"Is that normal? I mean, does this mean things are coming back?"

"It could," Dr. Crowell told him. "It's as though she's remembering the feelings before remembering the events that caused them. It would explain her sense of loss, of sorrow." She paused. "It could be her way of preparing herself to remember—dealing with fragments of memory a little at a time."

Coop sighed heavily, feeling the muscles in his stomach tighten into hard knots. "Then what do I do?"

"I'm not sure you need do to anything. You and I both know those are going to be very painful memories for her when they come back."

"So you think I should do nothing, just let her keep thinking everything is hunky-dory?" He blew out an angry breath. "I got to tell you, Dr. Crowell, even Kelsey isn't buying some of these lame excuses I've been giving her."

There was another pause, a longer one this time. "Believe it or not, I can appreciate the position you're in."

"Oh, can you, now." He snorted sarcastically. "I doubt it."

Dr. Crowell seemed unfazed by the sarcasm. "Until now, Kelsey had assumed certain things about her life—she was in love, she was married. What was there to be curious about? Now she's sensing something. She's got these feelings, she's starting to think maybe things weren't quite as hunky-dory as she'd thought. That sounds like progress to me. It sounds like something's happening." She paused a moment on the other end of the receiver.

"But I'm not going to lie to you, Cooper. Things could be rough ahead. There's nothing I can tell you that will help that."

He shook his head. Things were pretty rough already. "Then wouldn't it just be kinder to tell her everything?" he asked in a quiet voice. "Wouldn't it be better for her to know the truth rather than for me to be telling her everything is all right when she feels that it isn't?"

"Maybe," Dr. Crowell replied. "And maybe the shock would shove those memories away for good."

Coop closed his eyes again, drawing in a deep breath. "So you're saying there's nothing I can do."

"I'm saying that if she's going to remember, she's going to do it in her own sweet time, in her own sweet way. Coop, you've invested a lot of time in this, you've put your whole life on hold in order to give Kelsey the opportunity to remember, and now it's looking like it might work. Do you really want to risk all that by jumping the gun now?"

"You really think it is working?" he asked, his voice flat and unemotional. "You really think she's remembering, I mean *really* remembering, not just bits and pieces?"

"Everything I see points in that direction."

Coop felt a little like the bottom had dropped out of his world. "Okay, Doc, I get the picture."

"Tell me something, Cooper," Dr. Crowell said. "I get the feeling you might have some mixed emotions about the possibility of Kelsey getting her memory back. Has there been some changes between you two I should know about?"

Change? Coop closed his eyes. He'd been in love with Kelsey when she'd been his wife, he was in love with her now that she wasn't. Nothing had changed.

"I want her to get better, Doc," he said, his voice weary. "That hasn't changed."

"Anything you want to talk about?"

Coop had to smile. "You don't have to worry, Doc. There's nothing wrong with my memory. I remember we're divorced—and I don't have any illusions about what's going to happen once she remembers, too."

"You seem pretty sure about that."

He laughed, a rough, grating sound that had nothing to do with humor. "You forget, Doc, I've been through this before."

"It doesn't have to be that way."

"What is it with you doctors?" he asked, giving his head a shake. "You and Mannie Cohen run a lonely hearts club on the side or something? Advice to the lovelorn?"

The doctor laughed. "You don't believe in second chances?"

"I believe, Dr. Crowell, that you can't go back," he said, rubbing his eye with the palm of his hand. "I believe that history is history, and nothing can change that. You know what happened, you know what having kids and a family meant to her. When she found out that wasn't going to happen it nearly killed her." He stopped, pain swelling in his throat and making it difficult for him to continue. "And it killed her love for me."

"Yet you did this for her," she said quietly. "That means something."

"Yeah, it means I'm a real Boy Scout," he said with a tired laugh. "And it means I'm earning my merit badge in story telling and avoiding the truth."

"This is getting to you, isn't it?"

He released a long breath. "I'm just tired. I'm tired of the pretense, of piling one lie on top of the other."

"When she remembers," the doctor said sympathetically, "she's going to know the sacrifice you've made."

Coop's mind moved to the night she'd surprised him in the shower. She was also going to know he'd touched her and kissed her when he had no right. "When she remembers," he said quietly, in a voice barely above a whisper, "she'll be gone, so it's not going to matter, anyway."

"Surprise!" Coop slammed the car door and gazed across the roof of the car to Kelsey on the front walk. "Surprise?"

"Yeah," she said, lifting her arms out and turning around in a small circle. "Surprise."

"Hey, you don't have your crutches—" But he stopped abruptly as his eyes traveled the length of her. "The cast—my God, it's gone." He looked at her. "Your cast is gone."

"Are you surprised?" she asked, watching as he rushed around the car toward her.

He stopped when he reached her, giving his head a shake. "What do you think?" He reached out a hand, slipping it around her arm. "How—I mean, when? When did this happen?"

"This afternoon," Kelsey said in a burst of excitement. "Dr. Hamilton was in town on a consultation and came by to check up on me." She looked at Coop, the shocked surprise on his face making her smile even wider. "He took one look and said he might as well save me a trip up to Santa Ynez."

"And he took it off, just like that?"

"Just like that," she repeated, making a play of snapping her fingers.

He forced himself to smile, forced an enthusiasm he

truly didn't feel to cover the tension gnawing at his insides. At least with the cast on her leg he'd had an excuse to be cautious, a physical reminder to keep his distance. Without it, she looked fit and healthy and very, very appealing.

"Should you be standing on it?" he asked after a moment, his grip on her arm tightening a little. "I mean, is it okay for you to be up and walking around? Maybe you should be sitting down—"

"Of course it's okay," she insisted, cutting him off. "As a matter of fact, I should be up and walking—build up the muscle." She made a small, slightly awkward turn in front of him. "It's weak—but I start physical therapy on Monday." She turned again. "I'll be running marathons before you know it."

Coop gave her a bewildered look. "You want to run a marathon?"

She laughed. "Do I look crazy to you? Of course I don't want to run a marathon." She grabbed him by the arm and pulled him up the walk toward the house. "It's just that after dragging a cast around on my leg for six weeks, it's kind of nice to know I could, if I wanted."

Coop let her lead him up the steps and into the house. She moved with a speed and agility that seemed to defy her weakened leg, but it really didn't surprise him. Her recovery had been remarkable from the first, and looking at her now, it was hard to imagine that just six short weeks ago, she'd been fighting for her life. She was alive and bursting with energy. Anyone could see that.

It had become futile for him to try to convince her to slow down and take things easy, or that she needed him around twenty-four hours a day to take care of her, so he'd given up on both. In the past week, he'd felt a little like he'd been living in a time warp. With her no longer incapacitated by her injuries, there was no unusual circumstance, no special condition to cast him in the role of caretaker. Suddenly he was a husband again, and they were acting very much like a normal married couple.

Reluctantly, he'd returned to work, taking a few of his regular flights and—with Doris's help—clearing some of the details and paperwork that had piled up over the last six weeks. And while he almost welcomed the respite from lying to Kelsey, settling into the comfortable routine of married life hadn't made his life any easier.

Their days had fallen into a familiar pattern, familiar because it wasn't unlike the one they had followed when they had been married. Of course, with her memory loss still a problem and her job on hold, Kelsey stayed closer to home than she had before. She was always fearful she would run into someone she wouldn't know or wouldn't remember. Still, she managed to stay busy with her gardening and their redecorating project, and even though their sleeping arrangements hadn't changed, she was up with him for breakfast each morning and to see him off to work. They would then go their separate ways until dinner, when they would relax together and talk over what they'd done with the day.

He knew there was nothing exceptional in these activities, nothing that millions of other couples didn't do day in and day out. But after two long years alone, after the torment of the divorce, after the pain of separation, it was like breaking new ground, like sunlight after a storm. He'd been pretending to be her husband for weeks now, but in this past week, he'd begun to *feel* like her husband, too.

"Come on," she said excitedly, pulling him inside. "I've got dinner waiting."

"You cooked?" he said, closing the door behind them. She gave him a cool look, then breezed through the family room to the patio. "You don't have to sound so shocked. I do know how, you know."

He had to smile at the dry humor in her tone. "I just meant with getting the cast off and everything, I wouldn't have thought you had time."

"Well, actually, I didn't," she confessed, walking to the patio table she had covered with a checkered table-cloth. "I called Vince's. I thought we should celebrate."

Coop bent and lifted the lid of the covered casserole dish resting in the center of the table. "Hmm," he murmured, inhaling deeply. "Ravioli."

"Your favorite." She beamed, pulling out a chair and gesturing for him to sit down.

"*My* favorite?" he asked, giving her a skeptical look.

"Your favorite, my favorite, what's the difference?" she said impatiently, motioning for him to sit. "You want to argue details, or you want to eat?"

He looked at her for a moment, emotion swelling in his chest. What he wanted was for this never to end. "I want to eat."

"Good," she said, tugging on his arm. "This is a celebration, so let's celebrate. And I've got another surprise for you."

"Another surprise? I'm not sure how much more I can take."

"You can take this," she said breezily, walking around the table and sitting across from him. She leaned across the table and lowered her voice. "There's cheesecake for dessert."

He watched her as she dished out the pasta, an eerie sense of déjà vu nagging at him. How many times had they sat like this, talking casually while enjoying a meal together? He had that uncomfortable feeling again, like the last two years had been a bad dream.

"Dr. Hamilton said I was so good with the cast and crutches, I actually built up some of the muscles in my arms and thighs," she said, handing him a plate.

"So you were sort of *doing* physical therapy while you were *waiting* for physical therapy." He laughed. "Only you could be laid up for six weeks and come out in better shape than you went in."

"I wouldn't exactly say I was in *better* shape," she insisted, picking up the salad bowl and offering it to him.

"Maybe you wouldn't," he murmured, taking the bowl from her. "From where I'm sitting, you look great."

Kelsey looked up, blinking. "Really?"

He reached for the bottle of wine, uncorked it and gave her a deliberate look. "Of course you do, you know that."

"Maybe," she said, her smile broadening. "But it's nice to know you think so."

He poured her a glass of wine. "Oh, I think so," he mumbled, pouring himself a glass and gulping down a mouthful. Suddenly he felt restless and impatient, and looking at her in the soft light of the patio only made those feelings stronger. "There's never been any doubt about that."

"Well," she said, taking a small sip. "For an old married lady, that's nice to know."

"You're hardly old." He snorted and took another drink. She wasn't married, either, but he didn't want to think about that.

He also didn't want to think about how she had felt in his arms and how much he wanted her at that moment. Hunger gnawed at him, the kind of hunger the meal before him wasn't going to satisfy.

He finished his glass of wine and poured himself another, hoping it would dull his senses, take the edge off his need. Except that a warmth began to slowly seep into his system, heating his blood and easing the tension in his muscles. It did nothing to take the edge off the hunger—it only made it worse.

He drained the glass, then poured himself another. He felt relaxed and uninhibited, and everything about her aroused him even more. The movement of her hands, the motion of her lips...it was as if the meal became a performance, a demonstration that stirred and inflamed his already overworked and overburdened emotions.

"You're not eating."

Coop jumped. "I know," he said, taking another gulp of wine. "I'm drinking."

"I can see that," she said, lowering her fork to her plate. "You're not hungry?"

He glared at her over his glass, his voice barely above a whisper. "You have no idea."

"Coop, what are you doing?"

He looked around innocently, giving her a shrug. "What? I can't have a little drink?"

Her frown deepened. "Is...is everything all right?"

"Everything's just dandy," he murmured, draining his glass again and watching the little line between her brows deepen. To appease her, he reached for his fork and took several bites of pasta, but he had no taste for its spicy flavor. He wanted more to drink, wanted to make the hurt go away.

"Coop," Kelsey said as he reached for the wine bottle again. "No more, please."

"Just one more glass," he promised, giving her a theatrical wink.

He finished the glass in one gulp, watching the disapproval in her eyes and realizing right then what it was he had to do. He had to get drunk, had to make himself as offensive and unpleasant as he could. He had to do everything he could to anger and upset her, because it was all he had left. There was no cast on her leg. There were no internal injuries or bruised flesh to rely on, no physical barriers to distract him. But he had no right to want her the way he did.

He poured the last of the wine into his glass and lowered the empty bottle to the table. His judgment was a little off, and the bottom of the bottle hit the curved lip of his spoon, sending it flying through the air in a spectacular arc. It landed noisily on the terra-cotta tiles of the patio floor.

"Oops," he said with a grin, the word feeling thick and heavy on his tongue.

Kelsey didn't smile. She didn't even move. She just sat there, looking at him and lightly tapping her finger against the side of her wineglass.

Coop drained his wine, feeling the patio list toward the ocean. The alcohol was working, and it looked as though his plan to make her angry was working, as well. He wanted her so mad she wouldn't welcome his touch. Then maybe she'd stop him if he decided to do something stupid, if he decided to push the dishes to one side and pull her across the table to him.

"Maybe you'll think about eating something now," she said in a tight voice, nodding at the empty bottle on the table.

Coop looked at her, desire pounding at him like a drum, and slowly rose to his feet.

"No," he said, shaking his head. "I want more wine."

Chapter 10

Kelsey stared out through the French doors and down at the millions of tiny lights that dotted the Santa Barbara coastline below. She wished she could cry, wished she could summon tears and get rid of the emotion that choked her like hands around her neck. Except she was too angry to cry—angry or frightened, she couldn't tell which.

Her fists closed into tight balls, and she pounded them against her thighs. What had happened? What had caused Coop to drink like that? It was as though he'd been trying to be unpleasant, had purposely wanted to spoil the evening.

She closed her eyes to the magnificent nightscape, feeling a sense of dread start to build in her chest—that awful dread that lived in those murky black depths where her memories lay hidden. What was in all that darkness that frightened her so? What had happened in that time she had lost?

She opened her eyes, turned from the window and glanced across the room at the hospital bed. That bed had disturbed her from the beginning. It didn't belong there. It didn't make sense. Coop had given her an eloquent explanation about doctors' orders and providing her with the utmost comfort during her recovery, but it had been six weeks. Why were they still sleeping in separate bedrooms?

Anxiety rose in her throat, tasting bitter and vile. What was it she'd blocked out? He'd sworn to her there was no other woman, but there had to be something. Had their marriage been in trouble? Had Coop developed a drinking problem? What could have happened to explain why they weren't sleeping together?

She thought back over the past several weeks, thought of Coop's careful attentions, of his affection and his concern for her. The feelings had been real between them, she was certain of that.

She glanced at the faded T-shirt he'd given to her to use as a nightgown. She might have forgotten a lot about the past, but she still knew him, still knew her husband. When he'd told her he loved her, he hadn't been lying. She'd seen the love in his eyes, felt it in her heart.

She walked across the bedroom and ran a hand along the cold rail of the hospital bed. So why was this ugly thing still here? If there were problems, if there was something she'd forgotten, something wrong between them, why hadn't he just told her? Was there something he was protecting her from, something he didn't want her to know?

Pressure throbbed fierce at her temples, tension from a long, frustrating evening spent alone in her room. She had to stop this, had to stop guessing, had to stop letting her fears and anxieties get the best of her. There was a good chance tonight had nothing to do with her amnesia. It might have been nothing more than a wife getting annoyed with her husband—a common, ordinary marital dispute. Surely they weren't immune. She could certainly remember arguments they'd had in the past. Why did it have to be more than that?''

She ambled through the darkness, then flipped the switch in the master bath, bringing the room to life with light. At the moment, it really didn't matter what kind of argument they were having, or why. It had caused one hell of a headache—and it was making it difficult for her to think straight at all.

She rummaged through the medicine cabinet and pulled out the small plastic bottle of pain relievers. If she could get the throbbing to stop long enough, maybe she could fall asleep. After a good night's sleep, maybe things would look better.

"Oh, no," she moaned, slipping off the cap and looking into the empty container. She stared at herself in the mirror, frowning and feeling the painful pulsing inside her head grow worse. "No, no, no, *no!*"

She thought of the full bottle of aspirin on the cupboard shelf in the kitchen and cringed. Leaving the bedroom meant seeing Coop again, and she wasn't sure she wanted to do that right now, not when she felt so angry—or so vulnerable.

When he'd returned to the patio with a second bottle of wine, she'd decided she'd had enough. She had gotten up and—despite her weak leg—stomped down the hall and into the bedroom, slamming the door behind her.

It had been a brilliant exit, dramatic and theatrical, and she didn't doubt it had demonstrated to him just how displeased she was with him. Unfortunately, it also left her stranded with an empty bottle of aspirin.

Of course, it might have been different if he had come after her, had made some attempt to apologize or make amends, but he hadn't. She'd been left to while away the evening alone in her room, coping with her fears and letting her imagination run wild.

She looked at her reflection in the mirror, watching her frown lines deepen. How had Coop spent the evening? Had his been as long and as frustrating as hers had been? Did he regret what had happened, or had he finished that second bottle of wine and fallen asleep in front of the television?

"Forget the aspirin," she said to her reflection, deciding it wasn't worth it. The last thing she needed was to find him sprawled across the sofa sound asleep.

She switched off the bathroom light, feeling her way through the darkness to the bed. She would tough it out, would just force herself to forget about the pounding behind her eyes, forget about the tension crawling up her neck, and simply get some rest.

She pulled the covers back, climbed in and settled back against the pillows. It was, after all, just a headache. It wasn't as though she'd never had one before. How bad could it be? She would relax and use a little mind over matter, just concentrate on her breathing like women in labor did and—

She sprang into a sitting position. Something was clicking in her brain. Something had been triggered and was finding its way out of those lost regions in her memory.

Breathing. Relaxing. Labor. It was so close, so close. It was right there, right on the outskirts of her memory, right in back of her brain. She almost had it, she could almost remember...

Only as suddenly as it had come, it disappeared again, fading into the abyss.

Kelsey sank against the pillows again, her heart pounding furiously. She'd almost had it, had almost been able to grab it and to pull it back. Except now it was gone.

She closed her eyes tight and pounded her fists against the mattress. Just a few seconds more, that's all it would have taken. A few lousy seconds, and she would have had it.

"Mind over matter," she murmured again, feeling her heart pound in rhythm with the tension in her head. "Mind over matter."

She tried to relax, tried to fill her thoughts with all those things she'd been thinking of when the memory had started to surface. She stared at the dark ceiling, taking deep breaths and trying to figure out what it was about women in labor and breathing techniques that had seemed so familiar. Had it been because of her job? Something in pediatrics and working with newborns that she'd almost remembered?

She pounded her fists on the mattress again, straining to remember, hoping that faint spark of recognition would come back, that it would flame and grow and trigger something again. But nothing came, no glimmer, no hint of anything. Restless and frustrated, she thrashed about, trying to relax, and only succeeding in stirring herself up more.

"I can't stand it," she muttered, kicking the covers aside and sitting up. But the motion was too sudden, too harsh, and pain exploded at her temples and behind her eyes.

She paused long enough for the painful throbbing to ease, then slowly swung her legs off the bed and came carefully to her feet. She checked the time on the clock beside the bed. Eleven forty-six. Chances were Coop had gone to bed. Not that it mattered. Running into him was a chance she'd have to take, because she needed something for her headache, and she needed it now.

Pausing at the doors, she listened before she turned the knob. But there was no sound coming from the other side. Cracking the door, she peered out. The hallway was dark and deserted. The whole house looked dark and deserted.

She took a few hesitant steps forward, then paused and listened again. The door to his room was closed. No doubt he had gone to bed.

Relaxing a little, she quickly made her way down the hall, through the breakfast nook and into the kitchen. There wasn't any need for lights. She knew the way by heart. The small bottle of aspirins was just where she'd expected it to be, and she snapped the cap in one smooth motion. The tablets tasted bitter on her tongue, but she didn't mind. She just wanted them to dissolve, wanted the medication to start moving through her bloodstream and take the pain away.

"Better," she whispered, washing the tablets down with several sips of bottled water from the refrigerator. "Yes, better." The water tasted sweet and icy cold and very refreshing after the aspirin's acrid bite, and she took another long drink. "Much, much better."

She walked to the sink and looked out the kitchen window to Jonathan's house across the street. Despite the late hour, lights burned bright inside the house, making it look warm and inviting with its flower-lined walks and manicured lawns. It looked full of life, of happy times and children.

She followed the path of a car as it passed slowly along the street, wondering what her house looked like to an outsider. Did it look as dark and cold and empty as it felt to her at times? Would it ever have that warm, lived-in look? Would it ever be filled with children?

She thought of Coop, of the plans they'd made and the family they hoped to have. Was that the reason they were still sleeping apart? Did he not want to risk a pregnancy until she was completely over her injuries and her lost memories had returned? Or was it that he'd changed his mind, that a family wasn't something he wanted any longer?

"Kelsey?"

She'd walked right past him. At first he'd thought she was ignoring him because she was too angry to speak. Not that he blamed her. He'd acted like a jerk, sloppy and rude. He wouldn't be surprised if she never talked to him again.

Except as he watched her he realized she hadn't seen him sitting there in a dark corner of the breakfast nook. She wasn't ignoring him—she didn't even know he was there.

He took a moment, watching her as she pulled the aspirin bottle from the cupboard and popped several tablets into her mouth. He'd been stupid to drink the way he had, to think alcohol would do anything more than inflame his already heightened senses. He might have succeeded in making her angry tonight, might have been able to make himself so unpleasant that she'd locked herself in her room all evening. But it had done nothing to stem his desire, nothing to stop him from wanting her.

It had been hours since he'd had a drink, since alcohol had burned through his bloodstream. But sitting in the darkness watching her, he felt the same potent sensation. The moonlight through the window caught the locks of her hair, making it shine soft and silky. It made her look more like an angel than a flesh-and-blood woman, more like someone from a dream or a fairy tale.

Only she was real, she was flesh and blood. The faint outline of her bare breasts and slim shoulders against the thin fabric of his old T-shirt made that very clear. She wasn't an illusion. She was the woman he loved, the woman he wanted.

"Better. Yes, better. Much, much better."

Her soft words surprised him, and for a moment he thought she was talking to him, that she had become aware of his presence and was addressing him. But she had no idea he was there. The shadows of the dark corner had obscured him from her view completely.

He figured the wise thing would be to just sit there and let her pass him again, let her walk back to her bedroom alone and shut the door behind her. Except he wasn't feeling very wise tonight. He was feeling lost, miserable, and he couldn't just let her walk away.

"Kelsey?"

The sudden sound of his voice out of the silence made her jump violently, the plastic bottle of water slipping from her hand and falling clumsily into the sink.

"C-Coop," she stammered, spinning around and finding his shadowy silhouette in the murkiness of the breakfast nook. "You...you scared me to death."

"I'm sorry," he said, leaning back in the chair.

"How long have you been sitting there?" she asked, straining to see him in the darkness.

"An hour," he said with a careless shrug of his shoulder. "Maybe two—I don't know."

"Oh," she mumbled, unnerved to think how close he'd been all this time. "I—I thought you'd gone to bed."

He shook his head. "Couldn't sleep."

Her gaze narrowed, and she forgot about being angry for a moment. "Are you...all right?"

"You mean am I drunk?" He breathed out a cheerless laugh. "No."

"I, uh, came out for the aspirin," she said, lifting up the small bottle she still held in her hand.

"Headache?"

She nodded. "Yeah. You?"

"Oh, yeah—a killer."

It made her self-conscious that he could see her, but she couldn't see him. "Want some?"

"No, thanks. I gave up on aspirin hours ago."

She couldn't tell if he was looking at her or somewhere else, and it made her uncomfortable. "You had a lot to drink."

"Yeah," he murmured, watching how her breasts pressed tight against the T-shirt with every breath she took. "Too much."

"Is…everything all right? I mean, it isn't like you to drink like that—at least, not that I can remember."

"Don't worry," he said, crossing his arms over his chest and leaning back in the chair. The T-shirt just barely covered her torso, and with the cast gone, her legs looked long and smooth and seemed to go on forever. "I haven't become a drunk, if that's what you mean."

"It crossed my mind," she admitted, sensing his movements in the darkness even though she couldn't see exactly what they were. She pushed herself away from the counter, taking several hesitant steps across the cool tiled floor toward him. "After all, I've forgotten a lot."

"Yeah," he muttered, watching her move and feeling his blood start to heat. "A lot."

"Maybe…" She hesitated only briefly. "Maybe we should talk about some of those things I've forgotten."

"And maybe you should just go back to bed."

She shook her head. "No, I'm not going anywhere."

"Go to bed, Kelsey," he said again. "Just get out."

She stopped. "Is that what you want?"

"What I want?" He slowly leaned forward in the chair. "What *I* want doesn't matter."

She could see him better now, sitting in the dark corner with his shirt off and his feet bare. His face looked pale and gaunt, and his eyes had a raw, hungry look. Something stirred in her, knotting in her stomach and radiating like an ember giving off heat. "It matters to me."

He looked at her. "Don't do this."

"Don't do what, care about you? Love you?" She shook her head again. "Too late, Coop—I already do. You're my husband. I love you."

"Husband." He snorted, raking a hand through his hair. "Yeah, I'm some kind of husband, all right."

His voice sounded different, strained and tense, and she heard something so sad, so wounded in it. "Coop, what is it? What aren't you telling me? What's happening here?"

"Nothing," he insisted, slamming his fist on the table and glaring at her. "Nothing is happening here—and nothing *can* happen here."

His violent reaction made her stagger, shocked and surprised.

"I—I don't understand," she whispered. "I don't understand any of this. All you've done for weeks now is push me away. If something's wrong, Coop, just tell me. Tell me, because it couldn't make me feel any worse than I do right now."

"Kelsey, please," he pleaded, the pain in her voice tearing at his insides. How did he make her understand when he didn't understand himself? How could he explain that he wanted to do the right thing—even if none of this seemed right? How could anything be right when it hurt her so much? "Just go to bed."

"What is it?" she demanded, her lip quivering and tears glittering in her eyes. "What is it you're not telling me? What is it you think you're protecting me from?"

"You want to know?" he growled, the hurt and the fear on her face and in her voice causing something to snap in him. He stood, grabbed her by the arm and pulled her to him. "I'm protecting you from this." He crushed his body tightly against hers. "From me."

He found her lips and ravaged them, kissing her with all the emotion, all the longing and desire that had been building in him for weeks. Her taste invaded him, entering his blood, torching it until heat exploded through him like a brushfire out of control.

This was right, the two of them together, Coop and Kelsey, husband and wife. Not making up excuses, not living a charade, not cruelly rejecting her over and over again. It was what she wanted and what he was ready to die to have.

All he wanted was to love her. How could that be wrong?

"Kelsey," he gasped. Her name sounded sweet to his ears, as sweet and as pure as it tasted in his mouth. "God forgive me, Kelsey, I want you. I can't help myself."

Even as he captured her mouth again, even as he felt her hands clawing to get at him and the soft groans escape from her throat, he knew God would forgive him—he just wasn't sure she ever would.

Kelsey heard the need in his voice, felt his hard, strong body pressing against her, and a fireball replaced the knot in her stomach, twisting tight. This was what she wanted, what she needed—to feel him in her arms, to feel his need and to know he wanted her. If there were problems she'd forgotten, they didn't matter now. She still had Coop. Still had his passion, his fire, and most important, she still had his heart.

"I want you, too," she murmured against his lips, her hands moving around his waist and slipping beneath the fabric of his jeans. "I want you, too."

The feel of her hands at his sides and along the swell of his bottom made rational thought drain from his brain and hunger gnaw at his soul. He gave the civilized, thinking part of himself over to the primal being that shared his skin, the primitive, feral creature whose only purpose was to appease his appetites.

He pulled her closer, his hands wild in an effort to touch and caress. He found the end of the T-shirt, caught it and pulled it from her in one smooth motion. He found the waist of her panties and tore them free, leaving her bare and exposed before him.

"Beautiful," he murmured, his voice raw and tight in his throat. "So beautiful."

At the sight of her, the air stalled in his lungs, and his heart lurched violently in his chest. He took one moment—one brief, fleeting moment for reverence, for wonder, for admiration—but only that. He couldn't deny himself any longer. Desire pounded in his brain. There wasn't time for slow, careful exploration—not with the fire in him burning out of control.

He pulled her to him, bringing them body to body, flesh to flesh. He ravished her willing lips, heard a soft groan reverberate through him, not knowing if it came from his throat or hers. He lifted her up, trailing a path of wet kisses from her lips to her neck, then to the gentle swell of her breasts. She tasted warm and rich—like life and love and woman, and he paid tribute to her beauty with all he had.

Kelsey closed her eyes, giving in to his wild passion and feeling herself become wild, as well. His hands on her felt like fire, igniting her blood and sending it racing through her veins. They had been man and wife for years, had made love countless times before, but she felt as desperate, as hungry as if they'd been apart for years.

"Coop," she groaned, her voice sounding coarse and husky to her ears.

His lips on her breasts were driving her crazy. Tension coiled in her belly, and her legs trembled beneath her. She felt the hot, potent blasts of his breath against her skin, felt the strength and the power in the arms that held her. He was her anchor, her mainstay. She wanted to lose herself in his passion and find herself alive beneath his touch.

Her hands slid down, finding him hard inside his jeans. She tugged at the buttons until they finally gave way, opening the fly and freeing him to her unrestrained touch.

"I love you, Coop," she whispered, feeling the strength and the power of him. "I love you."

Coop moaned, the sound rising from his soul. What burned in his blood was hotter than fire, more blistering than desire—it was a maelstrom of emotion, encompassing all he wanted, all that was his, all he would ever need.

He half-dragged, half-carried her down the hallway, starting for the master bedroom that had once been theirs to share. But catching a glimpse of the double doors, he suddenly thought of the narrow hospital bed that waited inside, of the hard metal bars and adjustable controls. He wasn't going to make love to her on that—an ugly, institutional-looking hospital bed that only reminded him of the lie he'd been living.

Stopping suddenly, he swept her up in his arms, kicked open the door to the room he'd been using and carried her inside. Maybe there was a poetic justice in all of this, that they should make love there, on the low-lying futon bed where he had spent so many nights alone, knowing how close she was yet not being able to show her how much he cared.

He was touching her now. Like something out of a dream, he was holding her and kissing her and feeling her heat. Moving with her as he lowered her onto the bed, he was aware there would be a price to pay. But feeling her beneath him, hearing her soft groans of arousal and finding her moist and ready for him, there was only one truth that mattered. They were meant to be together. For a moment or for a lifetime, they were man and wife.

Kelsey felt the hard firmness of the futon along her back, felt the solid weight of his body pressing her against it. Anticipation surged in her belly, causing tension to build and the fireball inside her to burn white-hot. She had to have him, had to make him a part of her or she was going to die from the need. She'd survived a building collapsing, survived the forces of nature, but she wasn't going to make it without his love.

And then he was there, moving over her, bringing his body close, pushing deep. Everything within her reacted when he pressed into her—heart, soul, mind, body. There was a moment, one brilliant, clarifying moment when all she could do was lie there in wonder, but that was only a moment. After that there was only need, and yearning, and a desire that blocked out everything else.

Had it always been like this when they'd made love, the mindless need, the wild abandon? Because that's how she felt, mindless and wild, unaware of anything except the man in her arms and the hunger that clawed at her. She was ready to burst, grasping at him like a lifeline. She had forgotten a lot since the accident, but could she have forgotten this? Could she have forgotten what it was to be with him, to be filled by him, to be made desperate from the pleasure?

Suddenly the coil inside her snapped, and the fireball burst free, shattering apart in a brilliant explosion of light, sound and action. Every muscle in her body convulsed, hurling her past the boundaries of pleasure, past the confines of satisfaction and gratification. Clinging to him, she held on for dear life, letting his strong, powerful movements carry her over the edges of madness to the outer limits of peace.

Chapter 11

Coop felt her nails bite into his back, felt her body grow rigid and her muscles contract. He felt the rapture seize her and carry her away. Her soft groans filled his senses. Her short, rapid breaths blew energy into him. He felt empowered, invincible.

Following the path she blazoned, sharing her pleasure and experiencing her ecstasy, caused the fragile hold on his control to slip. He was, after all, just a man.

The climax began with a shower of lights, filling his head and blocking out everything else. There was no earth, no sky, no outside world. He was alone with only Kelsey beneath him and the life flowing between them like electricity through a wire. He felt his body surge forward, hurling him into that void, into that secret place where sanity blended with madness, reason with awareness.

"I love you."

He heard the words, felt them circle his consciousness

like a halo of light. He couldn't tell if he'd said them or if they had come from her—but it didn't matter. What was important, what mattered was love, and it was there between them.

Finally, the agony became too sweet and he surrendered, body and soul. He found what he'd been seeking, reclaimed what he'd once lost, and the pleasure proved to be the finest he'd ever known.

Kelsey heard his ragged breathing, felt his hard body erupt and his arms clutch her tight. She grabbed him, held him and let him sweep her away again. She crested, peak after peak, until, riding one wave after another, she was sure she would go mad from the pleasure. It was only when she heard him cry out, when she felt him collapse, spent, against her that she found her way back.

"I love you," he said in a breathless whisper in her ear.

I love you, too. The words formed on her lips, but she had no strength left to push them out.

Coop wasn't sure how long they lay there together, locked in each other's arms. It could have been an hour or it could have been days. Time had lost its importance.

It wasn't until he felt her shiver that he realized the night had turned cold. He moved then, but just enough to reach for the bed covers and pull them over their cold bodies.

"Better?" he asked, gathering her close. The room was full of shadows, but enough moonlight found its way in through the window so he could see her face in the darkness.

"Nothing could be better than this," she murmured sleepily, squinting at him through slitted lids.

He brought his hand up and ran his knuckles along the softness of her cheek. She looked so beautiful, content and fulfilled. He had no doubt she had wanted to make love with him, but the fact remained that she still believed him to be her husband. If she had remembered the truth, this never would have happened.

Like an invader storming the gates of a fortress, guilt nagged at him, but he couldn't bring himself to regret making love with Kelsey. Not with her looking beautiful and satisfied.

"I can think of something," he whispered, bending down and pressing a kiss against her mouth.

"Oh?"

"This," he murmured, planting wet kisses along her jaw, down her neck and over her breasts. "And this," he whispered as he trailed a path of kisses along her waist, into her belly button and over the swell of her hips.

Kelsey would never know where the energy came from, but it flooded her depleted system, revitalizing spent muscles and weary nerve endings. His bold caresses had her peaking again and again, sending her over the edge and into that chasm of lights. When he entered her again, she could do nothing but cling to him as they rode the wave together, journeying farther and faster than before.

Finally, she gave in to the exhaustion, feeling his heavy body above her and reveling in its weight. Her sleep was deep and peaceful, and her dreams—for the first time since the coma—were sweet.

"Eight, nine, ten, eleven." Kelsey stopped, a chill rumbling through her. The damp fog that had rolled inland and shrouded the dawn in a blanket of white had sent the temperatures dropping, and the sheet she held over her naked body offered little protection. "Twelve, thirteen." Her voice quivered, and the tiled kitchen floor felt like ice against her bare feet. Another chill caused her finger to tremble as it counted the days on the calendar.

Except she was too excited to think about the cold, was concentrating too hard on counting the days of the week to worry about her numb toes. Besides, Coop was in the bedroom asleep. He would be warm and would wrap his arms around her tight when she crawled into the bed beside him. His body heat would take the morning chill from her.

"Fourteen." She stopped and stared at the calendar, hearing only the soft, mechanical ticking of the kitchen clock hanging on the wall above the stove and the sound of her breath as it entered and exited her lungs.

There could be no mistake. She'd counted it out three times. It had to be right.

Still, she had to be sure, didn't want to take the chance that in her haste she might have gotten careless, might have skipped over something and made a mistake. This was too important. Too much was at stake. She wanted to be absolutely sure. Flipping through the pages of the calendar, she counted it out again.

Excitement erupted in her with a funny little giggle. Leaning forward, she rested her forehead against the wall, taking a moment and letting the implications sink in. Except the news was too good to keep to herself for very long—she had to share it. She had to share it with Coop.

Clutching the sheet around her, she turned and ran across the cold tiles and down the hall to the bedroom. At the door, she paused again. He was still sleeping, his body beneath the blanket looking big and long on the small futon bed.

At the sight of him, her body reacted, and she remembered their lovemaking the night before. It seemed hard to believe she'd doubted his feelings for her, because she had no doubts now. But even if the doubts had existed for a while in her mind, he'd alleviated them last night. She was his wife again—fully, completely, thoroughly.

Her gaze followed his form beneath the bed covers, and she remembered the hard feel of him against her. The sight of him started a chain reaction in her. Desire smoldered in her belly, and her blood began to heat. She felt more like a bride than a woman with five years of marriage under her belt.

Letting the sheet slip to the floor, she slid beneath the blankets and stretched out beside him. His skin felt warm and wonderful against hers, and she pressed a kiss along his back.

He stirred, turned and gathered her close. "Freezing," he murmured sleepily, finding the juncture of her neck and shoulder and nuzzling the silky sweetness with his lips and tongue. "Why are you so cold?"

"I've been up," she whispered, feeling the cold evaporate at every place he touched her.

"What time is it?"

"It's not even six yet."

He lifted his head, forcing his lids open. "Everything okay?"

"Oh, Coop," she sighed, seeing the concern in his sleepy face and thinking her heart was going to burst in her chest. Smiling, she pulled him close. "It's more than okay—it's wonderful."

He regarded her for a moment, wide awake now. "Have you been into the cold ravioli again?"

"Better."

"Better than cold ravs?"

"Better," she said again, laughing. "I've been counting."

"Say again?"

She laughed at his confused, bewildered look. "Days—on the calendar," she said, by way of explanation. "I've been figuring out my cycle—you know, since my last period."

Like an icy finger, a chill ran the length of his spine. "Your cycle?"

"My cycle," she said, nodding excitedly. "And you know what we might have done last night?"

He shook his head, his throat too thick with emotion for words to pass.

She felt tears sting her eyes. "We might have made a baby."

The ringing in his ears became so loud he began to think he hadn't heard her right. Only there had been no mistake. The smile on her face, the look in her eyes told him with unerring clarity that she'd said what he feared she had.

He cleared his throat loudly. "A baby? How—I mean, why? What makes you think so?"

At his look of utter shock, her smile widened. "I don't remember about before the accident," she explained. "But I can say without a doubt that I haven't been on the pill since I woke up in the hospital." She shrugged. "It's just math after that, counting the days of my cycle." She reached out, running a hand along his cheek. "Last night was one of the nights I could conceive."

Conceive. The word was like a knife in his chest, twisting, turning, tearing his flesh. Conceive. How did he tell her? How could he ruin her happiness, destroy her dream? He remembered all too well what had happened the first time she'd discovered the truth. It not only had destroyed their marriage, it had nearly destroyed her. How could he protect her this time? What did he do?

"Kelsey," he whispered, his voice coarse and raw in

his throat. Taking her hand in his, he shifted his weight, scooting into a half-sitting position. "Sweetheart, you have to remember you've been through a lot in the past several weeks. I don't think… Maybe it's not such a good idea for you to get your hopes up, at least not for a while, until we can be sure."

"I know, I know," she said, looking at him. "But it's okay to dream, isn't it? I mean, we've wanted a baby for a long time, we'd been trying so hard. Unless—" She stopped suddenly, the line between her brows deepening. "Unless that's changed, and I've forgotten."

He could feel every muscle in her body grow rigid. "No," he assured her, bringing her hand to his lips and brushing a kiss along her fingertips. "No, that never changed."

"Then what's wrong with hoping?"

He felt the tension slipping from her and watched the frown disappear from her face. It was wrong to give her false hope, it was wrong to let her go on believing in something that was never going to happen.

"Kelsey," he said, his fingers gently massaging her hand. "Kelsey, there's something…"

She looked at him when his words stopped. "What?" she prompted, giving him a little shake. "What is it?"

He pressed a kiss into her palm, excitement making her eyes sparkle bright in the gloom. How he wanted to share her excitement. How he wished he could just forget and dream the sweet dream. He'd pretended about a lot of things in the past couple of months, but he couldn't pretend about this. "There's something we need to talk about."

"Tell me," she insisted, scooting up and pulling the sheet around her. "Coop, you look so serious. What's the matter?"

"It is serious." He stopped, drawing in a deep breath. "It's about us—about you and I having a baby."

His expression made alarms go off in her head. She thought back to that moment the night before, that moment when she'd almost had a memory.

But this reaction was stronger and more vivid. Something was coming out of the darkness. Something was crashing through the din, climbing its way up out of that black hole of the lost and back to life again.

They had sat like this before. They had hoped and dreamed. They had celebrated. Images flashed through her brain, random and disjointed—maternity clothes, the hospital room and...

She squeezed her eyes tight. No, she didn't want to see, she didn't want to remember the tiny casket going into the ground.

"A baby," she whispered, her breath coming in short, quick gasps. "Oh, God, Coop." She stared up at him, frantically searching his face. "Coop—a baby. We had a baby."

Coop watched her reaction, watched recollection and recognition sink in and become reality. He hated this, hated to think of the pain and the misery there was for her to remember, all the hurt she would have to relive. He wanted to reach out, wanted to gather her close and spare her the pain. But how could he spare her the truth? The past was right there, and nothing he could do would protect her from it.

"A little boy," he said, his bottom lip starting to tremble and his voice cracking with emotion. "He...he lived only a few hours." He paused, tears stinging his eyes. "He was early—too early, and his little lungs, there was something wrong. There was nothing anyone could do."

"Oh, my God, Coop, I remember," she sobbed, her

face crumbling into tears. "Our little baby. Our little boy." She looked at him, his image blurred by the tears. The memory was suddenly as clear and as painful as it had been years before. "I remember, I remember."

It was a long time before either of them spoke again. It wasn't the time for words. It was a time for mourning. It was a time to hold and be held, to comfort and be comforted—together, always together.

They sat together for a long time on the futon, propped against the wall and in each other's arms. The tears had long since stopped, the shock had diminished, and the pain had become an arduous burden to carry. Yet still the need to hold, to comfort and be close was there.

"It must have been hard on you, knowing and not being able to say anything."

Coop closed his eyes. He didn't want to think about the things he hadn't told her. "It...it wasn't something that was easy to talk about."

"I can understand that," she said, her voice strangely devoid of emotion. "And it would be important for me to remember on my own."

He drew in a deep breath. "Everyone seemed to think so." He looked at her, feeling like a kid looking for someone to blame. "Now I'm not so sure."

"No, it was the only way," she insisted. "I can see why the doctors would have thought it best."

"I just wish it didn't have to hurt so much."

She turned her head and looked at him. "At least we have each other to lean on now. I'm grateful for that."

Coop nodded, his throat closing with emotion. She hadn't leaned on him before. She'd turned away.

"It explains a lot, though," she said, her voice thoughtful and quiet. She turned and settled against him. "A lot of things I couldn't understand."

Coop ran a hand along the length of her hair, stroking gently. He couldn't help wondering how much she had remembered. "Like what?"

"The fear, and those awful nightmares," she said, absently working the fabric of the sheet around her. "It was like I knew there was something awful in there, in those lost memories—something I wanted to forget, that I dreaded remembering." She shrugged. "Now I understand."

"It was a bad time," he whispered, the pain no less fierce now than it had been the first time around. He reached out, wiping one lone tear that slipped down her cheek. "Sometimes I've wished I could forget."

"No," she said, shaking her head. "No, it's better this way. It hurts—" Her voice cracked and failed, and she struggled for a moment. "God, it hurts so much, but I don't ever want to forget again. Our little boy, our baby." She turned and looked at him. "We had him for a little while. I don't ever want to forget."

He nodded, tightening his arms around her. He wanted to sit there and comfort her as long as he could, as long as she would let him. He hadn't been given the chance before. The doctors had delivered the devastating news that Kelsey's chances of conceiving again were next to impossible.

The news had been a fatal blow for Kelsey—first her child, then her hope. It had more than devastated her, it had demoralized her. She hadn't been able to bounce back, hadn't been able to pick up the pieces and go on. She'd pushed everyone away, her friends, her family and especially him.

He pulled her closer. He almost felt grateful for the second chance he'd been given, for the memory loss that enabled him to hold her and comfort her the way he had wanted years before. How much longer would it be before the rest came tumbling back, before it all was there before her, hitting her in the face? The gates had been opened. It was only a matter of time before the floodwaters swept him out of her life forever.

"It also explains a lot about us," she said, resting her head against his shoulder.

"Us?" He heard the tightness in his voice and cleared his throat. "What do you mean?"

"Just that I had this feeling there was something, you know? Something you weren't telling me. It would be so awkward sometimes, between us. So tense." She breathed out a little laugh. "I know you said there wasn't another woman, but I couldn't shake the feeling something was wrong." She moved a hand along his arm, touching the gentle dusting of hair. "Now I realize you were just trying to protect me, not see me hurt."

Coop felt sick. She was making him sound noble, like some kind of knight in shining armor, and it only made him feel worse. What was she going to think when she learned the whole truth? Would she be as understanding? Or would she see him for the imposter he was?

"How do you feel now?" he asked, weaving a long lock of her hair between his fingers.

"Sad," she said with a heavy sigh. She turned in his arms and slipped a hand along his neck. "But hopeful, and..." She stopped, pressing a kiss along his cheek. "Very, very happy."

He wanted to warn her, wanted to tell her not to be too happy, not to feel too secure, because there was still so much out there that could destroy her again. Only he couldn't—not yet, not now. She'd been through too much already.

After the baby had been born, they had been given no

opportunity to deal with the tragedy of his death before being hit with the rest of it. This time he wanted it to be different. This time he wanted her to have time to recover and cope with the loss, and selfishly he wanted to be there to help her.

It wouldn't be long before all the gaps in her memory were filled and the whole truth would be brought to light. He knew he was living on borrowed time. His day of reckoning was coming, and he wanted every moment he could have, every moment she would give him before the ax finally fell.

"Where were you?"

Coop sat on the futon and gently swept away a lock of hair that fell across her sleepy face. "I just had to make a quick call. I phoned Doris."

"You're going to work?" she asked, her voice husky from sleep.

"Thought maybe I'd take the day off," he said, brushing his fingers along the length of her bare arm. Leaning down, he lowered his voice. "If that's okay with you."

She smiled and rolled onto her back. "What do you think?" she murmured, slipping her arms around his neck.

Coop let her pull him down, stretching out on the futon next to her. After the emotionally charged scene earlier, they'd both fallen asleep, emotionally and physically spent. It had been nearly eight when he woke again, barely enough time to catch Doris before she left for the office.

Doris assured him she would manage without him, but not before giving him a lecture on spur-of-the-moment decisions and how they wreaked havoc with the smooth operation of a business. He'd taken her good-natured tongue-lashing, knowing that despite her grousing, he could trust her to see that flights were on time and obligations were met.

"Thank you," Kelsey murmured.

He looked at her, brushing a kiss along her jaw. "What for? For playing hooky or braving Doris's wrath?"

"Both," she said, slowly moving her hands along the hard muscles of his shoulders and arms. "And for staying home to baby-sit me."

He pulled away a little, looking at her. "Is that what you think I'm doing? Baby-sitting?"

"What would you call it?"

He smiled, holding her close and letting her feel him against her. "I'll call it anything you want, as long as we can stay like this all day."

Kelsey laughed, feeling better and happier than she had in a very long time. The memories of her pregnancy, of childbirth classes and nursery plans, of hours spent in labor and the delivery of her son were so vivid now, so crystal clear, it seemed hard to believe she'd ever been able to forget. But as painful as it had been to remember, she felt a peacefulness inside her, a calm she hadn't felt since waking up in the hospital. The black holes hadn't disappeared completely, but they didn't look quite so dark or frightening as they once had.

The sun streaked in bright from the window, the fog that had shrouded the dawn having rolled out over the ocean as quickly as it had rolled in. Kelsey could hear the sounds of the neighborhood coming alive, car doors slamming, children's voices calling in the distance. But despite the intrusion of light and sound, the real world felt far away and removed from their small room. It was just her and Coop and the past they shared.

"Well," she murmured, running her fingers down his

torso and unsnapping the front of his jeans. "If we're going to stay here all day, let's get you comfortable."

Comfortable. As Coop slipped out of his jeans and tossed them to the floor, he wondered why men always thought "comfortable" was the death of passion. That's not the way it was at all.

He slid into her arms, lowering himself between her legs and entering her slow and easy.

He heard her soft groans in his ear, felt her body come alive beneath his touch, felt her fire start a fever in him. Heat swept through him, carrying him out of himself, out of the real world and into the void to ecstasy.

"You know," she whispered, long after her breathing had returned to normal and the world had taken shape again, "I don't see how you do it."

"Do what?" he mumbled.

"Sleep on this thing."

He lifted his head. "What? The futon?"

"Yeah," she said, making a face. "It's a rack. How have you stood it for eight weeks?"

Eight weeks. What would she think if she knew he'd been sleeping on it for two years? "You don't like it?"

"Do you?"

He thought about the months he'd slept on the thing. After Kelsey had left, it hadn't mattered where he slept, hadn't mattered if he was comfortable.

Comfortable. Without her, nothing had been comfortable—not his house, not his life and certainly not this lumpy futon.

"Come on," he said suddenly, sitting up.

"What?" She blinked, surprised, and grabbed for the sheet. "Why?"

"Let's go shopping," he said, reaching for his jeans. "I want a new bed."

Chapter 12

"Don't do that."

Mannie Cohen pointed to the chair in front of his desk and gestured for her to sit down. "Don't do what?"

Kelsey closed the door behind her and walked across the carpeted floor. "Look at me like that."

"And exactly how am I looking at you?" Dr. Cohen asked, pushing his glasses down his nose and peering at her over them.

"Like that," she said, pointing an accusing finger. She sat, then straightened her skirt. "Like I've been a disobedient little girl."

"Well," he said, giving her a deliberate look. "We did talk about this."

"Oh, come on, Mannie," she chided. "Look at me. I'm fine—better than ever. No more cuts, no more bruises, my leg is getting stronger all the time." She smiled, clapping her hands and squeezing them tight. "And now I'm going to have a baby." She looked across the desk at him and leaned forward. "Don't scold me. Congratulate me—I'm so happy."

Dr. Cohen stared at the lab report in front of him. He hadn't believed the results the first time, and ran the test again. There was no doubt. She was indeed going to have a baby, and no one was more surprised than he was. He knew her medical history, knew about the first pregnancy and the problems she'd experienced during the birth, as well as the odds against her ever conceiving again.

He regarded her. She looked positively radiant, the picture of health, happiness and womanhood. If there was one thing he'd learned in his years in medicine, it was that nothing was set in cement. Certainly not when it came to the human spirit—or the determination of a woman.

She'd made a remarkable recovery both physically and mentally, and remembering the death of her infant son had been a big step for her. He was more convinced than ever that she would recover her memory completely. He just wasn't so sure how she was going to handle the rest of it.

He wasn't going to sit in judgment of anyone for the way things had worked out. He couldn't blame Coop for getting caught up in the charade, for behaving like a husband when she believed herself to be his wife. But there was a baby on the way, and as a doctor he couldn't help being concerned about how discovering she was divorced would affect her health, her pregnancy and the health of her unborn child.

"I know you're happy, and I'm happy for you, I really am," he said. "I'm also your doctor. Don't blame me for being concerned as to how all this is going to affect your recovery."

"I thought we agreed I've recovered—past tense," she argued.

"And I thought we'd agreed it would have been better to wait."

"No," she said, shaking her head. "*You* agreed it would be better to wait. I decided to live my life, to go after what I want."

"And what about the memory loss?"

She couldn't deny there were still gaps that needed to be filled in. But she was certain she'd faced the worst. Nothing could hurt more than the memory of losing her baby son.

And now there was life inside her again—life and hope and love. She felt like a phoenix rising from the ashes, and she didn't feel afraid anymore.

"You've talked to Dr. Crowell. You know things are coming back. Having a baby isn't going to stop that."

"And what about Coop? Did you tell him you thought you were pregnant?"

Kelsey thought back to that morning on the futon bed when she'd woken him up with the news. "I told him there was a possibility."

He could only imagine what Cooper Reed's reaction was going to be when he received the results of the lab reports. The situation between the man and his ex-wife was complicated enough. The news that a baby was on the way would no doubt be about the last thing he would suspect.

"Well," Dr. Cohen said, opening a drawer in his desk and pulling out a prescription tablet. "Sharon will make an appointment for you with Gary Marks before you leave. He's in Santa Barbara, and the best obstetrician I know of. In the meantime—" he scribbled on the tablet and tore off the page "—get this filled today. I want you on prenatal vitamins as soon as possible."

"Okay," Kelsey said, dutifully taking the prescription

from him and slipping it into her purse. "Whatever you say."

He peered over the top of his glasses. "Yeah, right."

His sarcasm made her smile grow wider. Besides, she felt so good right now, nothing was going to get her down. She stood, leaned over the desk and planted an kiss on his cheek. "Be happy for me, Mannie. I'm fine, and even if those other memories never come back, it doesn't matter. I've got everything I'll ever need right now."

"Hi, Coop."

Coop looked across the street, letting the car door slam behind him. "Hi, Jonathan."

Coop caught sight of Holly Harding in the doorway, holding her daughter in her arms, and gave her a quick wave.

"You're home early today, huh?" Jonathan shouted, letting the plastic baseball bat in his hands drop to the ground.

"Yeah, I guess I am." Coop knew he was early, but pacing in his small office had been driving him crazy.

He'd wanted to be casual about today, wanted to show Kelsey it was a day just like any other day, that it was no big deal. But it was a big deal. She was seeing Mannie Cohen, and the doctor was going to burst her bubble, tell her she wasn't pregnant, and he'd been on pins and needles all day as to how she was going to react.

She'd insisted on going to the appointment alone, even though she'd promised to call him at work afterward. Only she hadn't called, and she hadn't answered the phone each time he'd called—and that had only made him more nervous.

"Didn't you fly your hellupcupter today?" Jonathan asked, skipping to the end of the drive.

"Oh, yeah, I flew it," Coop said, heading up the walk toward the porch.

"You fly high," Jonathan said, standing on tiptoe and pointing up. "Way up there, huh?"

"Way up there."

"'Cause you're the pilot, huh?"

"That's right, I'm the pilot."

"Me, too," Jonathan said, making a motor sound with his cheek. With his hands clutching an imaginary steering wheel, he raced off across his front yard toward his mother and sister, giving Coop a backward wave.

Coop laughed and slipped his key into the front door lock. It had become almost a daily ritual between them—waving and exchanging a few words. It was just one of a dozen small things that gave his life a settled, almost normal feel.

He unlocked the door, heard Kelsey in the kitchen and felt his heart lurch in his chest. He couldn't bring himself to regret the last four weeks. They'd been the best in his life. He felt whole again, felt life was worth living. He woke up every morning looking forward to the day, and went to bed each night with Kelsey in his arms.

A miracle had happened. She had breathed life into him, rejuvenated and revitalized him. She wasn't the only one who had recalled memories—he had, too. He remembered what it was to feel again, to hope and dream and love. He remembered what it was to be married. He *felt* married, he *acted* married. How more committed could two people be to each other? They talked together, laughed together, ate together, slept together.

He thought of the brass bed that took up considerable space in the master bedroom of their home. He knew it hadn't been right to suggest they make such a purchase, and he never should have allowed it. But it had seemed like the right thing to do. After what had happened between them, after sharing a night of love and passion, it hadn't felt right that they continue to sleep in separate beds.

He thought of their crazy shopping trip—bouncing on mattresses, poking, prodding, testing them out. After the emotional trauma of remembering their lost baby, she'd been giddy, and she'd made him giddy, too. She hadn't questioned his lame excuse as to why he wanted a new bed and not the bed they'd shared during the four years of their marriage—the bed he'd gotten rid of after she'd walked out. She'd been too excited to notice his excuse didn't make sense. And it hadn't really mattered. They'd acted more like teenagers going steady than a couple who'd been married—and divorced.

He knew he should be preparing her for the future, knew he should be getting her ready for the truth, not perpetuating a fantasy. Except he loved her—they loved each other, and that was also the truth. If things had gone the way they should have, if life was fair and fate played by the rules, they would still be together, still be married—and they would have a family.

"Coop, is that you?"

The sound of her voice made the warmth spread through him like sunshine after a long, dark night. "It's me."

"You're early."

Something in her voice was different. He frowned. "Maybe a little."

"Maybe a lot," she called back, popping her head around the corner. "I'm not ready yet."

"Ready for what?" he asked, starting toward the kitchen.

"No, stop," she insisted. "Don't come in here yet. Go take a shower or something."

He opened his mouth to say something, but before he could get the words out, she had disappeared again.

"I don't feel like taking a shower," he said. If something was wrong, he wanted to hear it now. "Kelsey?" He waited a moment longer, feeling the impatience build inside him. "Kelsey? What are you doing?"

"Just a minute," she called.

His frown deepened. He had a bad feeling about this. Something wasn't right.

He turned, tossing his keys into the tray on the hall stand in the foyer. They hadn't talked about starting a family since that morning on the futon, but he knew Kelsey hadn't given up hope that she might have conceived that night—or any of the nights since then. He knew she hoped Mannie Cohen would confirm those hopes today, and he hated to think how disappointed she would be.

He turned and stared toward the kitchen, tapping a fist against the leg of his jeans. Had the test results triggered something? Did she know she couldn't conceive, that there would never be another child? Did she know they were divorced?

"Kelsey?" he called, apprehension building in his stomach. "Honey? Is everything all right?"

"Just a minute."

Her voice sounded strained, different, and he took a hesitant step forward. "Kelsey, this is making me nervous. What's going on?"

"Coop, please, just a minute."

She'd used her nurse's voice, the voice she used when she expected her orders to be followed. But he wasn't in the mood to follow orders. He wanted to know what was happening, and he wanted to know now.

He turned the corner into the breakfast nook and found her in the kitchen with her arms in a huge ceramic mixing bowl, working furiously.

"What are you doing?"

She jumped, her head snapping up. "Oh, Coop," she moaned, trying to cover the enormous bowl with her hand. "You're going to spoil everything. I told you to wait in there."

"I didn't want to wait," he said, walking into the kitchen. He glanced at the open canister of flour and the empty packages of yeast on the counter. He wasn't sure what he'd expected, but seeing her up to her elbows in bread dough wasn't it. "What are you doing?"

She straightened and sighed heavily. "I was trying to surprise you."

"By baking bread?"

She pounded at the dough in the bowl. "You used to love homemade bread."

"I still do," he said, remembering the perfectly rounded loaves she would make for special treats. "But why are you making it now?"

"I don't know," she said, tossing a damp dish towel over the bowl and setting it aside. "I was feeling particularly domestic today."

"Oh, yeah?" He rounded the counter and reached for her. Mindless of her flour-dusted apron, he slipped his hands around her waist and pulled her close. "What's got you in such a *domestic* mood?"

She looked at him, letting her hands find the front of his shirt. "I've got something to tell you."

He brushed a kiss along her lips. He wanted to be holding her when she told him the doctor had burst her bubble, wanted her to know it didn't matter to him that there would never be any more children.

"So tell me," he whispered.

Before she had a chance to say anything, a loud chirping sounded. "What's that?"

"My beeper," Coop mumbled, and reached for the small electronic device clipped to his belt.

He depressed a button on the top and recognized the number on the small screen. Mannie Cohen was calling him, and he had a pretty good idea why. The doctor would have had no choice but to tell Kelsey she wasn't pregnant, and if she'd pressed him, he might even have had to tell her she never would become pregnant again. No doubt he was calling now to give fair warning.

Fair warning, he thought, switching the beeper off. As if anything in this whole situation was fair.

"Something important?" Kelsey asked.

"No," he mumbled, shaking his head. There would be time later to talk with her doctors and figure out what to do. Right now she was going to need his support. "Nothing that can't wait." Tossing the beeper on the counter, he turned to her again. "So what is it you wanted to tell me?"

Kelsey looked into Coop's face, wanting to savor the moment. This was one memory she never wanted to forget.

He'd been afraid of her getting her hopes up, afraid of her being disappointed and getting hurt. But maybe he was just a little afraid of being hurt himself. She'd seen his face when he'd talked about their baby son. She'd seen the pain and the grief. But she could also remember how excited he had been at the prospect of becoming a father, how much he had wanted the baby she had carried for seven short months.

The death of their child had affected him, too. She understood why he hadn't allowed himself to hope, why he hadn't allowed himself to even consider the possibility that she might be pregnant.

Which was only going to make her news all the more joyous. He had no idea—despite the fact she had talked about the possibility, despite the fact that he knew she would be seeing the doctor today. He really had no idea what she was about to tell him.

"You know I saw Mannie today."

"Yeah, I know," he said, his voice sounding stiff and artificial even to his own ears. "You were supposed to call me when you got back."

"I know," she said, giving him a meek look. She hadn't wanted to. She'd been afraid if she heard his voice on the phone she would have blurted out everything—and that's not what she wanted. "I got home late, though, and then I got busy with the bread and... Time just got away from me."

"Okay," he said, accepting her explanation. Resting his hands lightly at her waist, he gave her a little twist. "But the bread's rising now, the work's all done. What did Mannie have to say?"

"Well," she said, feeling the color rise in her cheeks. "Everything that was broken seems to be fixed now. My leg is strong, the cuts and bruises have disappeared." She looked at him, feeling a little like the cat who'd swallowed the canary. "Basically I'm the picture of health."

"I can see that," he said matter-of-factly. He dropped his hold on her waist, walked to the refrigerator and yanked open the door. He tried to move as casually and as naturally as possible, but every muscle in his body felt tight. "Anything else?"

She shook her head, watching as he pulled out a pitcher of juice and reached for a glass. "No, not really. Just that he wants me to keep seeing Dr. Crowell and..."

He filled the glass with juice, lowered the pitcher to the counter and looked at her when her words drifted off. "And?"

"And he has another doctor he wants me to see."

"Another doctor?"

"Yeah."

"In Santa Ynez?"

"No, it's someone here in Santa Barbara."

Coop thought of the page Mannie Cohen had sent and wondered what the doctor might have had to tell him. "Another psychiatrist?"

She shook her head, slipped off her apron and hung it on a hook in the broom closet. "No, he's not a psychiatrist."

"Then what?"

"He's a..." She turned, drew in a deep breath and squared her shoulders. "He's an obstetrician."

Coop's mind worked furiously. Why would Mannie send her to a baby doctor? Was she having that much difficulty believing she couldn't conceive? Had she demanded the word of an expert? "Why would you need to see an obstetrician?"

Kelsey wasn't sure where the tears had come from, but suddenly they were there, streaming down her cheeks. But she didn't mind crying this time. "You don't know?"

"You're crying. What is it? What's wrong?"

"Nothing. Nothing's wrong," she insisted, smiling through the tears. "Everything's wonderful, everything's *great!*"

"Then why the tears?"

"I'm crying because I'm happy. I'm crying because—" She stopped, taking another deep breath.

"Because why?" he demanded impatiently.

She looked at him and shrugged. "Because we're going to have a baby."

"What?" Coop was sure he'd heard her wrong.

"A baby," she said again, taking a few steps towards him. "I'm pregnant."

Coop forgot about the glass in his hand, forgot about playing it cool. At the moment it was all he could do to move the air in and out of his lungs. He felt the glass slipping, felt it disappear from his grasp, but the ringing in his ears made it impossible to hear when it crashed against the tile floor and sent juice spilling in all directions.

"A baby?"

"Mannie ran the tests today."

Coop shook his head, pushed himself away from the counter, walked through the spilled juice and tracked it across the kitchen. "I—I don't understand." He spun around and looked at her. "You must have misunderstood."

Kelsey shook her head. "No, there's no mistake. We're going to have a baby."

"You mean Mannie told you? He actually said you're going to have a baby?"

She nodded.

"He ran tests and everything?" Coop asked, feeling breathless and a little light-headed.

She nodded again.

"And the results were that you're pregnant?"

She slowly stepped past the spilled juice and walked across the kitchen to where he stood. "Just to be sure, Mannie ran a second set of tests."

"And?"

"And there's no mistake." She slipped her hands around his waist. "We're going to have a baby."

"I—I don't know what to say," he stammered, gathering her close. "I—I can hardly believe it."

"Believe it," she whispered, pulling him close. "Believe it, and be happy."

"Are you sure?"

"I ran the tests myself."

Coop leaned forward, resting his elbow on his knee and cradling the phone against his shoulder. The bedroom was dark and quiet, with just the sound of the water running in the bathroom next door. Even though he knew Kelsey couldn't hear him while she showered, he kept his voice low. "So there's no mistake?"

"No, no mistake. She's pregnant, just a little over four weeks along."

Coop let out a long breath, feeling tension begin to build at the bridge of his nose. "Doc, I don't understand. How did this happen?"

"Well, it happened in the usual way," Mannie said with a snort. "But why it happened, that's a little trickier."

"Why *did* it happen?" he demanded.

"I've been reviewing Kelsey's file, reading the records from two years ago, after the first pregnancy. I've also faxed copies to Gary Marks, the obstetrician she'll be seeing." He paused. "Considering everything, I'd have to say I would agree with the diagnosis that was made at the time. The damage she sustained during the delivery was severe. It wouldn't have seemed likely conception could occur given the circumstances. And reports from the six-month postpartum check seemed to bear that out. Scar tissue in the Fallopian tubes was extensive. Of course, none of that ruled out pregnancy. It just made the probability unlikely—*very* unlikely."

Coop squeezed his eyes closed tight. "Then what happened?"

"Who knows?" he said. "Maybe the scar tissue wasn't as extensive as it was first thought. Maybe there has been some kind of reversal or regeneration. Maybe it was just meant to happen. And I can tell you, I never underestimate a woman's determination when it comes to getting what she wants—especially a woman like Kelsey. She wanted to conceive a child, and by God, she did it."

"But what about her recovery?"

"Physically she's in great shape. The memory loss..." He stopped, thinking of the conversation he'd had with her in his office. "She tells me she's remembering, and I believe her. And who knows, maybe now with her attention focused on a baby, it'll free up her subconscious to remember more."

"And the baby? What about the baby? Is there a chance what happened last time could happen again?"

"The baby was too early last time, too small to survive. There's a history of premature labor, and we're going to want to take extra precautions this time to make sure that doesn't happen. Still, there's no reason to think she won't carry this child to term, no physical obstacles that would prevent her from doing so. You know, if there's one thing I've learned in this business it's that life always manages to find a way, despite what we experts say. Sometimes you just have to accept it."

"So where do I go from here, Doc?" Coop asked in a weary voice. He was too tired, too drained of emotion for anger or frustration. He just needed help, needed direction, needed to know what to do. "Do I tell her everything now, or what? I mean, what will the shock do to the baby? Will it put Kelsey at risk? Should I wait?"

"Well, of course the risk of miscarriage lessens the

further the pregnancy advances, so in that sense, yes, waiting would be preferable.''

''And if she remembers on her own?''

''Then I'd say nature took its course.''

Coop sighed heavily. ''This isn't helping me much.''

''I know.'' The doctor sighed. ''But let me ask you something, Coop. What is it *you* want?''

''What do you mean?'' he asked irritably. He wasn't in the mood for word games. ''What does that have to do with anything?''

''Maybe nothing, maybe a lot. Just indulge me a little. What do you want?''

He ran a frustrated hand through his hair. ''I want my wife, Doc, and my child.''

''Then go to your wife, Coop. You love her, and she loves you. All the rest is just details. Congratulations, you're going to be a father.''

''Ex-wife,'' Coop muttered as he hung up the phone. He heard the water in the bathroom stop and the shower door open.

They weren't married. Mannie Cohen had a way of forgetting that. Coop only wished he could. Because no matter how he felt, despite their living arrangements and the love he felt in his heart, they weren't husband and wife. And yet now, with the baby, they were a family.

Chapter 13

Kelsey snuggled into the crook of Coop's arm, pulling the covers over them. The room was dark, making the lights of the city below shine even brighter.

"I thought it might be better if we waited," she said. "You know, before we tell anyone—my dad, the family."

Coop thought of Mo Chandler and sighed heavily. How was he going to explain this to his former father-in-law? "Yeah, that might be better."

"Just for a little while, until we're sure everything's going to be all right."

"Okay."

"It's going to be hard, though, to keep quiet." She laughed. "I feel like I'm going to burst—like I want to tell everyone."

"Yeah."

Kelsey turned her head and looked up at him. "You all right?"

"Sure, why?"

"I don't know. You seem a little quiet."

"Do I?" He made a show of reaching down, of rubbing a hand over his stomach and groaning, hoping to divert her attention from anything serious. "Must be all that bread. I finished a loaf all by myself. I'm stuffed."

"No, that's not it," she said, turning in his arms. It was too dark to see his face clearly, but his shadowy silhouette was outlined against the pillow. "Is something bothering you?"

He had to smile at the irony—a sad, solemn smile that almost hurt. There was so much bothering him, he wouldn't even know where to start, things like truth and lies, and how he was going to hold everything together long enough to keep both her and their baby out of danger.

"Not really," he lied, reaching out in the blackness and finding a long strand of her hair. "I'm just a little tired, that's all."

"Tired?" She leaned close, searching his face in the shadows. "Are you sure that's all?"

His hand stroked the length of her hair. Even in the darkness he could see that tiny line across her brow deepen. "Of course it is," he said, tapping his finger on her forehead. "Don't look so worried."

"But I am worried. I want you to be happy about the baby."

"Oh, sweetheart," he said, pulling her close. "I am happy—very happy. Don't doubt that—don't *ever* doubt that."

"Then what is it? What's got you so quiet tonight? Talk to me."

Selfishly he wished they could talk, that he could unburden himself once and for all, get everything out in the open. If only he could explain everything rationally, make her understand and not get upset and put herself and their baby at risk. It wasn't that he'd been quiet tonight. He'd just been too stunned to say much, too shocked by the day and its events, too afraid that if he opened his mouth, he'd say too much and lose everything.

"There's nothing to talk about," he insisted. "Not really."

"No?" she asked skeptically.

"No," he said, but the word held no conviction even to his own ears. He gave his head a shake. "Look, I'm just…just a little concerned, that's all."

"Concerned?" She pulled back. "About what?"

"About what? Kelsey, you're going to have a baby."

"And that concerns you?" She sat up. Her voice was loud in the darkness, loud and full of fear. "Now I *am* worried. Are you having second thoughts about the baby?"

"Don't be ridiculous," he said, sitting up, too. He rested a hand on her arm. "Kelsey, I almost lost you a few months ago—you almost died. And now this." He reached out and settled a hand on her abdomen. "A baby," he murmured, kneading her stomach lovingly. "There could be complications—for you, and for the baby, for…for us." He stopped, emotion tightening his throat and making it difficult to speak. "I just love you so much—if you only knew. I love you, and the baby." His voice cracked, and he cleared his throat. "I—I don't want to lose you, not ever, not again."

"Oh, Coop," she said, moving close and wrapping her arms around his neck. "Coop. Nothing's going to happen this time—you'll see. I'm going to be fine, and the baby's going to be fine—we all are. I promise." She brushed a kiss long his lips. "I promise."

Coop surrendered to her embrace and to her soft, wet kisses. He allowed her long, silky body to move over his, let her slow movements and loving gestures stroke and soothe his tense muscles and weary nerves. He wanted to lose himself in her lovemaking, wanted only to feel and respond, and not to think.

She was so sure, so hopeful. If only he could feel hopeful, too. If only he could block out the truth and believe it could be that simple—that they would be careful, that the doctors would take special precautions, that Kelsey would deliver a strong, healthy baby. It was what he wanted, what he dreamed of having—his wife, his child, his family.

Only the road ahead was a mine field, seeded with one disaster after another, any one of which could blow up in his face and destroy the dream forever.

She had to know the truth. It was no longer merely a matter of her recovery, no longer a question of whether she would retrieve what the amnesia took from her. There was a baby on the way—a new life they would share in for the rest of their lives. He had to find a way to tell her without risking her and the baby.

The lies nagged at him, plaguing his conscience, tormenting his soul. However, the soft, delicate stroking of her hands, the smooth, even motions of her body against him were like an oasis in the desert. Soon needs rose up in him, urgent and compelling. He wanted her, wanted to escape into the passion and let it take away the hurt, and pain and the fear—for just a while. Just long enough for him to catch his breath. Just long enough for him to dream the dream one more time.

"I love you," he whispered, bringing their bodies together and pressing deep. He reveled in the warmth of her, in the feel and the scent and the taste of her. "I love us together—like this."

"Coop," she murmured, her voice thick and raspy with

need and desire. "Be happy, Coop. Don't be afraid. I love you, that's all that matters. Don't be afraid."

Afraid. He could hardly imagine a life without fear, a life without guilt or remorse or regret. They had become a way of life for him in the past two and a half months. Except now. Now she was in his arms, now she belonged to him. She was his safe haven, his refuge where he could find peace. She was everything to him—his love, his life, the center of his universe.

But the respite and peace could only last so long. Soon desire burned out of control. His body exploded, and the world shattered.

It was a long time before he floated back, before his breathing became normal and the world took shape again. Unfortunately, along with the world, the rest of it—the lies, the guilt and the fear—came back, too.

"Everything's going to be all right," she whispered sleepily, snuggling close. "You'll see. I know it. We're all going to be all right—you, me, the baby. It's going to be great. I *know* it. Trust me."

Coop tightened his arms around her, holding her late into the night. He did trust her—he always had. The problem was, once he told her everything, she was never going to trust *him* again.

"Here, let me help you with that."

Kelsey glanced up from the armload of groceries she was struggling with, surprised to see her neighbor from across the street. She let Jonathan's mother relieve her of one of the heavy bags.

"Thanks," she said, giving the young woman a grateful smile. "I was trying to make it in one trip."

"I can understand that," the woman said, following her across the yard and up the walk. "I sometimes feel I put in a couple hundred miles a day—in and out of the house, the kids, the dog, shopping, preschool, doctor, dentist. If there was any real justice in life, I'd weigh ninety pounds after all that exercise."

At the door Kelsey stopped and slipped the key into the lock. "If there was any real justice in life, men would know the joys of PMS and chocolate would make you thin."

"Isn't that the truth." She laughed, following Kelsey into the house. She set the bag on the kitchen counter, then turned. "I've been meaning to come over and introduce myself." She held out a hand. "I'm Holly Harding from across the street."

"Hi, Holly," Kelsey said, taking her hand and shaking it. "I'm Kelsey."

"I think you already know Jonathan."

"Oh, yes." Kelsey laughed. "What a sweetheart he is."

Holly smiled proudly. "He's a character, all right."

"You also have a little girl?"

Holly nodded. "Sarah. She's two."

"That's a busy age."

"Oh, don't I know it—they don't call them the terrible twos for nothing."

Kelsey hesitated. She'd been reluctant to socialize much since the accident. With the gaps in her memory, she'd been afraid she would say or do something that would make it awkward and embarrassing for everyone. Only Holly Harding hadn't known her before, not really. Coop had told her that himself.

"Would you like to stay for a little while, have some tea? I was just going to make myself a cup."

Holly peered through the window toward her house. "Well, the place still looks reasonably peaceful. At least

Christian—my husband—hasn't come stomping out of the front door screaming yet or anything—which is what usually happens when I leave him alone with the kids.'' She turned to Kelsey. ''I'd love to.''

Kelsey filled the kettle and placed it on the burner. How long had it been since she'd stood chatting in her kitchen with a neighbor? How long had it been since she'd shared a little girl talk with a friend? Surely she'd done things like this before the accident, even if she couldn't remember.

She turned and opened the pantry doors, taking the groceries Holly handed her out of the bags and storing them on the shelves. She liked the comfortable feeling, liked the easy conversation and the relaxed atmosphere. It made her feel like a real person again, like a wife and a mother. Normal.

''Oh, my, do I ever remember these guys,'' Holly said dryly, pulling an oversize carton of soda crackers out of a bag.

''The crackers?'' Kelsey took the carton from her and slipped it on the shelf, thinking of the nausea and morning sickness that usually started sometime around noon and lasted well into the night.

''Yeah, I think I've eaten about a million of them,'' Holly said, folding the paper sacks and stacking them neatly on the counter. ''I practically survived on them when I was pregnant with Jonathan.''

The kettle whistled, and Kelsey switched off the burner. ''Morning sickness?''

''More like all-day sickness. I was green from the time I got up in the morning to the time I went to bed at night.''

''Ugh.'' Kelsey groaned, suddenly feeling grateful for the few good hours she had during the day. ''That couldn't have been too much fun.''

"Believe me, it wasn't."

"Same way with your daughter?"

"Actually, no. It wasn't nearly as bad. My doctor said my body probably was used to having been pregnant before and didn't rebel so much the second time around."

"So, how long did it last—the second time, I mean?" Kelsey asked, reaching into the cupboard and pulling down two porcelain teacups.

"I guess I actually started feeling human around my fourth month," Holly said, leaning against the counter. "I know it doesn't seem very long now, but at the time, I didn't think I was ever going to feel good again."

Kelsey dropped teabags into the cups and filled them with the bubbling water. "I hope herbal is all right. That's all I keep in the house."

"Herbal's perfect," Holly said, reaching for one of the cups. She followed Kelsey into the breakfast nook and sat down. "Tea was another taste I developed when I was pregnant. It used to help settle the crackers in my stomach."

"Tea and crackers," Kelsey mumbled, thinking that had pretty much been her diet.

"Tea and crackers," Holly repeated with a small laugh, taking a sip of her tea. "All the advances in medicine, and we're still eating tea and crackers like our mothers did."

Kelsey laughed, too. She liked Holly, liked her easy, friendly nature and her genuine humor. Why hadn't they become friends before? Had it only been because she'd been working before the accident, because she hadn't been home as much and had no free time for making friends?

She sipped her tea, listening as Holly talked about Sarah and Jonathan and the other neighbors on the block.

"You know, every time Jonathan sees a helicopter in the sky, he's convinced it's Coop," Holly was saying. "No matter where we are—the grocery store, the library, even visiting my mother in Oaji. We have to stop and everyone has to wave." Holly mimicked her son, waving frantically. "Hi, Coop—hi!"

Kelsey laughed, creating a picture in her head. "Well, I suppose when you're four years old, helicopters would be pretty interesting."

"Don't I know it," Holly agreed. "Poor Christian, he keeps trying to tell Jonathan about *his* job and what *he* does at work, but I'm afraid it's a little tough to get excited about authorized tax shelters and KEOUGH accounts."

"Well, maybe when he's a little older," Kelsey said, smiling. Suddenly, from somewhere out in left field, her stomach rolled uneasily, causing her mouth to go dry and head to spin. "Uh, maybe when…" She swallowed hard. "When he's a little…"

"Kelsey?" Holly rose from her chair and rushed around the table to kneel in front of her. "Is everything all right? You don't look too good."

"No, it's nothing," Kelsey insisted, reaching for her tea, but another debilitating wave of nausea came. "I'm just a little…it's just…"

"Oh, no," Holly said. She rose quickly to her feet, ran to the pantry and reached for the carton of soda crackers. She ripped open the box and pulled out a long, waxed-paper container of crackers. "I recognize that look." She dashed into the breakfast nook and shoved several small soda squares into Kelsey's hand. "Quick, get a few of these down. It'll help."

Kelsey munched on the crackers one after the other.

"Breath deep," Holly instructed. "Through your nostrils. Nice and slow."

"I feel so stupid," Kelsey moaned. "I'm...I'm really sorry."

"No need to apologize to me," Holly assured her. "I know how these things can strike right out of the blue." She picked up Kelsey's teacup and headed into the kitchen. "I'll put on some more water. I think another cup of tea might do it. Just keep breathing."

After half a stack of crackers and several more cups of tea, Kelsey began to feel better. "I am really sorry."

"Will you quit apologizing?" Holly insisted, sitting in the chair across from Kelsey again. She sipped her tea. "Now, maybe it was all my talk of morning sickness earlier, but I get the definite feeling there might be something more to that green face than just an upset tummy."

Kelsey hesitated. It didn't seem right that she should tell her neighbor before her own family heard the news. Still, it seemed foolish to try to make another explanation after what had happened.

"I'm only a little over four weeks along," she said, taking a deep breath. "We hadn't planned on saying anything to anyone—you know, for awhile yet."

Holly set down her cup. She leaned forward, a grin breaking wide across her face. "You're not going to believe this."

Kelsey stopped as she reached for another cracker. "What?"

"We weren't going to say anything for a while yet, either."

Kelsey's eye's widened. "You mean you're..."

Holly sat back in the chair and giggled like her two-year-old daughter. "Five weeks."

"Oh, my God," Kelsey shrieked, dropping the cracker

and covering her mouth with her hands. "You're right, I don't believe it."

They started comparing ailments and complaints, weight gain and sore breasts, leg cramps, heartburn, doctors and diapers—the kind of baby talk all expectant mothers engage in.

"This is almost too much of a coincidence," Holly said. "Do you suppose it was something in the drinking water last month? Or the phases of the moon? I mean, I don't know about you and Coop, but this sort of took Christian and me by surprise. We're thrilled, but surprised."

"Well, Coop was pretty surprised," Kelsey said, remembering the shocked look on his face. "Me, on the other hand—I know this sounds crazy, but I swear, I knew the moment it happened."

"I don't think that sounds crazy at all," Holly contended. "After all, a woman knows her body better than anybody."

"Yeah," Kelsey said. "I suppose you're right—but get a doctor to believe that."

"So tell me, how did Coop take the news? I mean, if he wasn't expecting it, he must have really been bowled over."

Kelsey thought back to that afternoon three days earlier. "He really was. We'd been so distracted by the…"

Holly looked up when Kelsey stopped.

"Distracted?"

Kelsey drew in a deep breath. The accident wasn't something she liked talking about, but it wasn't something she needed to hide, either. "I had an…an accident several months ago—during the storm. It was pretty serious."

"Oh, Kelsey, my God," Holly said, the smile fading

from her face. "I remember seeing the cast, but I had no idea."

"I'm fine now," Kelsey assured her. "Really, but I admit, it was touch and go there for a while. I scared my whole family pretty good—especially Coop."

"I can understand that."

"Anyway, he's been so wonderful since I was released from the hospital—taking care of me, doing everything. I don't think he was really thinking in terms of a baby."

"I'll bet he's walking on air now."

Kelsey smiled. "I think he's pretty excited."

"Well, take full advantage," Holly advised good-naturedly. "The first time around Christian didn't want me to do anything. He cooked, he cleaned, he shopped—it was wonderful. Now, if he lets me sleep in an extra hour on Saturday mornings, he figures he's done his part."

Kelsey paused, thinking. "Uh…actually this isn't the first time around for us."

Holly looked up. "Oh?"

"We had a baby before—a little boy," Kelsey said, her voice turning wistful. Despite how painful it was to remember, the memory was hers, and she never wanted to lose it again. "He came early and lived only a few hours."

"Oh, Kelsey, how awful for you," Holly said immediately. "I'm so sorry."

"It was pretty rough for a while," Kelsey confessed. Suddenly she had that breathless, funny feeling again—but this time it had nothing to do with morning sickness or the baby in her womb. A picture appeared in her mind. She saw doctors standing around her hospital bed, heard them talking to her, talking to Coop, and she remembered a terrible feeling of depression.

"Then it must make this baby all the more special," Holly was saying. "For you and for Coop."

"Yes," Kelsey whispered, the picture in her mind fading into blackness again. "Yes, it does."

"Was this long ago? The first pregnancy."

Kelsey drew in a deep breath, letting the feeling go and bringing her thoughts to the present. "A couple of years ago. Just before the divor—"

Holly glanced up when Kelsey abruptly stopped. "Before what?" she asked innocently.

It came back in a rush, hitting her in the face. "The *divorce*. Oh, my God."

"I've decided," Coop said, leaning back in the high-backed leather chair. "I'm going to tell her everything."

Gloria Crowell pulled a small spiral notepad from the center drawer of her desk. "Okay, let's talk about it."

"No." Coop shook his head adamantly, determined not to let the psychiatrist or anyone else sway him from the decision he'd made. "There's nothing to talk about. I'm going to tell Kelsey the truth. I've made up my mind."

"Yes, I can see that." The doctor tossed her pencil onto the desk. "I take it you've thought about this?"

"I've thought of nothing but this for the past four days," Coop pointed out.

"Okay," Dr. Crowell conceded. "So you think this is the right time, with the baby and everything?"

"I think it's the time *because* of the baby and everything."

Gloria Crowell turned to Mannie Cohen, who sat in the chair next to Coop perusing the thick file she'd given him. "How about it, Doctor? Physically, is she going to be able to weather this?"

Mannie Cohen closed the file and lowered it to his lap. "Physically she's fine—rested, healthy."

"And the risk to the baby if she's told the truth?"

Mannie rested his elbows on the arms of the chair, tenting his hands together, glancing toward Coop. "If you're looking for me to tell you that once she knows everything, no matter what her reaction is it won't hurt the baby—I can't do that, but..." He paused for a moment, flexing his fingers. "For what it's worth, I agree. I think it's time she knows."

"Despite the risk?" Dr. Crowell asked.

Mannie picked up the file from his lap, sliding it across the desk toward her. "Your own file charts the improvement. Emotionally she's much stronger, much less afraid."

"Well, I can't argue that," Gloria said, leaning back in her chair. "She isn't as frightened by the gaps in her memory."

"No, she isn't," Coop concurred, shifting restlessly in the chair. "She wants the rest of her life back—even if it is painful."

Gloria slowly sat up, turning to him. "And what about you, Coop? What do you want?"

"I want my life back, too," he said after a moment. "I want my wife, my child. I want my marriage, I want us to raise our child together."

"You don't think telling her about the divorce sounds a little counterproductive to that?" Gloria asked.

"Does it?" Coop snapped, rising to his feet. "What would you have me do? Let things go, continue to live like there's nothing wrong? Let the baby be born and then lie to them both? When would you have me tell her, Doctor? The day the baby graduates from college?"

"Look, Coop," Gloria said calmly. She made a nonchalant motion with her hand. "Sit down, please. I'm not the enemy—I'm really not. I'm just playing devil's advocate here. We need to look at this from all sides, try to make an objective decision."

"I'm telling you I've already made my decision," Coop insisted stubbornly, ignoring her request. "There's nothing to discuss. I'm going to tell her."

"Even if that means you'll lose her?" Mannie Cohen asked carefully.

Coop turned and looked at him, then slowly lowered himself to the chair. "I'm not going to let that happen."

"You weren't so sure of that a few weeks ago in my office," Mannie reminded him.

"A few weeks ago, there wasn't a baby. A few weeks ago we weren't living as man and wife."

"You think that's going to make a difference this time?" Mannie turned in the chair to look at him. "Don't get me wrong—I tend to agree with you. This isn't just about Kelsey and her recovery any longer. It's gone way beyond that. There's a new life to consider. But you said yourself you thought once she remembered, once she knew the truth, she would leave again. Are you prepared for that?"

"No." Coop released a long, slow breath. He wasn't angry any longer, just tired. "But I'm not going to let it happen that way this time." He pushed himself to his feet and walked to the large credenza. He leaned against it, staring at the two doctors. "I've had a lot of time to think about this, a lot of time to go over what happened two years ago. I'm beginning to think I gave up too easily, that I didn't fight hard enough to change Kelsey's mind. She was in such pain after the baby, angry and confused— in a state of shock. She didn't know what she wanted."

"And you think she does now?" Gloria asked.

Coop looked at her. "I know what we now have between us. I know it's real. And I know I'm going to fight like hell before giving it up again."

Chapter 14

She pulled the cord furiously, sending the drapes flying and closing out the dull gray light of the late afternoon. She wanted it dark, as dark and as black as she could get it, so dark she couldn't see what was in front of her, so dark she wouldn't have to look at the truth.

She remembered all of it now—the baby, the complications, how poor her chances of conceiving were.

And the divorce.

Kelsey squeezed her eyes tight, feeling hot tears burning down her face. She still had trouble believing, still couldn't accept what she knew was true. It was as though the earth had shifted and thrown everything off kilter, as though everything she had believed in had suddenly been thrown asunder. Only this morning she'd thought she had everything—a home, a husband, a baby on the way. Now what did she have?

She turned from the window, her gaze stopping at the new bed just a few feet away. She and Coop had shopped for that bed together. They had tested mattresses, compared prices and chosen just the right one. It was their bed, the bed they slept in, made love in—the bed they shared as husband and wife.

Except they weren't husband and wife. They were divorced, had been divorced for over two years. This wasn't her home. He wasn't her husband. Coop had been deceiving her all this time—acting out, pretending, letting her believe they were still married. They all must have been in on it—Gloria, Mannie, her father, her family. What kind of nightmare was this?

She closed her eyes, feeling the burn of tears. Why did she have to remember? Why now, when she had been so happy, when she thought she was finally going to have what she always wanted? Why couldn't the memories have stayed buried just a little while longer? Was she destined to always lose what she wanted most?

She squeezed her eyes even tighter, her hands balling into fists. She wanted to run, wanted to hide in the dark, to block out everything and forget again. She'd thought remembering the loss of her baby had prepared her to face the rest of it, that there could be nothing that would shock or hurt her again. How wrong she had been. Cooper Reed wasn't her husband any longer, and that cut to the quick.

Coop. Her friend, her lover. He'd been so wonderful since the accident—so attentive and kind. What had he thought when he heard she believed they were still married? How shocked he must have been, how surprised and astonished. The wife who had turned him out of her life was now calling for him and needed his help.

She could almost chart in her mind how the events had progressed, how Gloria and the others had talked with him, convinced him of the importance of her remembering on her own. Why would he have agreed to such an elaborate charade? How could he have pretended all these weeks? Out of a feeling of obligation, out of pity?

Like segments of her scattered memories, the pieces were finally fitting into place. The empty house, the lengthy hospital stay, the separate bedrooms and that damn futon bed. Oh, God, she understood it all now. It hadn't been a matter of adhering to doctor's orders. It hadn't been concern for her health or anxiety over her recovery. It had been the fact that they were no longer husband and wife.

She thought back to that night in the shower, thought of her bold actions and foolhardy attempts to seduce him. She wanted to die. How awful that must have been for him then, and how humiliating it was for her now. Time after time he'd rejected her, had let her down as gently as he could. The feeble excuses, the unreasonable concerns—they all made a pathetic sort of sense now.

She turned and walked out of the bedroom and down the long, dark hall, feeling humiliated. She passed the empty bedrooms, one after the other, remembering the plans they'd had, the children they'd anticipated. Only those hopes and dreams had died with their infant son. Their lives had taken a different direction after that, a different course.

The past had found her again. She could remember everything in detail now—the crushing blow of the baby's death and the terrible depression she'd felt when the doctors had delivered the news about her slim chances of ever conceiving again. It had been more than she could take.

Coop had wanted a family. She knew how disappointed he'd been. On top of everything else, on top of the grief and the guilt, she'd felt like a complete failure, eaten up with self-pity. He'd wanted children, lots of children, and that could never happen because he'd been stuck with a barren wife. He'd deserved better. He'd deserved a wife who could give him what he wanted, a wife who could give him children, and she'd thought she never could.

"Oh, God." She groaned, the tears tasting bitter on her tongue. Her hand drifted to her belly. What kind of perverse joke was being played on her? What kind of grotesque farce was being carried out? She'd been given the child only to discover she no longer had the man.

Staring through the gloom of the empty living room, she thought of the furniture that once had been there, the furniture that was now crowded into her small apartment in Santa Ynez. This house wasn't her home, wasn't *their* home—and hadn't been for a very long time. She couldn't stay here any longer. It felt cold and empty—as cold and empty as she felt inside.

She rushed into the bedroom, yanked open the closet doors and pulled her clothes to the floor. They were her clothes, her belongings. She remembered wearing them, buying them. They belonged in the cramped closet in her bedroom in Santa Ynez, not here, not in Coop's house, not in the house where he had taken pity on her and lived out a lie for the last two months.

She pulled out a large suitcase from the back of the closet and carried it to the bed. Slowly, she began to gather up her clothes, folding them and stacking them neatly inside. She remembered the first time she'd packed to leave this house, remembered how lost and angry she'd felt. Her baby had just died, she'd disappointed her husband, and her hopes had been dashed.

She had practically pushed Coop into a divorce after that, had wanted him away from her and out of her life. It had never been a matter of not loving him, but rather a matter of loving him too much. She'd loved him too much to saddle him with a woman who could never give him what he wanted.

She sat on the edge of the bed. The child inside her was still too small for any outward sign to show—the child she and Coop had made, the child her doctors had said would never be. The marriage might be over, the charade at an end, but the baby inside her was real, and it was growing.

She remembered Coop's reaction when he learned about the baby, remembered his stunned silence and look of shocked surprise. No wonder he'd been speechless and confused. Pregnancy wouldn't have even been a consideration when he'd taken her to bed. He might have agreed to pretend being her husband, but a baby hadn't been part of the bargain.

Coop. Maybe he'd only been trying to help. Maybe he had been concerned about helping her regain her memory, but she couldn't help feeling betrayed. How could he have kept the truth from her all this time? How could he have told her he loved her, made love to her, made her believe she was his wife? How could he have made it all up?

"Kelsey?" Coop slipped the key out of the lock and shut the front door behind him. "Kelsey? Sweetheart, where are you?"

He'd headed right home after the meeting in Gloria's office, feeling better than he had in a very long time. He knew what he wanted, knew what he had to do to get it, and after so many weeks floundering in uncertainty, the certainty was almost liberating.

He tossed his keys on the hall stand and he headed for the kitchen. "Kelsey?"

It wasn't even five yet, but the thick, heavy fog hanging low to the ground had blocked what little sunlight remained, making the house dark and full of shadows. He peered into the breakfast nook, seeing the teacups and crackers on the table.

"Kelsey?" he called again, glancing through the nook and into the empty kitchen. "Babe? You home?"

He glanced at the dishes on the table again, feeling the skin at the back of his neck start to tingle. There were two cups. She'd had tea with someone. Who, and where were they now?

He turned, walked to the entry, turned and scanned the empty gloom of the living room. He thought of the story he'd told her the day he'd brought her home from the hospital, about getting rid of furniture and plans to redecorate. It was just one of the lies he wanted to be rid of, one of the long list of distortions and misrepresentations he'd been drowning in.

He headed down the hall, walking in long, urgent strides. Passing one bedroom after the other, he couldn't shake the rising feeling of uneasiness. The house was too quiet. It felt too empty. Maybe it had lacked furnishings for over two years, but there was a vacantness that didn't feel right.

He stopped at the doors to their bedroom. There was no trace of light, no hint of movement from inside. The tingling at the base of his neck had become a prickle, ominous and uncomfortable.

"Kelsey?" He pushed the door open and stepped over the threshold.

It was dark in the room, but he could feel her presence as surely as if the sun was shining through the windows. He felt for the wall switch.

"No."

His hand stilled at the sound of her voice. "It's dark."

"I want it dark."

He could make out her faint profile silhouetted against the draperies. She was standing in the corner with her arms crossed over her chest. The sight of her standing there in the darkness gave him a bad feeling.

"Oh, God, what is it?" he asked without preamble. "What's happened? Is it the baby?"

"The baby," she murmured, her hands dropping to her abdomen. "The baby is fine."

A wave of relief washed over him, but it did nothing to calm his sense of dread. Something had happened. It might not be the baby, but it was serious.

"I saw the cups in the kitchen," he said, trying to think what could have gotten her this upset. "Somebody came by today?"

She nodded her head. "Holly, from across the street."

"Oh, yeah?" He started slowly across the room toward her.

She turned and stared at him through the shadows. "Yes."

Her stance, the tone of her voice, everything about her made him stop in his tracks. "Kelsey, what is it? What's happened? Did Holly say something to upset you?"

"No, Holly's terrific. She's pregnant, too, as a matter of fact."

"Then for the love of God, tell me what is it," he pleaded, hearing the panic in his voice. "Kelsey, please, you're scaring me. What's wrong?"

"*I'm* scaring *you?*" She laughed, a harsh, sneering sound. "What have you got to be afraid of, Coop?"

Coop started toward her again, but his knee collided painfully with something in the darkness and he stopped. He fumbled for the lamp beside the bed. The tiny bulb flooded the room with a dim glow. "A suitcase?"

"My suitcase," she corrected. "It's heavy. I'd like you to put it in the car for me."

"A suitcase," he murmured, feeling as though he'd been punched in the stomach. "Why? Where are you going?"

"Home," she said in a flat voice.

Coop swallowed hard, his mouth feeling as dry as a desert. "Home? What are you talking about?"

"Look, Coop, you don't have to do this any longer," she said, pushing past him and heading for the door. "It's over. I know." She stopped at the door and turned to him. "I remember."

Her words shot across the room like a bullet, hitting him straight in the heart. The blood drained from his hands, from his heart, from his brain.

"You remember?"

"I remember," she repeated, her voice void of any emotion. "Everything."

"Kelsey," he murmured, rushing to her. "Kelsey, I don't know what to say."

"You don't need to say anything, Coop," she insisted. "I remember. There's no need to keep pretending any longer."

"You don't understand—"

"Yes, I do," she interrupted. "You forget, I'm a nurse, I've seen cases like this before. I know how these things go. Don't overwhelm the patient with too much too soon, don't force them, allow them to recall on their own." She held out her hands in a mocking, careless shrug. "And look—it worked, I'm cured. You did a good job, all of you. Gloria, Mannie, the whole family. I appreciate the effort, I really do, but it's not necessary anymore."

He didn't believe her nonchalant words or her casual gestures. She was hurt and in shock. He could see it in her eyes, hear it in her voice. Her whole world had been torn apart—their world together. He longed to go to her, to gather her in his arms and comfort her, but every movement she made told him she wouldn't welcome anything from him at the moment.

"We…we need to talk," he said, struggling to keep his voice steady. "I want to explain."

"There's nothing to explain," she maintained, giving her hair a toss.

"But there is," he insisted, his voice turning desperate. "I want you to understand. Everyone was so worried about you. And then, when you woke up, you didn't remember. They—the doctors, your dad, everyone—we just wanted to do the right thing. I just wanted to do the right thing."

"The right thing," she repeated, nodding. "Yes, well, I can understand that. You wanted to help. I appreciate it."

"Please, Kelsey," he said, stepping forward and reaching for her. "Sweetheart—"

"No," she snapped, dropping the calm facade for an instant. "Please, don't touch me."

He could see her composure slip, could see her lips quiver and her eyes turn shiny with tears. "God, Kelsey, I'm so sorry," he said, reaching for her again.

"I *said*," she snapped, jerking away from him, "don't touch me." She glared at him, a tear spilling to her cheek and cascading to her chin. With an impatient hand, she batted it away. "I don't want you to ever touch me again."

Coop's heart twisted painfully in his chest. He'd come home determined to tell her everything. He'd been ready for her shock, anger and outrage, but he hadn't been prepared for this. This had come right out of nowhere, something out of his worst nightmares, and he wasn't sure what to do.

"Kelsey—God, Kelsey," he beseeched, his voice cracking with emotion. "Please…don't do this."

"Don't do what, Coop? Don't be honest? Don't face reality? Keep pretending?" She took a step forward. "In case *you've* forgotten, we're not married anymore. I know that now—I've remembered. There's no need to keep up the act. It's time for me to leave."

"I know you're upset," he said as she started for the door again. "Please just stay for a little while. Talk with me."

"Talk? About what?" She looked at him. "I know you think you have to explain, that you have to help me to understand, but it's not necessary. I understand, honestly, I do. I just want to leave now. I want to be alone, to go back to my real life." She started down the hall. "Let's just forget about this, about what happened."

"You want to forget me? Forget us?"

She stopped. "There is no us."

"Bull," he said, moving across the carpet and down the hall toward her. "You're just going to waltz out of here, forget the last two months ever happened?"

She spun around, her chest rising and falling with rapid breaths. "The last two months weren't real. They were made up, just another part of my recovery—like taking a pill or going to physical therapy."

"You can't believe that."

"Of course I believe it," she shouted, her voice echoing down the empty hall. "I believe it because it's the truth."

"Kelsey," he said in a tightly controlled voice. "You're upset, you're not thinking straight. I mean, when it started out you were in the hospital—I wanted to help, wanted to do whatever I could to help you get better. But you can't believe that everything after that was—''

''Was what?'' she demanded. There were no tears, no trembling lips or quivering voice. ''An act?''

''You know better than that.''

She stopped, drawing in a shaky breath. ''You should have told me. I can understand in the beginning, but all this time, letting me go on believing…'' She shook her head. ''Once the memories started to come back, you should have told me the truth.''

''I wanted to, hundreds of times.'' He hesitated, searching for the words. ''I…I was just so afraid.''

''Afraid? Of what?''

''Of losing you.'' He reached for her, catching her by the upper arms. ''I love you, Kelsey—you have to know that.''

''No.'' She shook her head, pulling away. ''No, no, no. Don't say that to me.''

''I say it to you because it's true.''

''I don't want to hear this,'' she said, turning and running for the door. ''I'll send my father down for my things. I've got to go.''

He caught her at the door, pressing his palm flat against the wood, making it impossible for her to open it. ''I love you, Kelsey—I always have, I always will.''

''Let me go, Coop,'' she pleaded, looking at him.

''How can I?'' He let his hand slide down the door. ''You're my wife, Kelsey, in all the ways that matter— and you're carrying my baby.'' He let his hand settle on her abdomen. ''This child—this child is a miracle.''

''This baby was more than you bargained for.''

The harshness in her tone made him pull his hand away. ''What are you talking about?''

"I remember what the doctors said. They hadn't given us much hope another pregnancy would be possible."

"Which only goes to show you nothing is for certain—a diagnosis or a divorce."

"Look, Coop, I—I don't blame you about the two of us...being together," she stammered. "I take responsibility, too. I mean, I wanted...well, I thought we were..." She shook her head, and took a deep breath. "You had no way of knowing there could be a child."

Coop stepped back. "You think that's what this is all about? The baby? You think I want you only because of the baby?" His gaze narrowed. "Are you forgetting who walked out on who?"

"I'm not forgetting anything," she said, pulling the door open. "Including the fact that you let me go."

"It's been two weeks, don't you think it's time we talked about it?"

Kelsey glanced up from the spot on the carpet she'd been studying for the better part of the hour. "And what good do you think that would do?"

Gloria poked at the small pile of paper clips on the blotter with the tip of her pencil. "Well, if nothing else, it would make me feel like I was earning my fee."

Kelsey made a face. "I thought this was supposed to be about what *I* was feeling?"

"Okay," Gloria agreed affably, leaning back in her chair. "So tell me."

Kelsey had to laugh, although there hadn't been much to laugh at in her life for the past few weeks. She'd left their house—Coop's house—and driven to the small apartment in Santa Ynez. The building had looked neat and clean with its fresh paint and carefully manicured lawn, just as she'd remembered leaving it. She parked at the curb out front. She could see the door to her unit, apartment 2B, but for some reason she hadn't been able to bring herself to go inside.

She knew what waited for her in there. She remembered the TV dinners alone, the extra shifts at the hospital, the lonely existence before the accident. She lived her life through others, borrowed their joys, not really having anything of her own. It seemed so bleak now, so barren after the months she'd had with Coop, after all she had and all she'd lost.

Life with Coop had been an illusion. Maybe his intentions had been good—maybe his intentions had been the best—but the fact remained what she thought she had, what she thought was real didn't exist.

"What do you want me to say?" she asked Gloria, taking a deep breath. "I'm disappointed? I'm hurt? Fine, I'll say it. I *am* disappointed, I am hurt." She sat up in her chair, cocking her head to one side. "Are you satisfied?"

"Why don't you tell me about the hurt."

Kelsey rolled her eyes, reaching for her purse on the floor next to the chair. "Forget it, Gloria, I don't want to do this now."

"Okay," the doctor said, nodding and slowly leaning forward. "So if not now, when?"

"So...maybe next time," she said, imitating Gloria's voice as she stood up.

"Kelsey, I think you're making a mistake."

"How, by dealing with my own problem?"

"If that's what you're doing, that's great. Is it?"

"Look, I know everyone was just trying to help me get better. I understand that, I don't blame anyone—you, Mannie, my dad, Coop—I really don't. But that doesn't mean it didn't hurt. How would it make you feel if you woke up tomorrow and found out that all this time you really weren't a shrink at all?''

"It would shake me up pretty bad," she admitted, tossing her pencil onto the blotter. "So tell me, what shook you up more, finding out about the divorce or finding out you maybe didn't want it?''

Kelsey shook her head, laughing as she rounded the chair and headed for the door. "Gloria, Gloria, Gloria. Spoken like a true shrink—so many questions."

The doctor shrugged, letting the barb bounce off her. "My questions wouldn't bother you so much unless you had a problem with what the answers might be."

"I've got no problem answering questions," Kelsey claimed, turning at the door and walking several steps toward the desk. "Ask away."

Dr. Crowell pushed her chair back from the desk and slowly rose to her feet. "Are you in love with your husband, Kelsey?''

Kelsey's smile quickly faded. "You blew that one, Dr. Crowell—I don't have a husband."

"You have Coop," Gloria pointed out, walking slowly around the desk. "And you're going to have his child."

"You're wrong," Kelsey said, her hand unconsciously settling over her stomach. "I lost Coop—twice."

"You're sure about that?"

Kelsey held a hand up. "I don't want to talk about this.''

"I thought you said you weren't afraid of the answers."

Kelsey drew in a deep breath. "I just...don't want to talk about Coop."

"He loves you very much."

"No," she said, shaking her head, turning for the door again. "I don't want to hear this."

"No, I don't suppose you do." Gloria sighed, leaning against the edge of her desk.

Kelsey stopped in her tracks. "What's that supposed to mean?"

"Oh, come on now, Kelsey," Gloria said, crossing her arms. "You and I have gotten to know each other pretty well in the last couple of months. We've talked a lot about your feelings for Coop during that time."

"I thought he was my husband."

"And so now your memory has come back and you *remembered* you don't love him?"

Kelsey's shoulders slumped, and she slowly walked to the chair. "I never stopped loving Coop," she said, slinging her purse into the seat. "Never."

"And the divorce?"

"Coop wanted a family. I didn't think I would ever be able to give him that." She looked at Gloria, tears stinging her eyes. "How could I tie him down, keep him from what he wanted?"

Dr. Crowell reached for the box of tissues on her desk and offered it to Kelsey. "Maybe he wanted you more than he wanted a family."

Kelsey shook her head, pulling several tissues from the box. "No, I didn't want him to stay with me out of pity."

"So you believe he just felt sorry for you, is that it?"

"Something like that."

"And what about now? He tells you, me, anyone who will listen that he loves you. Is that just pity?"

Kelsey frowned. It sounded so...so different when Gloria said it. "He loves the baby," she said lamely, trying to focus. "It's the baby he wants."

"Okay, let me make sure I understand this," Gloria said, nodding and making a play of mulling it over. "Coop doesn't love you, he's just saying that, but you love him enough to set him free, only he doesn't want you, what he wants is your baby." She gave her head a confused shake. "Is that it?"

"Yes—I mean—" Kelsey let out an impatient breath. It sounded so silly the way Gloria put it, so ridiculous. "I mean, no—"

"Tell me something, Kelsey," Gloria said, pushing herself away from the desk. "I'm curious. What would have happened two years ago if you had found out Coop was sterile?"

"What?" Kelsey blinked.

"Children mean a lot to you, don't they?" Gloria challenged. "You want a family, isn't that right?"

"Well, yes, of course."

"So if you found out Coop couldn't impregnate you, would you have wanted to stay married to him?"

"Oh, no, you don't." Kelsey shook her head. "No, you don't. I know what you're doing. You're taking everything I say and twisting it, making it sound ridiculous, and it isn't going to work."

"It isn't?" Gloria asked skeptically.

"No!" Kelsey straightened her shoulders indignantly and snatched up her purse again. "I let Coop go because I loved him." She took a step forward, her chest rising and falling with emotion. "And you're forgetting, Doctor—he let me go. He didn't stop the divorce. You don't let go of someone you love."

"Well, I'm confused then." Gloria shook her head, walking slowly around the desk and sitting down again. She shrugged. "I mean, isn't that what you're doing right now?"

Chapter 15

"Hi, Coop."

Coop automatically raised a hand to wave. "Hi, Jonathan."

"You were flying hellupcupters today, huh?" the little boy shouted from across the street.

"I sure was," he said, slamming the car door shut. In the distance, he saw Holly in the shadows of the open garage and picked up his pace. He'd been lucky, had managed to avoid her for the last couple of weeks, and he'd just as soon keep it that way. He wasn't in the mood for conversation or questions about Kelsey and the baby.

"Hello, Coop—how's the prospective daddy doing?"

He stopped as he rounded the car, gritting his teeth. His luck had run out. "Pretty good, Holly, how are you?"

"Tired," she said, putting a hand on her tummy. "And round." Jonathan tried to pull his hand away, but she held tight. "Tell Kelsey I found that wallpaper pattern I was telling her about.'' They turned and started up the drive. ''Tell her I'll be over tomorrow to show her.''

''Yeah, I'll…tell her,'' he mumbled, giving her a small nod. He watched as they walked into their garage.

He made his way slowly up the front walk, looking at the empty house and dreading the long evening that lay ahead of him. The place had become a tomb again, a collection of empty rooms, empty space. A silent reminder of all he had—and lost.

He'd thought of moving out, of getting a small room somewhere—a hotel, an apartment, any place he wouldn't see Kelsey at every turn. Except it didn't seem to matter where he was or what he did, he missed her constantly.

He'd called her numerous times in the past fourteen days, leaving messages at her apartment, at Mo's, even at the hospital where she'd worked before the accident, but she hadn't called him back. Mo had assured him she was all right, that the baby was fine, and had encouraged him to hang tight, that she would contact him when she felt the time was right. But Coop had a feeling that as far as Kelsey was concerned, the time was never going to be right again.

He shoved his key into the lock, twisting it in the slot and remembering what it was to have her waiting for him when he got home. Knowing she was there made coming back to the house at the end of the day a homecoming.

Everything was so different now, he thought as he pulled the door open.

He stepped into the entry and tossed his keys into the small dish on the hall stand. He had just started down the hall when a smell finally penetrated his olfactory nerves. He stopped in his tracks.

The smell of bread baking, its rich, warm aroma, filled the air.

He shook his head, trying to shake off the sudden and unsettling sense of déjà vu. He remembered the day Kelsey had told him about the baby, remembered the bread she had baked and the wonderful aroma that had filled the house.

He breathed deep. It couldn't be. It was impossible. His mind was playing tricks on him. His memory was causing some kind of malfunction in his brain, prompting his senses to go haywire.

He shook his head again, calling himself a fool, and started down the hall again. He'd taken only a few steps, though, when he stopped again.

He walked back to the entry. He put his hands on his hips and inhaled deeply. Damn it, he wasn't crazy. He could smell bread baking.

As he headed for the kitchen, his mind raced, searching for explanations. Had he left something on the stove or in the toaster? Was a window open somewhere and odors from around the neighborhood were drifting in? Was this some kind of phantom scent? Had the house suddenly become haunted? Had aliens landed?

However, as he rounded the corner of the breakfast nook and looked into the kitchen, he came to an abrupt halt. Standing before the open oven, Kelsey reached for a loaf of bread from a rack inside, turned it out of the pan and set it on the counter next to several others.

Coop blinked, feeling a little like he'd been transported into another time. At that moment, he could have believed aliens from another planet had landed sooner than finding her there.

"Kelsey?"

She jumped at the sound of his voice, spinning around. "Coop—hi, you're home. I didn't hear you."

"What's…" He took a few hesitant steps forward, gesturing to the loaves of bread lined neatly along the counter. He still only half-believed she was there, still half-believed his longing and loneliness had caused him to start hallucinating. "What's all this?"

She slowly closed the oven door and lowered her hands to the counter. "A peace offering?"

"I don't understand," he said, thinking this had to be a dream. She looked too beautiful to be real, too perfect for flesh and blood. "Are we at war?"

She reached back and untied the apron wrapped around her waist. "I think I sort of acted that way when I stormed out of here." She slid the apron onto the counter beside the loaves of bread. "For a modern woman, it's not very original—baking bread—but I wanted to apologize."

"Apologize?" he stammered. He wasn't sure what to say. He could hardly believe she was there, actually standing in their kitchen like she'd never left, as if the awful solitude and loneliness of the last two weeks had never happened. "To me?"

"Of course, to you," she said, walking slowly around the counter toward him. "You certainly deserve one." She walked to the table, touched the back of a chair to steady herself, hoping he wouldn't notice how she was trembling. She'd taken a chance just showing up, a big chance, but she'd come this far, and there would be no turning back. "What can I say? I was upset and I took it out on you." She looked at him, giving him a small grimace. "I seem to have a rather nasty habit of doing that."

"You shouldn't be the one apologizing."

"Oh, yes, I should," she said fervently. "For so many things." She let go of the chair and took a step closer to him. "I lashed out at you just like I did two years ago—after the baby."

"Kelsey," he said, closing the distance between them.

"No," she said insistently. "Let me get this out. It's taken me too long as it is." She drew in a deep breath. "I was wrong about so much. I can see it now, thanks to Gloria and her incessant questions." She paused for a breath, shook her head. "I hated those damn questions, but you know, they finally made me see, finally helped me to understand." She took another step forward. "I was wrong about leaving you, about wanting the divorce. I knew what we had together, knew how we felt about one another." Emotion swelled in her throat, making it difficult to speak. "It's just...when I thought I couldn't...when I saw how hurt you were, I couldn't think straight. I hated myself for disappointing you, hated that I couldn't give you what you wanted. I thought if I let you go, I thought maybe someone else..."

"Oh, God," he groaned in a raw, low voice. "All I ever wanted was you."

Tears swelled in her eyes, blurring his handsome features. "I know that now. I think I must have blocked out the past two years on purpose, because I wanted to do them over again. I wanted you back," she whispered, her lips trembling. "Tell me it isn't too late, Coop. I've made so many mistakes, been mixed up for so long, but I never stopped loving you—never." Her hand drifted to her stomach. "And now I feel like I've been given a second chance at a family. Please, give me a second chance with you, too."

"Kelsey," he murmured, catching her in his arms. If this was a dream, he hoped he would never wake up. If it was real, he would spend the rest of his life being grateful. "Kelsey, I love you."

"I love you, too," she whispered against his lips. "Tell me I can stay, tell me you forgive me and that you'll marry me—again."

He pulled back, suddenly feeling as though the sun was shining bright. "Is the bread part of the deal?"

She looked at him, smiling despite the tears. Everything was going to be all right now. "We can negotiate."

"Then, lady, you got a deal." He laughed, pulling her close and bringing his lips to hers. "You know, this is the kind of peace offering I could get used to."

Epilogue

"Time for breakfast."

Kelsey scooted up against the pillows and reached for the top button of her nightshirt. "Somebody sounds hungry this morning."

"Be nice to this guy," Coop said, carrying his little son in his arms. "He slept six hours straight." He handed the baby to Kelsey. "Of course, he woke up wet to the gills and ready to eat my finger, but that's not bad for a little guy who's only four and a half weeks old."

"Good morning, my precious," Kelsey cooed as she took the baby in her arms. Smiling, she looked at Coop. "How long did you have to wait?"

Coop gave her an innocent look. "I don't know what you mean."

"You know exactly what I mean," she said dryly as her son began nursing hungrily at her breast. "I heard you stub your toe on the nightstand when you got up."

"I just took a peek," he said, rubbing his sore toe.

"A peek?" She gave him a skeptical look.

"To make sure he was all right," he insisted. "It was his first night in the nursery, and that's a whole room away."

Kelsey gave him a stern look. "Coop, you have got to stop standing over that crib all night long—you need your sleep."

"I can always sleep," he said with a sigh, laying down across the bed and running a finger along his son's full cheek. "But he's only going to be like this a short time." He leaned close and gave the baby a kiss on the top of his head, then kissed Kelsey, too. "I just like looking at him."

Kelsey smiled, looking at the child in her arms. Chandler Cooper Reed—or CC as his daddy called him—was indeed a sight to behold with his big brown eyes and wispy brown hair. At eight pounds, two ounces, he'd burst into the world kicking and screaming—round, healthy and six days overdue. "Yeah, I know what you mean."

"I sort of like looking at you, too," Coop murmured, pressing his mouth to hers again. The kiss was far from a peck this time. "How did I ever get so lucky?"

"You wouldn't give up," she whispered, her heart filled with emotion. "Even when I wanted to."

"Well." He sighed, feeling more content, more comfortable than any one person had a right to feel. "I guess it just goes to show if you keep at something long enough, you finally get it right. Marriage, babies, they just take a little practice."

Kelsey lifted CC to her shoulder and patted him gently on the back. "And maybe a good bump on the head."

CC let out a yelp and pulled a loud burp up from his toes. Kelsey and Coop looked at him, then at each other and laughed.

"Oh, no," Coop assured her as he took the baby from her. "I've learned my lesson good." Holding CC in one arm, he reached for Kelsey with the other, pulling her close. "A building doesn't have to fall on me to know how lucky I am. This marriage is forever this time—I'm never letting you go again."

"That's good," she murmured, snuggling into the crook of his arm and lazily buttoning her pajama top. "'Cause I'm afraid you're both stuck with me."

"Yeah, stuck," Coop repeated, holding his whole world in his arms. "And don't you forget it."

* * * * *

Next month, Silhouette Sensation®
brings you the first book in a thrilling new series

THE STARS OF MITHRA

by

New York Times bestselling author

Three mystical blue diamonds place three close
friends in jeopardy...and lead them to romance.

Turn the page for a taster of
HIDDEN STAR
available July 1998, in Silhouette Sensation

HIDDEN STAR
by
Nora Roberts

"Excuse me." Her voice sounded rusty, as if she hadn't used it in days. "I must have the wrong office." She inched backward, and those big, wide brown eyes shifted to the name printed on the door. She hesitated, then looked back at him. "Are you Mr. Parris?"

There was a moment, one blinding moment, when he couldn't seem to speak. He knew he was staring at her, couldn't help himself. His heart simply stood still. His knees went weak. And the only thought that came to his mind was *There you are, finally. What the hell took you so long?*

And because that was so ridiculous, he struggled to put a bland, even cynical, investigator's expression on his face.

"Yeah."

"I see." Though she didn't appear to, the way she continued to stare at his face. "I've come at a bad time. I don't have an appointment. I thought maybe..."

"Looks like my calendar's clear."

He wanted her to come in, all the way in. Whatever that first absurd, unprecedented reaction of his, she was still a potential client.

She was blond and beautiful and bewildered. Her hair was wet, sleek down to her shoulders and straight as the rain. Her eyes were bourbon brown, in a face that—though it could have used some color—was delicate as a fairy's. It was heart-shaped, the cheeks a gentle curve and the mouth was full, unpainted and solemn.

She'd ruined her suit and shoes in the rain. He recognized both as top-quality, that quietly exclusive look found only in designer salons. Against the wet blue silk of her suit, the canvas bag she clutched with both hands looked intriguingly out of place.

Damsel in distress, he mused, and his lips curved. Just what the doctor ordered.

"Why don't you come in, close the door, Miss...?"

Her heart bumped twice, hammer-hard, and she tightened her grip on the bag. "You're a private investigator?"

"That's what it says on the door." Cade smiled again, ruthlessly using the dimples while he watched her gnaw that lovely lower lip. Damned if he wouldn't like to gnaw on it himself.

And that response, he thought with a little relief, was a lot more like it. Lust was a feeling he could understand.

"Let's go back to my office." He surveyed the damage—broken glass, potting soil, pools of coffee. "I think I'm finished in here for now."

"All right." She took a deep breath, stepped in, then closed the door. She supposed she had to start somewhere.

Picking her way over the debris, she followed him into the adjoining room. It was furnished with little more than a desk and a couple of bargain-basement chairs. Well, she couldn't be choosy about decor, she reminded herself. She waited until he'd sat behind his desk, tipped back in his chair and smiled at her again in that quick, trust-me way.

"Do you— Could I—" She squeezed her eyes tight, centered herself again. "Do you have some credentials I could see?"

More intrigued, he took out his license, handed it to her. She wore two very lovely rings, one on each hand, he noticed. One was a square-cut citrine in an antique setting, the other a trio of colored stones. Her earrings matched the second ring, he noted when she tucked her hair behind her ear and studied his license as if weighing each printed word.

"Would you like to tell me what the problem is, Miss...?"

"I think—" She handed him back his license, then gripped the bag two-handed again. "I think I'd like to hire you." Her eyes were on his face again, as intently, as searchingly, as they had been on the license. "Do you handle missing persons cases?"

Who did you lose, sweetheart? he wondered. He hoped, for her sake and for the sake of the nice little fantasy that was building in his head, it wasn't a husband. "Yeah, I handle missing persons."

"Your, ah, rate?"

"Two-fifty a day, plus expenses." When she nodded, he slid over a legal pad, picked up a pencil. "Who do you want me to find?"

She took a long, shuddering breath. "Me. I need you to find me."

Watching her, he tapped the pencil against the pad. "Looks like I already have. You want me to bill you, or do you want to pay now?"

"No." She could feel it cracking. She'd held on so

long—or at least it seemed so long—but now she could feel that branch she'd gripped when the world dropped out from under her begin to crack. "I don't remember. Anything. I don't—" Her voice began to hitch. She took her hands off the bag in her lap to press them to her face. "I don't know who I am." And then she was weeping the words into her hands. "I don't know who I am."

* * *

Hidden Star
*by Nora Roberts is available
in July 1998, in Silhouette Sensation®.*

COMING NEXT MONTH

HIDDEN STAR Nora Roberts

The Stars of Mithra

She didn't know who she was, but she had a loaded gun, a diamond and more than a million dollars in her bag. Private investigator Cade Parris had to unravel this mystery fast. He needed to know just what sort of trouble she was in, because she was the woman he'd been waiting for.

THE BACHELOR PARTY Paula Detmer Riggs

Always a Bridesmaid

Sheriff Ford Maguire was curious about and attracted to single mum Sophie Reynolds. But she clearly had no intention of getting romantically involved with him. He wondered why... Ford wasn't the kind of man a woman could resist for long.

MACNAMARA'S WOMAN Alicia Scott

Maximillian's Children

Tamara Allistair was trying to find out what had really happened ten years ago, but someone clearly didn't like it. Her car had been sabotaged and all that saved her was her own skill and handsome renegade CJ MacNamara. CJ became her self-appointed protector; with him on her side, Tamara might be able to give love a try after all—if she lived long enough!

THE TAMING OF REID DONOVAN
Marilyn Pappano

Southern Knights

Reid Donovan was the original bad boy, but Cassie Wade didn't see him that way. Everything he wanted was suddenly within his reach. And then he was asked to walk away from it all. And when the FBI asked, he wasn't sure he had a choice. Would Cassie wait for him?

On sale from July, 1998

COMING NEXT MONTH FROM

▼™ SILHOUETTE®

Intrigue
Danger, deception and desire

HER DESTINY Aimée Thurlo
RIDE THE THUNDER Patricia Werner
BEFORE THE FALL Patricia Rosemoor
BEN'S WIFE Charlotte Douglas

Special Edition
Satisfying romances packed with emotion

WHITE WOLF Lindsay McKenna
A COWBOY'S TEARS Anne McAllister
THE RANGER AND THE SCHOOLMARM Penny Richards
HUSBAND: BOUGHT AND PAID FOR Laurie Paige
WHO'S THE DADDY? Judy Christenberry
MOUNTAIN MAN Doris Rangel

Desire
Provocative, sensual love stories for the woman of today

THE GROOM CANDIDATE Cait London
THE OFFICER AND THE RENEGADE Helen R. Myers
THE WOMEN IN JOE SULLIVAN'S LIFE Marie Ferrarella
BOSS LADY AND THE HIRED HAND Barbara McMahon
DR HOLT AND THE TEXAN Suzannah Davis
THE BACHELOR NEXT DOOR Katherine Garbera

On sale from July, 1998

Three mystical
blue diamonds
place three close friends
in jeopardy...and lead them
to the adventure of a lifetime

SILHOUETTE SENSATION® brings you a thrilling
new series by *New York Times* bestselling author

Nora Roberts

In JULY: HIDDEN STAR

Bailey James can't remember a thing, but she knows
she's in big trouble. And she desperately needs the help
of private investigator Cade Parris.

In SEPTEMBER: CAPTIVE STAR

Cynical bounty hunter Jack Dakota and spitfire M.J.
O'Leary are handcuffed together and on the run from a
pair of hired killers.

In NOVEMBER: SECRET STAR

Lieutenant Seth Buchanan's murder investigation takes
a strange turn when Grace Fontaine turns up alive. But
the notorious heiress is the biggest mystery of all.

LAURA VAN WORMER

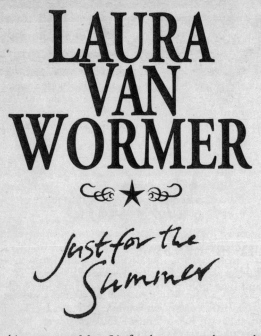

Just for the Summer

Nothing prepares Mary Liz for the summer she spends in the moneyed town of East Hampton, Long Island. From the death of one of their own, Mary Liz realises that these stunningly beautiful people have some of the ugliest agendas in the world.

"Van Wormer,...has the glamorama Hampton's scene down to a T. (Just for the Summer is) as voyeuristic as it is fun."
—Kirkus Reviews

MIRA®

1-55166-439-9
AVAILABLE FROM JUNE 1998

4 FREE

books and a surprise gift!

We would like to take this opportunity to thank you for reading this Silhouette® book by offering you the chance to take FOUR more specially selected titles from the Sensation™ series absolutely FREE! We're also making this offer to introduce you to the benefits of the Reader Service™—

- ★ FREE home delivery
- ★ FREE gifts and competitions
- ★ FREE monthly newsletter
- ★ Books available before they're in the shops
- ★ Exclusive Reader Service discounts

Accepting these FREE books and gift places you under no obligation to buy; you may cancel at any time, even after receiving your free shipment. Simply complete your details below and return the entire page to the address below. *You don't even need a stamp!*

YES! Please send me 4 free Sensation books and a surprise gift. I understand that unless you hear from me, I will receive 4 superb new titles every month for just £2.50 each, postage and packing free. I am under no obligation to purchase any books and may cancel my subscription at any time. The free books and gift will be mine to keep in any case.

S8XE

Ms/Mrs/Miss/Mr...................................Initials ....
BLOCK CAPITALS PLEASE

Surname ....

Address ....

....

....Postcode..................................

Send this whole page to:
THE READER SERVICE, FREEPOST, CROYDON, CR9 3WZ
(Eire readers please send coupon to: P.O. BOX 4546, DUBLIN 24.)

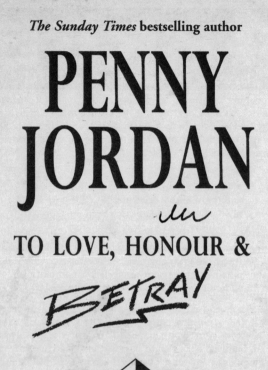